"We are offered a tantalizing glimpse into the private life of one of America's greatest poets, but for me, the real triumph is the character of Ada, Emily's young Irish maid. She's as beautifully realized as the gingerbread she so meticulously bakes with Emily. I can't wait to read what O'Connor writes next."

—NATASHA SOLOMONS, *New York Times* bestselling author of *The House at Tyneford*

"This vivid portrait of Emily Dickinson examines her humanity, complexity, and profound relationship with words. Told in her own eloquent voice and that of her trusted maid, *Miss Emily* deftly braids together the stories of two intriguing women in this highly accomplished novel."

—CATHY MARIE BUCHANAN, *New York Times* bestselling author of *The Painted Girls*

"My goodness—what a wonderful, wonderful book. I feel so privileged to have read it; I honestly cannot praise this book enough. Nuala O'Connor's beautiful writing sings from every single page as Emily and Ada's fascinating story unfolds. An absolute joy to read."

—HAZEL GAYNOR, *New York Times* bestselling author of *The Girl Who Came Home*

# More Praise for
## *Miss Emily*

"A jewel of a novel, *Miss Emily* by Nuala O'Connor is a fascinating, heartfelt, and captivating glimpse into the mind and heart of Emily Dickinson, one of America's most beloved poets, interwoven with the story of her spirited, witty, and devoted Irish maid, Ada. With its luminous prose and sympathetic, realistically drawn characters, you will feel yourself irresistibly drawn into Emily's and Ada's private worlds with every turn of the page."

—Syrie James, bestselling author of *Jane Austen's First Love* and *The Lost Memoirs of Jane Austen*

"Like a Dickinson poem, *Miss Emily* seems at first a simple story of friendship, but gradually reveals itself as a profound meditation on the human condition. O'Connor accomplishes this unfolding, just as Dickinson did, with her exquisite use of language. I lost myself in the beautiful detail of 1860s Amherst, a cast of characters that leapt off the page with life, and the constant reminder that words, properly wielded, can transcend time, transmit love, and, above all, inspire hope."

—Charlie Lovett, *New York Times* bestselling author of *The Bookman's Tale*

"An absorbing and provocative take on the inner life of a brilliant poet and her increasingly shrinking universe. The Dickinson household of Amherst, Massachusetts, is complex and very odd indeed and the tension builds toward shocking consequences for all involved. Nuala O'Connor's prose skillfully and lyrically creates Emily Dickinson's voice and that of her young Irish housekeeper, who chronicles the poet's harrowing struggle to find the freedom to write while living a cloistered life at home. A novel you won't want to put down."

—Jennifer Kaufman and Karen Mack, authors of *Freud's Mistress*

"The structure of the book is reminiscent of one of Emily Dickinson's poems, a lyrical dialogue between two distinct voices. Ada and Emily are divided by class, ethnicity, learning, circumstance; but a deep empathy and shared humanity unite them as women. This is a bittersweet story of repressed passion, thwarted opportunity, and the selflessness that is the essence of love."

—Stephanie Barron, bestselling author of the
Being A Jane Austen Mystery series

"*Miss Emily* presents its readers with a version of Emily Dickinson for the twenty-first century: an intensely private and reclusive woman who was as determined to live according to her own idio-syncratic rules as she was to engage on her own terms with the world outside her Amherst home. In the spirit of her beloved Elizabeth Barrett Browning and George Eliot, this fictionalized Dickinson crosses class, national, and religious lines to reach out to her Irish maid Ada with compassion, empathy, and humanity. In eloquent prose, O'Connor has depicted a life-changing encounter between two very different women that celebrates their complexity, passion, and strength."

—Dr. Paraic Finnerty, professor of American literature,
University of Portsmouth, and author of
*Emily Dickinson's Shakespeare*

"*Miss Emily* is an intricate, intimate novel that, in its careful attention to language, pays homage to our most American poet's extraordinary work. There are references to that work, rewards to true Dickinson aficionados, secreted in O'Connor's prose, but this novel achieves a broader aim too: it tells a story of friendship that keeps us turning the pages."

—Kelly O'Connor McNees, author of *The Lost Summer of
Louisa May Alcott* and *The Island of Doves*

"An original portrayal of Emily Dickinson seen here not just as a lover of words but as a heroine and friend to a plucky Irish maid who casts a new and sympathetic light on the Belle of Amherst."

—Sheila Kohler, author of *Becoming Jane Eyre*

"Secrets will always out. In the same way that Emily Dickenson's poems were once the best-kept secret in Massachusetts, Nuala O'Connor's luminous prose has long been one of Ireland's most treasured literary secrets. Now, through her superb evocation of nineteenth-century Amherst, an international audience is likely to be held rapt by the sparse lyricism and exactitude of O'Connor's writing. Through a fusion of historical ventriloquism and imaginative dexterity, O'Connor vividly conjures up—in the real-life Emily Dickenson and the fictional Ada Concannon—two equally unforgettable characters who pulsate with life in this study of the slowly blossoming friendship between a delicate literary recluse and a young Irish emigrant eager to embrace the new world around her."

—Dermot Bolger, playwright, and author of
*The Journey Home* and *The Venice Suite*

PENGUIN

*Miss Emily*

NUALA O'CONNOR is a well-regarded short-story writer and novelist in her native Ireland, writing under the name Nuala Ní Chonchúir, and has won many fiction awards, including RTÉ radio's Francis MacManus Award, the Cúirt New Writing Prize, the Jane Geske Award, the inaugural Jonathan Swift Award, and the Cecil Day Lewis Award, among others. Her short story "Peach" was nominated for a Pushcart Prize and she was shortlisted for the European Prize for Literature for her short story collection *Nude*. She was born in Dublin in 1970 and lives in East Galway with her husband and three children.

# Miss Emily

## NUALA O'CONNOR

PENGUIN

an imprint of Penguin Canada Books Inc., a Penguin Random House Company

Published by the Penguin Group
Penguin Canada Books Inc., 320 Front Street West, Toronto, Ontario M5V 3A4, Canada

Penguin Group (USA) LLC, 375 Hudson Street, New York, New York 10014, U.S.A.
Penguin Books Ltd, 80 Strand, London WC2R 0RL, England
Penguin Ireland, 25 St Stephen's Green, Dublin 2, Ireland (a division of Penguin Books Ltd)
Penguin Group (Australia), 707 Collins Street, Melbourne, Victoria 3008, Australia
(a division of Pearson Australia Group Pty Ltd)
Penguin Books India Pvt Ltd, 11 Community Centre, Panchsheel Park,
New Delhi – 110 017, India
Penguin Group (NZ), 67 Apollo Drive, Rosedale, Auckland 0632, New Zealand
(a division of Pearson New Zealand Ltd)
Penguin Books (South Africa) (Pty) Ltd, 24 Sturdee Avenue, Rosebank,
Johannesburg 2196, South Africa

Penguin Books Ltd, Registered Offices:  80 Strand, London WC2R 0RL, England

Published in Penguin paperback by Penguin Canada Books Inc., 2015.
Simultaneously published in U.S.A. by Penguin Books.

1  2  3  4  5  6  7  8  9  10   (RRD)

Designed by Elke Sigal
Manufactured in the U.S.A.

Library and Archives Canada Cataloguing in Publication data
available upon request to the publisher.

Print ISBN 978-0-14-319245-9
eBook ISBN 978-0-14-319247-3

American Library of Congress Cataloging in Publication data available

Visit the Penguin Canada website at **www.penguin.ca**

Special and corporate bulk purchase rates available; please see
**www.penguin.ca/corporatesales** or call 1-800-810-3104.

*For Emily, for poetry*

She was not daily bread, she was star dust.

—MARTHA DICKINSON BIANCHI,
*The Life and Letters of Emily Dickinson*

*Miss Emily*

# Miss Emily Dickinson Demands a New Maid

JULY AND THERE IS CRISIS. FATHER THROWS DOWN HIS CUTLERY and says he will not eat one more burnt potato.

"And I will not baste another seam," I say, glancing at Mother.

"Margaret O'Brien is all but irreplaceable," Mother says, taking a sip of currant wine. "And there are only four of us, with Austin gone. We are a small household. Yes, Margaret may be missed, but we will manage."

I think of Margaret, snug now in her marital chambers with her beloved Mr. Lawler, a competent mother to his four orphans. The Lawler house no doubt gleams all around them, and beautifully cooked potatoes steam on their dinner plates. I am silenced by Margaret's defection. Because she toils no more here, I must toil. Am I put out? Yes, I am. Am I anguished? I find that I am.

"Some of us miss Margaret O'Brien dreadfully," Father says.

"Housework is regularizing, Edward."

I stare at Mother. I do not wish to be regularized. Or regular. My desire is to be free to pursue the things that please me. And why say it to Father anyway? He is only required to enjoy the spoils of others' labor.

"Well, replace the irreplaceable Margaret we must, my dear," he says. "Emily is permanently floured to the elbows, Vinnie is never without a sweeping brush, and you are becoming too often ill from the weight of the household. Even the hens refuse to perform their duty since we lost Margaret. I shall see about a replacement forthwith."

I smile around at them all, from Father to Mother to Vinnie. My sister winks at me above the head of the puss she dandles on her lap.

"Do not look so triumphant, Emily," Mother says.

I change my facial expression to a more Mother-pleasing one but allow myself to feel exultant. I know that when Father decides on something, he applies himself to its execution with vigorous care, and I have privately wheedled, cajoled and begged him to right the situation. Father lives and loves ferociously, and, for me, there is little he will not do. We shall soon have our new maid-of-all-work. My shriven hands will look robust once more. No more hauling scuttles or trying, vainly, to get chicken and mushrooms and gravy to magic themselves ready at the same time. No more will I scrub, peel, milk, feed, wash, lift, scrape and polish. I will bake when the want overtakes me, not when Mother desires a rye loaf or her callers an apple pie. And I will be able to write anytime I please, for as long as I wish, not only in the dull snatches of time between this chore and the next.

I could rise from the table and kiss Father, here and now. Instead I eat the meal before me, knowing that soon we will sample beautifully cooked potatoes again.

# *Miss Ada Concannon Is Banished to the Scullery*

❦

I LOWER MYSELF INTO THE LIFFEY, FIRST TO MY THIGHS AND then waist-high. It is not too cold; the June days have heated the river, and the water has held the warmth all night. I flop onto my back and push away from the bank with my toes. My underclothes bloom like seedpods. Rose stands at the water's edge, guarding my dress and boots, the swamp stretching behind her. Her eyes are fixed to where I loll in the murky river; she is making sure, I suppose, that I am not about to slip from her life as I so often threaten to do.

I look toward the swamp, then spin on my back so I can see our house, a few fields off. While I float on the water, the village of Tigoora stirs much the same as it does every day. In our house Daddy puts on his jacket and thinks, maybe, about his time on the shivering ocean waves. The baronet and his lady snooze on, no doubt, knowing that the live-ins toil already and the rest of us will arrive shortly. Light seeps upward, diluting the ashen sky. The small ferryboat rocks, waiting to take us across the river to the Big House to begin our work.

"Ada, get out now," Rose calls. "I can see the ferryman coming. And Daddy, too. He told you not to go in the river."

I wave to Rose and swim a few strokes on my back. My sister looks like she might weep, so I haul myself out and pull my dress over my soaked underthings. The cloth drags against my wet skin, and Rose tugs at my sleeves and skirt to fix them. I wipe mud from my feet with wads of grass and pull on my stockings and boots.

"Look at your hair," Rose says forlornly, catching the rope of it and squeezing out drops.

"It'll be hidden under my cap," I say. "Don't fret, Rose."

❦

"Once more you stink of the Liffey, Ada." Mrs. Rathcliffe, the housekeeper, watches while I put on my apron. "And your hair is a shambles. I told your father to warn you not to arrive in that state to this house. Did he speak to you?"

"He did, ma'am."

"And?"

"And I won't do it again, ma'am."

"I cannot have you traipsing through the place like a muddy rat."

Cook joins us in the stillroom. "Lady Elizabeth is coming down this morning to do the menus. You'll need to get *her* out of here." Cook tosses her head in my direction.

Mrs. Rathcliffe looks at me, and I am chastened by her stern face. "Ada, from today you will join your sister in the scullery."

"Yes, ma'am."

"And you will not converse with each other. If I hear one speck of chatter or, God forbid, laughter from the scullery, I will be very, very cross. There will be consequences. Do you understand?"

"I do."

I leave the stillroom and stand in the passageway. The scullery, I think. I have had my warnings, but I am taken aback. I am diligent in my duties in this house, and the scullery is a step down.

They mean me to go backward through this life, it seems. What will the other girls say? And Mammy? Cook and Mrs. Rathcliffe continue to speak, thinking, I suppose, that I am already ensconced with Rose.

"That Ada Concannon is a peculiarly restless girl," Cook says.

"Her father might do better finding her a husband."

"I'll hand over a golden guinea to Concannon if he can find a husband for any of his girls. The men are all dead of the Hunger or gone on the boat. Good luck to him nabbing one man between the eight of them."

I hear the rustle of Mrs. Rathcliffe's skirts, and I run along the passageway. Rose smiles when I enter the scullery, her cheeks already glistening from the steam. The room is small, and though Rose is, too, she seems to fill it. I put my finger to my lips.

"I'm to work here with you," I whisper. "We're not allowed talk."

Rose grins. "That will hardly suit you, Ada." She takes a dolly tub from its rack and readies it for soaking clothes.

"What will I do, Rose?"

She points to a hare that is stretched out in the cold-water sink. "That needs skinning."

I grab the hare by the ears and lay it out on a board. Using a small knife, I slit the animal behind the ear and stick my finger inside; I pull the fur off its back and go at the legs.

"I'd rather be laying out the morning tea in the servants' hall or blacking the grate in Lady Elizabeth's parlor than doing this."

"Of course you would, Ada. But Daddy did warn you. You wouldn't be told."

I throw the hare onto its belly and fillet the back, my knife skimming its backbone as I cut. "God Almighty, will I be stuck here forever?"

"I'm stuck here. It does me no harm."

"But you're content in yourself, Rose. You know what I'm like—restless as a pup."

"What's Daddy going to say to you, Ada? And Mammy?" She puts a bundle of chemises into the tub. "Will you be paid the same as me now?"

I shrug, but I wonder if that is what will happen; the thought of it shames me. I would be better off finding a new position elsewhere if they mean to make an example of me altogether. I curse Mrs. Rathcliffe. I curse myself for my morning dip in the river.

"I don't know what's next for me, Rose. I don't know at all."

I cut in under the hare's ribs, then drag the rest of the meat off with my hands, enjoying the sinewy rip of it. Each pull of the flesh tugs a fierce grunt from my throat. I glance up to see my sister watching me, and though I smile at her, her look in return is doubtful. *I'll show them,* I think—Cook and Mrs. Rathcliffe and Daddy and them all. They'll see that I was made for more than the scullery. I'll do something that will shake the lot of them, and though I have no idea yet what it might be, it will be big.

# Miss Emily Surveys Amherst

THE JULY AIR IN AMHERST ALWAYS HUMS WITH HEAT AND promise. The conservatory is too greenly stuffy today, so I climb up and up through the house to the cupola. It is warm too and smells of the camphor gum I scatter to deter moths; I like this place to be truly my own—not even insects are welcome. It is my lamp atop the house, my spy hole.

I peer down onto Main Street, hoping to see Susan walking out from the Evergreens with little Ned, thinking she might pass on her way to the Hills' house. Alas, she is not abroad. Looking down into the garden, I see that the top of Austin's *Quercus alba* is rich with foliage; how proud he is of that oak. Across the meadow the factory churns out the palm hats that adorn heads from Maine to Oregon. And far off, the Pelham Hills are a lilac shimmer under the haze. I wonder what it would be like to be up on the hills now, looking back at Amherst, all snug and industrious in the summer heat.

I think of yesterday and the sweet afternoon I spent with Susan in the garden of the Evergreens.

"Do you realize, Sue," I said, "that we know each other twenty years this summer?"

"Truly, Emily? Can it be that we first met in '46? Why, yes, it must be so." She smiled one of her glorious smiles, and the lamb hairpin that Austin gifted her on their marriage seemed to smile along with her. "How wonderful to have remained such steadfast friends through all of life's ripples." She took my hand in hers and pumped it; we both laughed.

Dear, radiant Sue. Whatever would I do without her? She has a patient, committed ear. She is the only audience my heart trusts, and to her alone I gift my deepest thoughts, my most profound self. For sure we have had our bumps; she is somewhat unknowable and changeable, and I am perhaps a little too needy for her at times. And when she and Austin kept their engagement secret—and for so many months—I was undone. But we jog along, and all those years ago I soon realized that her being wedded to Austin was an opportunity. What better way to retain a loved friend than through matrimony with one's own brother? Ten years on from their marriage, it is one of my greatest blessings to have her next door.

Sue lifted her face to me. "I really liked the poem you sent me yesterday, Emily. There is such joy in it. I could not say I understood it all, but the image of the bee was rather beautiful. You find poetry everywhere, my dear."

I can send Sue a note or poem on any old scrap—she does not expect gilt-edged formality. She is as hungry to read my words as I am to write them. It is our small conspiracy: I show all my writings to Sue, and she makes remarks that I mull over and accept or reject. Her wish is to help me to accomplish the best possible poem, not mold my words to her desire, which is what I fear from others.

Several women pass on the street below the house, parasols shielding their faces from the sun. I think to let out a cry or make a birdcall, but they might look up to the cupola and see me, catch me in my silliness. It would achieve nothing but to give them fodder with which to discuss me. Austin says I am much gossiped about already, and clearly it displeases him. But what is there for me to do about it? I have my own ways. I opt not to whistle or startle the parasol women, and they walk on unawares, leaving me free of their glances, their disapproval. But I still ponder that of my brother. He has become stern over the years; he was such a blithe boy. The demands of marriage and upright citizenship have stiffened him somewhat, but surely not completely? He won the prize—Susan! Perhaps he tries too hard to be manly, to be more like Father, and, in trying, he chooses Father's worst traits to emulate. I know not. I only see that the soft brother of our youth hides himself well now.

It is stifling in the cupola, though the full views of Amherst please me; I am an eagless in her eyrie. I look across at the tower atop Austin and Sue's house and wonder if we will talk again soon, if she will come to me, to sit awhile and tell me of new books she has read or people she has recently met. When we sat together yesterday, we hardly spoke of now; we let ourselves linger in our younger days, recalling hours spent at her sister's house when they first moved to Amherst.

I am eager to let Sue know that we will shortly have a new maid and therefore I shall be able to spend more time composing notes and poems to her and maybe, if I am up to it, sitting in her company. Sue's face is rounded out these days because of the baby that makes a small mountain of her front. The extra flesh on her cheeks suits her, as everything does. Sweet Sue, my own Dollie, my nearly-sister. She is as good as any true sister and more besides.

I take one last look from each of the four windows and descend to my room. My desk sits forlorn by the window; a swath of peach light crosses its cherrywood like an invitation. I look at Elizabeth Barrett Browning and George Eliot in their frames on the wall and know that they understand my distress at my enforced absence from words.

At night, when I am not too bone weary, I dream. I would love to live in the softer planet of dreams. But if I cannot live in dreamworlds—those palpable fantasies that are conjured from fancy, as much as from the stuff of life—then I am content to invent parallel worlds. Places of the imagination that I alone can inhabit. And these destinations are made of words.

"Emily! Emily, come now."

It is Vinnie calling, and I go down to her in the kitchen. She is sweating over a mound of crockery, and it is my duty to help, it seems. One of her menagerie strolls along the table toward the butter dish, tail cocked like a lord.

"See how Mr. Puss preens," I say to Vinnie, who smiles the indulgent, motherly smile reserved for her charges.

I grab a cloth and begin to dry and stack the dishes. I lean into Vinnie's side and chant into her ear:

> *"—His porcelain—*
> *Like a Cup—*
> *Discarded of the Housewife—*
> *Quaint—or Broke—*
> *A newer Sèvres pleases—*
> *Old Ones crack."*

"Less poetry, more drudgery, please, Emily." She flicks water droplets at my face, and I muss her curls, then pick up another plate to dry it.

"The opposite is my life's hopeful refrain these days, Vinnie. 'More poetry, less drudgery.' Perhaps I could compose a verse on that."

## *Miss Ada Leaves Ireland for the New World*

❧

IT IS THE NIGHT BEFORE I AM TO GO, AND MAMMY SAYS TO ME, "Ada, this is the last time we will speak. A girl like you won't have any wish to come back to a place like this."

"Ah, Mam," I say, taking her hands in mine, but we both know the truth of it. Once I close the door on our house in Tigoora, I will be gone for good and all. No one comes home from the New World once they go to it.

Mammy thinks it is just a figairy I took, to leave my Dublin home and my position with the baronet and sail for America; she says I have too many notions. But ever since my Auntie Mary Maher and her family left Tipperary to go across the sea, I have thought about going myself. My Auntie Mary's letters spill with Massachusetts, Washington and Connecticut, and the names of these places have always been like songs in my ear. At night, I whisper to myself the spots she mentions; they are lullabies to help me toward sleep: the District of Columbia, Hartford, Amherst.

"Massachusetts," I often say to Rose. "Massachusetts. What do you suppose a name like that means?"

Today I am up before everyone else. I sit at the table alone and spoon cold stirabout into my mouth—Mammy left a bowl out for me. She never likes a lingering good-bye, so I bade farewell to her before we turned in. Rose lay deep into my side in our shared bed, sobbing for hours until she drifted off. I was awake most of the night listening to the sleep sounds of my sisters and wondering what might lie ahead.

Daddy comes into the kitchen, stands by the stove and sighs. "You're off so," he says.

"I am, Daddy."

He takes me the five miles to the train station in the baronet's trap. He does not speak until we are on the platform.

"Godspeed, Ada." He hugs me close.

"Good-bye, Daddy. I will write."

"You'll write to your mother, I suppose," he says. "Stay amidships if the swells bother you. And keep your eyes on the horizon."

I step back to look into his face, but he turns from me and is gone. I take the train to Kingstown and board the first of the boats that will ferry me across the seas. The gangway is jammed with people, and a ship's officer shouts at us not to break it.

"Go easy, go easy!" he roars.

But in the throng we have no choice whether to move forward or back to save his gangway, with all the pushing and shoving and trick-acting that is going on.

Up on the deck, I grip the rail and watch the harbor shrink as we move away; Dublin lies like a big dozy cow, not able to shake the sleep off herself. I wrap my hands around the rail and rock back and forth; my palms come away dappled with salt grains, and I hold them up and watch them glint in the early sun. I laugh aloud, feeling happier than I ever remember in my seventeen years on this earth. I have never been on a big boat, and though every-thing is rumbling and strange, I feel as if I have done it all before;

it is like adventure comes natural to me. The coast of Ireland gets smaller and smaller—it cannot disappear quick enough. It is possible, I think, to throw off one life and glide toward another so easily that it is barely noticeable. When Dublin is no more than a blurred line, I put my back to it and turn my face forward.

# Miss Emily Hides in the Garden

THE GODDESS POMONA HAS BEEN AROUND THE ORCHARD SCATtering her goodness: everything is floral and abundant, while the apple maggots and cabbage worm do their best to undo it all. I sit under a pine, listening to the sounds of the earth, the turn of the beetle and the bone song of the crickets; above me a jay chimes her good fortune to the sky. Moody Cook, the blacksmith, is by the barn tending to the horses with the Irish boy, Byrne, who sometimes comes. Their voices lilt across the garden to me, though I cannot hear what they say. Byrne is a big, well-put-together young man, steady, gracious and capable. Father talks of him in an avuncular way, as if he has made Byrne the fine fellow he is.

The smells are summery: leaves, blossom and rich marl. I would like to push my hands deep into the clay and savor its deathly cool around my fingers; I would enjoy the corpsy feeling of it. I fix my spine against the tree trunk and stretch my chin skyward. There is true peace here for those of us who crave it.

I am hiding from Mother and Vinnie, who are determined to pin sheets while the sun shines, but the wet slap of linens is not what I want to feel today. There is a poem forming in my gut, and in order to release it, I must be alone. I have a chocolate wrapper and a pencil in my pocket, and as soon as the words crystallize in my mind and push to my fingertips, I will write them down. For that I need the shelter of the garden; I am too easily discovered in the house.

Mother's voice—in the imperious tone she uses for the help—slices through the air. "Mr. Cook! Mr. Byrne! Has my eldest daughter passed this way?"

The men saw me indeed, for they stopped their fussing around Dick, Father's favorite horse, as I passed the chaise-house. They stood to watch me go by, both raising a hand in salute. I had put my finger to my lips and shaken my head, knowing they would take my meaning.

"No, ma'am," I hear Moody say, "I have not spoken to Miss Emily this day."

"Nor I," says Byrne.

They did not even lie. Bravo, Moody Cook! Bravo, Daniel Byrne! I rise and slink under cover of trees to the farthest reach of the Homestead's rim and prop myself behind a large chestnut where there is no chance of Mother unearthing me.

Words begin to jostle, then settle, in my mind; they play out before me as if already written. I see them in the inked curlicues of my own handwriting; I see them in pencil, blocky and spare. Words behave differently depending upon what I need them for. Writing a poem is not like writing a letter; the addressee is my soul—myself. Yes, I write for myself, and if the thing I write ends up shambolic or spasmodic, then what of it? Is it not the nature of all humankind to be unruly and contrary? To be uneven and to do things in uncharacteristic ways? Words are my sustenance: they are bread and wine. I flex my fingers and press my palms together. I flatten the yellow chocolate wrapper across my knees, take my pencil in my hand and begin to write.

# Miss Ada Arrives in Amherst, Massachusetts

My Uncle Michael sits beside me as the train rolls toward Amherst.

"Massachusetts is greener than Ireland," I say to him.

"Only parts of it, girleen, and only for some of the year." Uncle pats my arm. "It's August now, but let me tell you, come winter there will be snow thicker and higher than you have ever seen." He clicks his tongue in pace with the train's skip and jolt. "Now, tell me all about the passage."

"My stomach never rose into my mouth once," I say, "though it was often wild at sea. And they served a gray slumgullion to us three times a day. I was the only girl on deck most of the time. The men seemed hardier than the women."

"And did you find people to talk to?"

"Not really. There was an English girl bound for Boston, but she could hardly speak she was so sick."

I don't tell him about the woman with the oranges. Every night she sat alone at the long table in steerage and peeled an orange. Never having eaten an orange before, I couldn't take my eyes off it. She dug her nails into the skin and broke the fruit into pieces; she popped the slices into her mouth, and the juice dribbled from her lips. I had never witnessed the like, and the sweet, strange smell tickled at my nose. The cut of her, I thought, my mouth filling with spit. There was something obscene and lovely about the woman, and I would have given my two ears for a nibble of that orange.

"Wait until you see where we live," Uncle Michael says. "Annie's husband set us up nicely. He's a decent man." He sounds proud. Mammy always said that my cousin Annie's good marriage had benefited them all. Annie married a Kelley from Tipp; she met him in America and not in Tipperary at all. Tom Kelley bought a large property on Main Street in Amherst, and all his family, and the Mahers, live on it in different houses. Tom named it—rather grandly, I think—Kelley Square.

Auntie Mary is at the door of her house when we walk up from the train station, our legs unfixing after sitting so long. Auntie cries, shakes her head and looks at me as if I am something Uncle Michael has charmed out of the clouds.

"Ada!" she calls, arms outstretched. "Ada Concannon, come here and let me wrap myself around you. I declare to God, it's like looking at my own sister. You're the spit of Ellen, the walking head off her."

All life throbs outside their door; the center of Amherst is not far. While Auntie Mary crushes me to her breast and sobs into my hair, I look farther up the way. Horses and men fill the street; women stroll, and children run. The smells in the air are sharp but welcome: oil and dung and a clear autumn-ness that is made of leaves. This is a town of light and brick; it hasn't the gray drear of Sackville Street back home; it hasn't the endless green of the land around Tigoora, though there are hills off in the distance. Auntie smells of butter, and her dress is stiff and new; she is a different shape to Mammy, but there is something of Mammy in her, too.

"Mary, you're holding that girl like you'll never let her go. Bring Ada inside and let her take her rest. Feed her. She must be wall-falling with the hunger."

Auntie steps back and looks at me. "How was my darling Ellen when you left, *a leana*? How are they all?" I go to speak, but she shushes me. "We'll get you settled first."

❦

I startle awake to the sound of a long, sharp whistle, and it takes a minute for me to realize it is coming from outside. It is the factory whistle, I learn later, calling the men to work. It takes me another minute to let the shape of the room settle around me, to know where I am. My cousin Maggie's bed is neat and comfortable, and I can't say I miss the snorting and farting of my sisters. Maggie is in Connecticut, doing for the Boltwood family, which is lucky for me, because I get her room, never mind her bed, all to myself.

I can hear Mammy's voice saying, "Look at you lying there, Ada Concannon. You think you're a cut above buttermilk."

"That's right, Mammy," I say aloud. "I do think that. Because I am."

Light slants through the sides of the shutters, and I get up and open them to see what I can see. The house is already awake—I can hear them below—and I don't want Michael and Mary to think I am a lazy strap, so I haul myself into my petticoat and dress and go down.

# Miss Emily's Father Pleases Her

❧

FATHER IS TRIUMPHANT. HIS VOICE BOOMS THROUGH THE OPEN back door, and I stand and listen from the yard.

"She starts Monday next. She does not need to live in."

"And her experience?" Mother says.

"Vast experience. She worked for a baronet in Dublin before coming here, as a scullery maid and in the stillroom."

"She will find our household modest in comparison, no doubt."

"I daresay she will find us easier." Father allows himself a laugh. "Now, my dear. You may congratulate me on such an early and spectacular success."

I step through the door into the kitchen. "Success, Father?"

"Yes, indeed, Emily. I have found you a neat little person, a cousin of Maggie Maher's, who does so well for the Boltwoods. Do you see how determination brings dividends? This girl is fresh off the boat from Ireland and keen to work. Am I pleasing you thus far?"

I go to him and kiss his cheek. "Yes, Father."

"Emily, you will be doubly pleased when I tell you that she is an accomplished baker."

"I am glad of that, to be sure," Mother says.

"Does she possess a name, this Irish cousin?" I ask.

"She is called 'Miss Ada Concannon.'" Father chuckles and shakes his head. "Now, Emily of the Words, does that not charm you greatly? Concannon! Such a name. And, Miss Concannon tells me, she is from a small Dublin townland called 'Tigoora.' Tigoora!"

The variety of Irish names always amuses Father. When Austin—who was ever the bravest of our fold—would come home from teaching the Irish immigrants at the Endicott School in Boston's North End, one of the first things Father did was have him recite the family names of the boys. Austin would proud his chest and rattle off as many as came to mind: McLoughlin, O'Gorman, O'Donoghue, Murray, O'Connor, Considine, Foyle, Cooney, O'Brien, Egan, Finley, Griffin, Kerrigan, McIlhargey, Sullivan, O'Neill.

Father laughed at the preposterous Mc's and O's, and this delighted Austin, who was contemptuous of his charges and would thrash them frequently, according to himself. And perhaps rightly so, for they were a rambunctious crew, accustomed to the North End's Black Sea area and its brawls and riots.

Austin told Vinnie and me of the houses of ill repute in Boston, which scattered half-clad women onto the streets at all hours of the day. We loved to hear of the ladies' painted faces and slovenly manners; Austin imitated their talk and their swagger, and we egged him on, thirsty for every detail. He called them doxies and streetwalkers, and we liked to imagine their sordid lives. North End is a place of taverns and stygian slums, and every Dickinson said a prayer of thanks—even the ungodly ones such as me—when my brother tossed away the schoolroom key and came home to Amherst for good.

# *Miss Ada Makes an Early Success*

"WE'LL GIVE YOU A FEW DAYS' GRACE, ADA, AND THEN WE'LL find a position for you." Auntie Mary sets an egg before me, and I bash it on the head and scoop out its lovely golden heart.

"The eggs in America are much prettier than the ones at home," I say.

Mary smiles. "You'll be queen of Amherst in no time, Ada. I can see that already."

"The Dickinsons are looking for a new maid-of-all-work," Uncle says. "Mr. Frink mentioned it to me when I said our niece was coming to live with us."

"That's welcome news," Auntie says. "The Dickinsons are a decent family, and you would have only four to do for: himself, herself and their two spinster daughters. And they live nearby."

"Are they very grand? Is the house large?"

"Oh, they are not *very* grand, but they are well-to-do. Diligent, devout people, I would consider them. Popular in the town. The Squire is an attorney, and he bought back the family home on Main Street—the Homestead, as they call it. His father, they say, squandered money—well, he was a bankrupt anyway. The house is modestly large, and the Dickinsons are serious, proper people. The unmarried daughters live with their parents, as I said. Generous, nice young women, though the elder one, Miss Emily, does not go out much anymore, which is remarked upon." Auntie Mary frowns. "She prefers her own company, I daresay."

"Enough blather now, Mary," Uncle says. "They are fine people, that is all. I will call on Mr. Dickinson today."

But he doesn't have to, because Mr. Dickinson and his son, Mr. Austin, come to the house on Kelley Square. Auntie Mary receives them in the parlor, and after a while I am brought in to be observed. Mr. Dickinson has a flat, serious mouth, and he is dressed like an undertaker, but he is a stately-looking man. His son is a wild-haired, younger version of the father, and he stands by the window, holding himself apart from us all. Auntie Mary glances at Mr. Austin while she speaks, as if she doesn't trust herself not to say anything foolish in his presence.

"Ada is a strong girl, Mr. Dickinson." Auntie holds me by the shoulders in front of the older man. "You couldn't ask for a hardier lassie. My own family are long-lived, but the Concannons are powerful people. Ada's father is round as a hog, but he can lift a rain barrel."

Mr. Dickinson holds up his hand. "You have convinced me, Mrs. Maher," he says. "We will receive Miss Concannon on Monday. Where do you hail from, miss?"

"Tigoora in County Dublin, sir."

"Tigoora? Very well," Mr. Dickinson says. "Come, Austin. The lawbreakers of Amherst await us."

The son walks from his spot by the window and surveys me. He grunts, and I take it for some sort of approval. "Good day to you, Mrs. Maher," he says, and his voice is solemn but not unpleasant. Both men tip their hats and are gone.

Auntie Mary takes me by the shoulder. "Well now, Ada, isn't that marvelous? I will write to your mother immediately and tell her what a success you have made of your very first day in Amherst."

"Am-erst," I warble, imitating her pronunciation. "Am-*erst*." Auntie looks at me as if I am half mad.

# Miss Emily Dickinson Finds a New Companion in the Kitchen

❧

It is a very real possibility that I will remain always and forever under my father's roof. I am, of course, happiest in my home circle—this is where I bloom—but something in me also longs for the peace of a place of my own, somewhere to withdraw to completely. I do not wish for travel or brave new lands, only a house surrounded by a sprawling orchard that holds orioles and bluebirds that trill for my ears alone, a cozy home with a kitchen uncluttered by others. I do not desire a man or babes; a husband would demand too much, I fear, of my time, of my very self. And there is no doubt that I would make an opinionated, quarrelsome wife.

The new Irish girl started some weeks past. I have not seen much of her, as I have been scratching ink across pages, but she seems lively and capable. She is a compact person, tidy in her dress, and has dark hair and icy eyes. Mother complained today that Ada is "prone to speechmaking," which makes her appeal grow tenfold for me. Not that I mentioned this fact to Mother. I allow myself so few companions that I do enjoy a person who likes to talk.

I entered the kitchen last week, and Ada stopped dead.

"Miss Dickinson?" she said.

"I am a regular here, Ada. Loaves of bread have been born into the world under my guidance." She stared hard at me. "I like to bake," I said.

"*Like* to, miss?"

I had to hold back a laugh so as not to wound her. I suppose for her baking is mere work, whereas for me it is ease and alchemy.

"Perhaps we might bake together soon," I said, and left her alone.

Now it occurs to me that she will have fresh methods of fashioning cakes and breads to share. What new tricks will she have brought from her mother's table to ours? I lift my eyes to the window to see rain falling; I love the kitchen on a dreary day. I put down my pen and go there to question Ada about what she knows of cake making.

Rain sleets against the kitchen window, but all is warmth and industry. Ada is scraping the leavings of a stew from a pot into a bowl.

"The birds use their wings as umbrellas on days such as these," I say.

She stops midscrape. "Is that so?" She fills the bowl, lays down her spoon and looks at me. "Begging your pardon, miss, but you talk a lot about birds. You must be very fond of them."

"Do I talk about birds so much?" I ask.

"The other day you said something about a nightingale."

"'*It was the nightingale, and not the lark, / That pierced the fearful hollow of thine ear.*'" I was quoting Shakespeare to amuse Mother. We need nothing else when we have Shakespeare, Ada."

"That's as may be, but your mother didn't look very amused, miss, if you don't mind my saying. And I have pots to scrub."

Ada has a superior, petulant face, but when she smiles, she glows like a window opening on a bright day. I want to make her smile.

"I hear that you Irish love rain," I say. "My sources tell me you are not happy unless soaked through by a torrent."

"We're used to rain, miss—it is constant in Ireland—but that doesn't mean we welcome it." She turns toward the scullery, and I have to stand in her way to stop her going.

"Margaret O'Brien brought variety to our table, Ada. I wonder if you have any particular things you like to bake? Cutler's store can order in even the most unusual items. We have an account there, of course."

"I know that. Miss Vinnie has already instructed me." She smooths her apron with one hand and looks at me as if she would like to be left alone. "The Concannons, the same as most Irish people, are plain eaters, Miss Dickinson. My mammy looks at salt as if the devil himself brought it to her table. If you like unfussy food, then I'm happy to share what I know with you." She wriggles past me, a saucepan held out in front of her like a chalice.

"My Indian round bread took a prize at the Amherst Cattle Show, you know," I say to her retreating back, and even as the words leave my lips, I know how silly I sound.

Ada turns. "Do cows like the taste of rye bread, Miss Emily?" she asks.

Is she teasing? The Irish employ a canny innocence that has fooled me before. Then she smiles, that lit-up grin of hers, and winks slowly.

"Oh, Ada."

"I think you should get out from under my feet, Miss Emily, and let me move on with my day."

"Let me perch here. I will be quiet as a nestling, and you won't even know that I am in the room."

She tuts. "Miss Emily, you're more of a turkey than a wren, truly, and I will know quite well that you're here."

But she smiles again, and I know that, like Margaret O'Brien before her, she welcomes a chance to chatter as she goes about her work. The Irish put great store in spinning a narrative around every small thing, and although I may view life New Englandly, I think I must be somewhat Irish at my core, for I love to do the same.

☙

Sue comes to me; she rolls in the door, her front a muslin-draped melon, and I lead her by the hand to the library, our favorite spot for conferring.

The first time I ever saw Sue, a cascade of sun fell from her head to her shoulders to her feet. She was entirely lit up, standing in the hallway of her sister's home when we came to call. She was Susan Gilbert then, a new face in our orbit, and we all loved her instantly. Her composure, her china-white skin and her even features all drew me to Sue, before I knew of her boundless intelligence. She was as luminous then as she is now.

"You cultivate possessiveness," Vinnie once told me. "You smother Sue, and every other acquaintance, with friendship."

She meant it kindly—in an instructional way—but it set me thinking about Vinnie and whether she knows the real me, the me of my deepest desires. Vinnie has never been a good character judge; she runs with a lot of sillies who care more for Holland lace and ensnaring men than the finer things of the mind and heart. It strikes me that perhaps it is not possible ever to know another, no matter how much we long to. Sue is bridled to Austin, but he does not know her as I do. Before they married, he complained to me that she did not respond to him as he might have liked.

"Dollie is filled with sawdust," he declared one day, a moment of extreme exasperation, surely, for the Susan I know is wholly flesh, with a heart that pumps hot blood. There is nothing dry or inert about her; she has passion for poetry and every fine thing. She is of the world in a way that I could never be, and I love that she brings the world to me.

On this day Sue occupies her seat elegantly, as if her stomach is not full with a wriggling babe. "It is so hot," she says, flicking a pamphlet in front of her face as a fan.

"What will hell be like?" I ask, and we both laugh.

"What news, Emily? Entertain me, for I cannot quite entertain myself these days. My brain has dried to biscuit."

"The chartreuse zinnia we planted in the conservatory has come up."

"How lovely."

"And I have been itching to tell you all about our new maid."

"Austin mentioned you had taken another Irish girl."

"Yes, and she is a darling. Her name is Ada Concannon. Does her name not sound like a peregrine fruit, Sue? Something meaty but sweetly exotic?" Sue nods uncertainly. "Ada talks about Mother as if I were not related to her and then hastily excuses herself. But she means every word she says. There is something of the scamp about her."

"Is it wise to engage so? Certainly do not encourage her to have a loose tongue, Emily. It may deliver trouble to your door."

Sue settles back into the chair and folds her hands across her high belly; she sighs and retreats into that space expectant women go to—a covert, mystical place of the mind with room for only one: the soon-to-be mother.

"Father was speechifying yesterday, Sue."

"Oh, yes? I do love when he sits atop his highest horse. What was his subject, Emily?"

"The usual: 'Intellectual eminence should not be woman's goal. Do not read too much, Emily.' And then he handed me a parcel of new books, though he fears they 'joggle the mind.'"

"Books are always welcome indeed. Was the latest Dostoyevsky among them?" I shake my head. "You must read it, my dear. It is about brilliance and murder—you will love its pathos."

"But is it *dignified*, Susan?" I say, imitating Father's sternest voice. "We must read only what is *dignified*!"

Sue laughs and tells me more about *Crime and Punishment*, about its treatise on intellectualism and its fluid, squalid nature. "Dostoyevsky seems almost casual about death, Emily. It is shocking. Wonderfully so."

"Just yesterday Ada found a hole in a loaf of bread she had baked. She held it up to me in dismay. I assured her it was all right and that a hole did not make the bread inedible. 'You don't understand, miss,' she said. 'It's a coffin. It means a death before long.' And she was so crushed by the idea that I had to go along with it and console her for a demise that has not yet taken place!"

"Oh, the Irish," Sue says. "Everything is low and sad with them. Those Pocumtuc girls make adequate domestics, and they don't talk much. And certainly not out of turn. You should hire one of them instead."

"I like Ada. She brings spirit with her. She enlivens me. And the entire house."

Sue waves her hand. "Emily, you want for company—that is why this girl amuses you. You must go forth from this house on occasion. Come to me, to one of my soirées."

I see a crowded room in my mind, and I feel dizzy. "I think not."

"People ask after you all the time." She whisks her hand over her hair. "And it injures me a little, Emily, that you do not come anymore."

I do not wish to wound Susan, but one as sociable as she perhaps cannot fully understand why strangers discombobulate me so much. I simply do not feel comfortable in a throng; my head gets addled, and I long for peace. And Sue may not comprehend either the writer's absolute need for quiet and retreat, the solace of it. I am so entirely happy in my own company that I rarely feel the need for anyone else, and when I do, I like to choose my companions wisely.

Sue looks at me, expecting a response. Though her face is the gentle one I love, there is a firmness to her, too, an insistence.

"You know that I quake before prying, inquiring eyes," I say. "It has always been so. Even when I seemed gay and giddy as a girl, I was uncomfortable. Deeply."

Sue softens. "People are not necessarily prying when they look at you, dear Emily. The average man is interested in his fellow man and in conversation, nothing more."

I slip from my chair and kneel before her. "When I talk too much, everything I think and feel is wrung from me. I have nothing to write about when all is spent. It takes me so long to restore myself. It is as if I must heal a wound after each party where all is chitchat and glances and *fun*."

"I do not wish you to be upset, Emily. I merely want to introduce you to people. I would like my guests to experience *you*, not only the poems of yours I share with them."

"I know you mean your invitation kindly, Dollie. But we are

here together now." I put my lips to her cheek and tell the curl of her ear, "I prefer to have you alone. That way you are all mine."

Sue dips her head to my breast, and I place my hand to the back of her sweet neck. I study the chevrons of tiny hairs that grow there, pointing their way down into her bodice.

## Miss Ada Is Upset by a
## Visitor to the Homestead

THE DICKINSON KITCHEN IS PAINTED GREEN AND YELLOW. Every time I walk into it, I think of apples and daffodils. It is bright and calm, the very opposite of the soot-blackened clutter that makes up my mammy's fireplace and table at home in Tigoora. And here the entire house is mine: I am cook and housekeeper and lady's maid, all in one. If Mrs. Rathcliffe could see me!

Yesterday Mrs. Dickinson came in and asked if I was able to read and then seemed affronted when I said I was. She handed me a neat, whey-colored book.

"Think of this as your second Bible," she said.

I looked at the cover: *The Frugal Housewife* by Mrs. Child. I opened it and recited, "'Dedicated to those who are not ashamed of economy.' I will read it, ma'am."

Mrs. Dickinson looked at me solemnly. "Mrs. Child urges prudence at all times and for every person." The twin sets of sausage curls below her ears jigged up and down as she spoke. I wanted to slip my finger into one of her shiny ringlets, to see what it would feel like. "Economy, Ada," she said, nodded and went away.

Like her husband, the missus is an austere bird; I don't think a smile would ever crack her lips. But Miss Emily is spry as a colt for someone more than twice my age, and she has a mouth full of words to match. From time to time, she appears like a ghost behind me in the kitchen, knocking the heart crosswise in me. Her manners are contained at first, but soon she starts to joke and jest. She certainly loves to put things in the oven and coodle over them when she takes them out. Then she gives them away: Federal Cake to this one, rye bread to that one, gingerbread to the local children. Miss Vinnie said the other day that Miss Emily single-handedly fattens up the Sweetser family every winter.

I stoke the stove to heat the hob for the potato scones I have ready. Grabbing a knob of butter, I rub it all around the pan with my fingers, enjoying its milky squelch. The door opens, and Miss Emily comes in.

"Ada," she says, "please put wine in the decanter." Her hands flutter to her face like stray moths. "I will need two glasses."

"Only this morning I dropped a spoon first and soon after a knife, so I knew that a visitor would be calling before the day was out."

"Is that so?" she says. "The rose decanter, Ada."

I hold up my buttery fingers so that she sees it will take a few minutes.

I have never known such a house for comings and goings. If it is not the letter carrier, it's Governor Banks, and if it's not him, or some person from the college, it is the sister-in-law from next door.

"Two glasses," Miss Emily says again. "Serve some of Mother's sweet malmsey wine." She seems ruffled, and I wonder if the wine is a balm meant to soothe her.

I go to the wine cellar and fetch a bottle. I hold a hot, wet cloth around the decanter stopper to loosen it up; I pull firmly, but the thing won't budge. All this time I know that Miss Emily is waiting.

Finally the stopper eases out, and I fill the decanter and place the lid back in the neck. The wine is brandy-colored, and it smells rich like chocolate. I take the tray carefully to the parlor, and I am surprised to find its red velvet sofa empty. I stand for a few moments, tray aloft, and hear voices drift down the hall. They are in the library. When I enter the room, I am further surprised to find that Miss Emily's guest is not her brother's wife, or a man from the college, but Mr. Austin. He is a bit of a harridan, if you can say that of a man; he goes around with a cocky set to his face. He frightens me a little, truth be told. It is only a blessing that his sisters are so warm.

"This is our new girl, Austin: Miss Ada Concannon. She's from Dublin, Ireland. Isn't that right, Ada?"

"It is," I say, setting the tray on the table by the fire. I stand back and let my eyes wander to the spines of the Ticknor and Fields books, rows of them in blue, brown and green jackets.

Mr. Austin steps near to me. "We met already, in Miss Concannon's uncle's house." He turns away and unstoppers the decanter. "Dublin. Home of Swift the satirist. Though I do believe he despised the place."

"Ada is preparing to instruct me on the making of soda bread and currant cake and other things. Are you not?"

"I am, miss."

"What shall we make first?"

I would like to leave the room, but Miss Emily seems determined to rope me to her. "Well, I'm fashioning potato scones today, miss."

"Potatoes?" Mr. Austin says. "Didn't the Irish all but extinguish themselves over the potato? I am surprised you can look at the things."

"We have had two great famines, sir. The country was devastated by them."

"So you are a famine survivor, Miss Concannon. Well done! Well done indeed." He sips the wine, and I stand there and resent his fingers cradling Mrs. Dickinson's lovely rose glass.

"I will come to you in the kitchen by and by, Ada," Miss Emily says, and I take my leave.

Something makes me linger outside the library door, and I hear Mr. Austin say, in his booming, scratchy voice, "We do not see enough of you, Emily. Susan wishes you to come to our house more often. We both feel it would enliven you to leave the Homestead."

"Dear Austin, you know that Sue and I have had this conversation. Many times. Are you her emissary sent to force me out the door?"

"I care little for Susan's soirées, Emily. I am merely performing a husbandly obligation. Come, let us talk of other things. I shall amuse you with the tale of the Northampton man who was trampled by a wild bull. You will laugh, Emily."

I turn away from the door and go back to the kitchen.

❦

"Famine survivor! What does he know about famine?" I thump the broom around Auntie Mary's floor, and she yelps when I catch her ankle.

"Pay him no mind, Ada. You're only annoying yourself." She sits at the table and holds her head, then shakes it.

"It's an insult to those who did not come through the famine. Who *could* not."

"I'm sure Mr. Austin didn't mean it like that, *a leana*. More than likely he was trying to be kind."

I go and stand by her. "Granny Dunn made sure our family survived, didn't she? Mammy always said so."

"She did. My mother never went begging to any man. She kept a crop of turnips safe and barley besides, and she got us all through. And weren't there fat trout in the Clashawley?" Mary takes my hands in hers. "Now, Ada. These people don't even need to look at you, never mind talk to you. You're lucky with the Dickinsons, they're gentlefolk. Margaret O'Brien always speaks very highly of them. But watch your step. Be mindful. Now, why don't you go for a walk along Main Street and up to the common? Clear the cobwebs from your mind. Go and take a look around. See if you can make a friend."

"Well, I will so," I say, slipping on the new gray wool coat that cost Uncle Michael twenty dollars and that I intend to wear until my feet slide into the grave.

Mrs. Child says in *The Frugal Housewife* not to let the beauty or cheapness of things tempt you to buy anything unnecessary. Well, my coat is both beautiful and necessary, and it certainly wasn't cheap, but Uncle said I needed it. I wear it with pride against the chill that creeps into the air each evening.

I walk toward the center of Amherst. Daniel Byrne, who helps with Mr. Dickinson's horses and more besides, passes me on Main Street; he tips his cap and smiles.

"Mr. Byrne," I say, trying to be a little formal, but something about him makes my mouth twitch and beam.

I glance backward after he has passed and find that he is looking behind at me also. I whip my eyes forward, and my heart batters in my chest. I walk on, finding that I am very glad of the decent look of my new coat. I say a silent thanks to my Uncle Michael for gifting it to me.

# Miss Emily Takes to Her Bed

SOME UNNAMABLE GLOOM HAS SETTLED ON ME, AND I HAVE retreated to my room to deal with it alone. But Vinnie does not approve of such withdrawals, and she hovers, trying to oust me. She goes to my window and settles the curtain pleats; this is my sister, always fixing, always soothing, the eternal housekeeper. She fattens my pillows with swift thumps.

"What is it, Emily? You must aim to be less pensive."

"It is nothing, Vinnie. I feel weary and restless, a little over-burdened. That is all."

"You will always be the same old sixpence," she says, wiping the tears that fall from my eyes, though I don't wish them to. "Try to think cheerfully, Emily. 'Be light in thought,' as Mother says."

"I shall try," I say. "I will take my rest now." I lie back.

"Emily, you mustn't wallow for long. Ada was quite put out this morning—she was ready to instruct you on the making of potato scones. She stomps around the kitchen now like an angry sprite."

"Send her my apologies. Tell her I am tired. But tell her I will be as right as Irish rain tomorrow. Say that, Vinnie, won't you?"

"Yes, Emily, I will use those exact words," she says, kissing me and taking her leave.

Under its foliage and roses, my wallpaper is filled with arrows, each of them pointing the same way around the walls of my room, from east to west and on eastward again. The arrows tell me to complete my circle as I begin it. For life—and writing—is a never-ending loop of begin, push on, end, begin again. I usually take comfort from the arrows' instruction on the inevitability of beginnings and endings, but today has not been like any day I have had before. Once this malaise descended upon me, the hours attained a stillness that I would like to preserve.

It is mild for an October day, and the sky is pink-bright. I get out of bed and push the window up to let the world into my room. But it does not come. The day is like an illusion hovering over me; it is as if I am the only person who exists. Nothing goes forward or backward—it just is. And I know that all of this stillness is something to do with my heart; it pulses, pushing me forward, but yet I am unable to move. I often wish I were a sparrow or a blade of grass so that problems of the heart and humanity might not bother me. And yet my mind is always at its clearest when something is off balance in me.

I cross the room and lie on my bed and think about words. When my heart or my head hurts, when my body betrays me in sickness, I have words to play with. But, more than play, they own me. I am their servant, and I serve willingly, with as much grace as I can muster. I have so little power over them, in truth. Words—all words—chill and scorch me.

Each dash I create is a weight, a pause, a question. I select them with care. The exclamation point is juvenile, while the dash is much more promising—a mature mark. Each dash interrupts, emphasizes, connects and pushes apart the words around it. The dash is a waiting beat—*dah—dah—dah*.

My lexicon bulges, but my picks from it are slender: I favor the blunt and the simple. I prefer one syllable to two. I like curt words: death, bird, pearl, bee, stone, crown, stab. These to me are the words that sing and that deserve their place in a poem, as surely as the nightingale deserves her perch in the wild.

With words I question, I complain, I code. I love to riddle.

> *Riddle-me, riddle-me,*
> *Riddle-me-ree,*
> *Perhaps you can tell*
> *What this riddle may be:*
> *As deep as a house,*
> *As round as a cup,*
> *And all the King's horses*
> *Cannot draw it up.*

Words lie in me like water in the riddle's well. They tempt me, like nothing else. Not man, not God, not even dear Dollie, in all her exquisiteness. And what is temptation but a forestalling of joy? And what is joy but the thing that we most desire? Yes, words tempt and tease me, and they send me teetering forward. Vital, immortal words.

Vinnie styles me "mad" sometimes; she loves to flit from person to person like a bee sucking nectar, and she does not understand my need to retreat to words. And Austin thinks me wild, in my ideas, in my notions. But convention never has been, and never will be, my first choice. I have not chosen to live as woman is supposed to live. The choice is mine, so who can object when I push it further and dwell in lands that exist only in my mind and on paper? Vinnie would take exception if she knew the extent of my escape into writing and words.

But those landscapes of my invention—poem lands—are

more real to me than Amherst. More real than the Homestead and all who dwell in her. The rustling passions of life are contained more truly for me in the words of poetry than in the everyday world. Life, as lived, is so desolate at times.

And why do I write? I ask myself daily, for the answer differs at every dawn, at every midnight. I write, I feel, to grasp at truth. The truth is so often cloaked in misleading speech. Sometimes I let words fall carelessly from my lips when I am with people, but alone I make them settle carefully onto paper. There they must be accurate, and they must work as a choir works to sing a tune well. I like to hear my own words in my own voice, and there are days when I sit at my desk and read aloud to myself from my word hoard. The words please me, the hymnal beats, too. And when they displease me, I take my pen and change them and start again. Read, cross out, read. Send to Sue. Adapt, choose, cross out.

Oh, chimerical, perplexing, beautiful words! I love to use the pretty ones like blades and the ugly ones to console. I use dark ones to illuminate and bright ones to mourn. And when I feel as if a tomahawk has scalped me, I know it is poetry then and I leave it be.

## *Miss Ada's Head Is Turned*

❧

IT IS AN ENTIRE WEEK SINCE MISS EMILY DARKENED THE kitchen door. I miss her, even though half the time she gets in my way. She sits, draped over the stove, jotting words on the back of sugar wrappers, lost in her head.

The only visitors to my kitchen these past days were Mr. Austin, for a few moments, and Daniel Byrne, who came in to sharpen all the knives at Mr. Dickinson's request.

Mr. Austin flung open the back door, strode in and stood in the middle of the kitchen. I stopped trimming the chops I had in hand and stood before him.

"How goes it, miss?" he said.

"Grand, sir." I looked up into his face. He is handsome to be sure, I thought, but his red hair is as bedraggled as a scarecrow's; he would not look out of place in a field of corn. Or footing turf on an Irish bog.

Mr. Austin glanced around the kitchen, as if trying to find something to fault, but all was neat and ordered. "Very well," he declared, and he was gone as quick as he came.

Daniel Byrne was a less alarming intruder; I welcomed the sight of him when I opened the back door to his shy knock. Like myself, he is from Dublin. He is a big fellow, with straw-colored hair and an easy manner.

"How long have you been in America, Daniel?" I asked as he took the knives he had come to sharpen from the drawer and laid them out.

"Since I was fourteen years old." He may be in Amherst a few years, but he still sounds like the boy from Ringsend that he is.

"You surely didn't come alone?"

"No, my father and my brother were with me. But after a spell they went west, like so many more. I like it well enough here, so I stopped."

"And your mother, did she stay in Dublin?"

He dipped his head. "My mother died when I was a baby."

"I'm sorry to hear it." I felt bad for asking, and I wanted to say or do something to cheer him. "Will you have some coffee or tea when you're done with the sharpening?"

"I will." He hissed a knife blade back and forth along the leather strop and tested its bite with a scratch of his thumb. "I'll be able to vote soon, Ada," he said.

"Is that your way of telling me you're nearly a man, Daniel Byrne?"

"It might be." A hint of scarlet rose in his cheeks. I busied myself scalding the pot and wetting tea leaves. Daniel finished the work quickly. He checked each knife against his skin and gave them all to me to return to the drawer. "There you go," he said, as if it were I who had asked him to do the job.

"Thank you, Daniel. Will you eat something with your tea? I made a sponge cake with blueberry jam."

"I had better get on, actually, but thank you. Next time." His eyes lingered on my face until we both turned our heads away. "I'll go," Daniel said, and he went quickly back out to the yard, but he left a part of himself behind in the kitchen, a sort of warm space that I found I welcomed very much.

❦

Mrs. Dickinson comes in and asks me to make an Irish soda bread—she fancies something different, being more used to yeast bread—and I am happy to oblige.

"A change is as good as a rest, Mrs. Dickinson," I say.

"Indeed." She turns her back to me and leaves the room. Sometimes I wonder why I open my beak to the woman at all.

In her book Mrs. Child says that water for bread should be warmed during chilly, damp weather, the very type these October days bring. I am busy wondering if I should heat up the buttermilk—against my normal action—when Miss Emily slides into the room.

"Miss, you have returned to me." She smiles, and I ask her to measure out two cups of flour and a teaspoon of pearl ash. "Or do I have to do everything myself?"

She takes her utensils from the cupboard—a big glass to measure by and a large silver spoon that she likes to stir with. These are her bits, and no one is permitted to touch them; she guards them shyly.

"Two cups," she says, and I nod. She begins to scoop; her face is as washed out as the flour.

"Now, miss, we'll get on with it." I heat the buttermilk. If Mrs. Child says it should be done, it must be so.

"I have been a little low, Ada," Miss Emily says in a quiet voice.

"There's no need to explain yourself to me, miss. I'm glad to see you back on your feet." The milk froths, and I take it off the hob. "You're maybe like me, Miss Emily. I feel one way one minute, and the next I feel the very opposite. I find it hard to keep up with myself at times. Is it like that with you?"

"Yes, Ada, I daresay it is."

"Now, miss, I'll show you how to make a good Dublin soda bread."

"Thank you, Ada."

I set her to mixing and then let her knead the dough. Once the round is ready, I have her cut a deep cross in it.

"That'll keep the devil out of the bread, miss."

Once the loaf is in the stove, we sit together, and I can see her spirits rise as sure as the bread is rising in the oven's heat.

"There are only a few places I ever seem to want to be, Ada. Here in the kitchen, making magic with flour and milk, and up in my room, scribbling words onto pages. Or, indeed, in the company of Susan. Is it wrong of me to want little more but these things?"

"How could it be wrong, Miss Emily? We must do exactly as we please in life. How else are we to be happy?"

"When I was a girl, I loved to gad about. But now sugaring parties and teas with ladies don't interest me. In fact, they unnerve me. I have a dread of being looked at. It has always been so, as long as I can recall. Mother blames herself for this. She sent me away as a two-year-old to stay with my Aunt Lavinia. She worries that I developed a fear of people when I was so rudely removed from all I knew. It may or may not be so. How can we know?" She leans forward and speaks intently. "Vinnie, Susan and I were at tea lately in town, and the cacophony struck me dumb. The din was hideous, and I did not feel I belonged. I felt sickened by probing eyes, as if I were an object with few dimensions. I knew that those strange to me did not see me *rightly*. Rather than be misinterpreted, I prefer not to be seen at all. I have concluded that the outside world—the one of people—does not bring me joy." She flutters a little, looks at me. "But what about you, Ada? Are you happy? You are so very far from your home, your family."

"I am content, miss. I've taken to America very well. These past few months have been a wonder to me. And my uncle and aunt are more than kind."

"Did your life in Ireland not suit you?"

"It suited me well enough, miss, but I always had a question about what lay far off. I couldn't rest until I answered it for myself. And Ireland has changed, miss. There aren't prospects like there used to be. A lot of people are leaving."

"I cannot imagine being so removed from my family."

I take out the bread; it is as golden and perfect a loaf as Mammy would make. Miss Emily hands me a broom straw—her favorite method for testing—but I take the knife I habitually use and stab it into the bread. It comes out clean. Then I knock on the bottom of the loaf and hear its hollow answer.

"If I didn't know you, Ada, your skill with that blade would perturb me."

"Mammy used to say I would frighten the crows out of the trees when I was in a thundering mood." I laugh. "But there's no fear of me with the knife."

"Ada, you are like a breath from Madagascar."

"You say the queerest things, miss." I take the loaf and cut it into quarters. We have a slice each, the butter dribbling off it onto our chins. It pleases me to see Miss Emily content, eating a lump of soda bread, with something like a smile lurking around her mouth.

❦

Miss Emily says November is the Norway month, but it has arrived in a burst of sunshine to thwart her. In the brightness of the day, the yellow bricks of the Dickinson Homestead glow beside the gloom of the Evergreens, Mr. Austin's villa. I look up at its dour walls as I pass; how his wife and son can stand the dark of the place is beyond me. Though Miss Susan has a haughty air, I see how soft she is around Miss Emily, and that makes me warm toward her. She is devout, too, and goes often to church. Her husband is another thing entirely; he is what Mammy would call "a wicked-faced gent." Who dreamt them up as a pair? I ask myself.

A cotton day moon lurks behind the trees as I walk toward the town. I am taking Auntie Mary to the Amherst House for a treat; she has not been feeling the best, and I mean to get a good dinner inside her, one that neither of us has had to cook. I have arranged to meet her at the inn. I walk across the common toward Amity Street, and I spot Auntie standing stiffly at the railing on the porch of the inn, waiting for me; she looks like the figurehead on the prow of a boat. I follow her gaze to the tiered water fountain and frog pond behind me.

"Ada! I thought you weren't coming at all. I was about to go home." She trots down the steps to meet me.

"I'm not late, Auntie."

"No, maybe you're not." She sighs and rips off her gloves.

I link her arm, and we ascend the steps and enter the lobby. The restaurant smells sweet and bready; I squeeze Auntie's elbow. "This will be lovely now, Auntie Mary. It's not often you're waited on hand and foot."

"There's a reason for that, Ada—I don't like being waited upon." She unpins her hat, and we take our table; she smooths the linen with her hands and looks around, appraising the other diners. "Did they enjoy the bareen brack at the Homestead?"

"They did. Mr. Austin found the ring in his slice, which was a shame, as he's already married. I was hoping Miss Emily or Miss Vinnie would come upon it in theirs."

"Ah, I don't think either of them is for marrying. Sure Miss Emily barely goes out anymore. Wouldn't it have been grand if *you* had found the ring, Ada?" Auntie Mary grins at me.

I snort. "Sure who'd have me, Auntie?"

"Well now, you'd be surprised. A girl like you doesn't go unnoticed in a place like Amherst."

I shrug, but truth be told I am as pleased as a dog with two pockets. And I hope that whoever it is she is thinking of is the same person I am thinking of myself.

We eat our meal with gusto, and Auntie Mary seems to fill out her clothes a bit better by the time we have enjoyed our soup, chicken and bread. I feel full up and glad, as if I have achieved something small but good.

# Miss Emily Intervenes
## in a Family Matter

Since Ada arrived, the hens have been laying again. Father styled her a sorceress recently, and he may be right. He was alarmed when she carved a grimacing face into a rutabaga and stuck a candle in it. She called it a "turnip lantern" and sat it by the stove. There it sent eerie shadows around the kitchen walls.

I feel that Ada has bewitched the hens with her Irish charm; she has used her sorcery to cajole them into laying, for since June they have done nothing so crude as produce an egg. I have heard her scold the fowl, calling, "Come out of that, you little slieveens," to coax them from their boxes.

This morning I encounter Ada scouring through the deepest grass in the garden, her behind cocked like a bantam's. A light rain falls, but she dips and lifts, moving from patch to patch. I stand to watch. Before she places each egg into her basket, she raises it to her mouth and puts her tongue against the shell.

"Ada, what are you doing?" I call.

"Gathering a clutch of eggs, miss," she says, with that guile-lessness that all her kind use, though there is a certain sly element to it.

"You're licking them!"

"I'm making sure they're all right, miss. Mrs. Child says that if you hold the large end of the egg to your tongue and it feels warm, it's fresh. If it feels cold, it's bad." She shrugs.

"Our beloved Mrs. Child."

"It's a very good book, Miss Emily," Ada says, a chiding tone to her voice.

"Well, I am glad of the abundance of eggs, as I mean to make a coconut cake for Susan, to comfort her in the last of her confinement. Women like to eat sweet things toward the end."

"They certainly do, miss. My mammy spooned sugar into her mouth right before each of my sisters was born. She couldn't even wait to sprinkle it on her bread."

I sit on the stone bench, though it is damp. "Ada, join me."

"You'll get your end, Miss Emily, sitting in the rain with no shawl or bonnet."

"And you, Ada, won't you get *your* end?"

"Not at all, miss. I'll go at the house like the hammers of hell shortly, and I'll be warmed up in no time." She tilts her face skyward. "I like a soft day, miss. I can't get along with all that sun. My skin's not used to it."

"I, too, love a drizzly day, Ada."

"I had a letter from my mammy."

"Was it a good letter? Did she send you news?"

Ada frowns. "Ah, Mammy is not great at the writing. It was mostly about her hope that our Lord will preserve me and that my workload is not too heavy. I wanted to hear stories of my sisters. Of the neighbors. Of home."

"How many sisters do you have, Ada?"

"Seven. I'm the eldest."

"How lovely! When I was a girl, I longed for more sisters, dozens of them. I made friends at school, of course, but Father feared for my health and dragged me home so often that I could never settle into my friendships."

"I was only a couple of years in school myself. Long enough to learn to read and write, I suppose."

I spy Austin barreling toward us from the Evergreens. Ada sees him, too, and stands up. My brother stops in front of us, his face pinched.

"Hello, Austin," I say, but he ignores me.

He looks down on Ada. "You are not in my father's home that his family may purchase leisure," he says. "You are here to assist, and for that reason I do not wish to find you idling on my parents' time."

Ada picks up her basket of eggs, and I rise to defend her, but Austin holds up his hand to me, so I do not speak. He turns and marches back toward his own house. My brother's eruptive nature pains me when it spills over in this way.

"I had better get back," Ada murmurs.

"Little Emerald Ada. Do not look so morose." Though Austin has maddened me, I defend him. "My brother is preoccupied with family matters and with work. His clients are demanding, and that makes him disagreeable, which in turn causes him to lash out. You were in his path, that is all."

"No, Miss Emily, it is true that I was idling."

Ada takes her basket and walks off; she prods again in the grasses. I watch her for a time, her deft bend-and-lift. I go to find Mother to urge her to tell Austin not to poke in our household affairs.

※

Mother, of course, defends her son. And what is worse, she castigates Ada for sitting outside "chitchatting."

I seek Ada out in the cellar. "Try not to dwell on Mother's reprimand, Ada."

"I've been taken up before for being too much of a talker," she says, carefully laying the eggs into a straw-lined crate for storage.

"Ada, Mother was never a successful youngster, so she does not understand the youthful. Bear that in mind, and you will make better sense of her."

"She is my mistress. There's not much need for understanding between us."

I wish that Mother would have a care, and Austin, too; what need has he to march over from his house to ours? Ada executes her work with grace and efficiency. She is stronger than Margaret O'Brien ever was, being ripe and flushed with energy. Mother should be more appreciative, more thoughtful toward Ada; she knows how arduous the work of the entire house can be. It is a lot to expect, but sometimes I wish Mother would *think* more. Her mind is not as elastic as it should be, as it *could* be—if she bothered to stretch herself. It is a sorry thought, but the act of thinking seems to be one that evades my mother most days.

❧

I scrape the meat from two coconuts and measure out the sugar, flour and butter. Ada helps me to separate the eggs; their yolks are bright as marigolds. She is subdued, and I fear that Mother's chiding has injured her.

"Ada, Mother suffers at times with neuralgia. You mustn't think that she is angry with you. Her head hurts wildly, and that makes her temper short."

She lifts her blue eyes to mine. "It's not that, miss. My Auntie Mary seems very down in herself. She didn't get out of the bed the last few mornings, and it's not like her at all. She normally jigs around the place. She loves to be busy."

"Has the doctor been called?"

"She won't hear of it, miss, and that is what is worrying Uncle Michael and me."

❧

"Mrs. Maher—that is, Ada's aunt—is not well, Father."

He removes his spectacles and looks up from his papers. "And you mean to fix her with cake, Emily, and I am to be its messenger."

"No, Father. I think she needs to see Dr. Brewster. She has not as yet seen a physician."

"Illness should never be ignored." Father lays down his pen. "I will see that Brewster visits Kelley Square today."

I knew that Father, the chief guardian of health, would not let me down. I go to the garden and drag it for winter roses. I give them to Ada for her aunt with my kindest regards.

"Your countryman Moore wrote of the last rose of summer," I say. "These blooms are that rose's children." Ada drops her nose into their pink heads and thanks me. Her heart lies so exposed; I can see that she is immensely touched by the flowers. "Give my very best to Mrs. Maher."

"Will you not come over and see my aunt yourself, miss?"

"I will come soon, Ada," I tell her, knowing as I say it that I am uttering a lie.

But how can I explain that each time I get to the threshold, my need for seclusion stops me? The quarantine of my room—its peace and the words I conjure there—call me back from the doorway. Ada could not truly appreciate that the pull on me of words, and the retreat needed to write them, is stronger than the pull of people. Yes, words summon me to the sacramental, unsullied place where my roaming is not halted or harnessed by others. My mind and heart are only free in solitude, and there I must dwell. I take her hands in mine and wish her Godspeed and her aunt a full and hasty recovery.

## Miss Ada Is Laid Low by Grief

EVERYTHING HAS LOST ITS SHINE, AND MY HEART IS DOWN ON the floor. Auntie Mary is dead, and what useful thing can be said about it? One day she is sitting in the Amherst House eating a fine dinner with me; a week later she is laid out to be waked in the parlor of the house she loved so well. She lies below with two pennies on her eyes that she brought all the way from Tipperary for the purpose.

I don't own a black dress, but Miss Emily has fashioned silk mourning ribbons to pin to my red merino, and she lends me her pendant of basalt and gold to wear at my throat. She comes from the Homestead to Kelley Square to help me get ready, though I know it pains her to leave the house.

"I can't believe Auntie Mary is gone," I say, looking out at the train tracks from my bedroom window, which now feels like the bleakest spot in the world. "There's something so very sad about dying far from the place you were born. To not be buried from the church you were baptized in. It's like Auntie's life went in a line, not a circle, as it should have."

Miss Emily fastens the clasp of the mourning pendant at my neck. "Angels have borne your Aunt to that country in the white sky, of which we know little," she says.

"But where is she really, miss? That's the question that rattles in my head. Where is the whole of my Auntie Mary gone, the ins and outs of her?"

"I cannot say. But the birds keep singing, Ada, and perhaps that is the hardest thing."

"Yes, they do keep singing. And Auntie Mary would have approved of that."

We go down, and Miss Emily stands with me at the coffin. I squeeze her hand.

"Auntie Mary talked less in the last week, as if words didn't matter anymore. I should have known she was getting ready to leave us altogether."

"Death comes stealthily, Ada. He doesn't wish that we catch him in the act." She sighs. "You will grieve, Ada, and sometime soon will come a new beginning in your grief, and it will be like a bloodletting. Then, only then, shall you go on again with grace."

I nod and think about what she says; I have not had to deal much with family death, and it fills me with a great loneliness for my own people, my own place. The parlor hums softly with the noise and warmth of all who have gathered. Daniel Byrne stands by the wall, and when he sees me look at him, he half raises his hand and knots his brow. But it's a well-meant frown, I know that. I smile, though my cheeks are stiff, making it hurt a little to do so.

Mrs. Sweetser has sent her girl to make the tea and serve it, so that I won't have to do it myself, or my cousin Annie either. I am sure Miss Emily is behind that, and it unburdens my heart to think of her kindness. She takes her leave after a short stay.

Uncle Michael, Annie and I stand over Auntie Mary, keeping watch until my cousin Maggie, who has yet to come from Connecticut, arrives. Uncle won't close the coffin until she gets here.

The boys will not come from California; Uncle has written to them but his letter will not have reached them yet, of course.

Some of Annie's children run and trip about the house—it is just another day to them, and so it should be—but Uncle finds their noise distressing. He throws sharp glances at them, and more than once he covers his ears with his palms. Daniel Byrne sees this and takes the children in hand, bustling them out onto the street. I am grateful to him, as is Cousin Annie, though she would not stoop to thank him. I link Uncle Michael's arm to continue our vigil by Auntie.

"She is looking her best," I say. "Her own gentle self is to be seen on her face."

"My heart is in smithereens, Ada. I miss her," Uncle Michael says. "She's still here, and I miss her."

I press my hand to his arm and gaze on Auntie. She is quiet and gathered, free now from the pain the doctor said she must have endured a long time. Poor Auntie Mary. She called for my mammy—her darling Ellen—at the end.

"Ellen," she said. "Ellen, *a leana*, will we go now? I feel I am ready to go."

And poor Mammy, three thousand miles away in Tigoora, doesn't even know yet that her sister is gone.

The house empties out, apart from some of the Tipperary people who will keep Uncle Michael company long into the night. I go in search of Daniel Byrne. I find him, still outside with the children, tossing a ball. He cups his hands around the hands of the littlest ones, to show them how better to catch. They do well under his guidance, whooping when they make a success of it. His patience with them touches me.

"Daniel."

The children scatter, and Daniel comes to me. "Ada, how are you now?"

"I'm grand, I suppose."

"What words of comfort can I offer? It's a sad thing to lose one so dear."

He holds out his hand, and I take it, surprised to find it is hot when he has been in the cool air for such a long spell. His hand is large around mine; he presses the skin of my palm with his fingers, and there is immense comfort in his touch.

"Thank you for taking the children out. Their noise was upsetting my uncle."

"I could see that."

Daniel pulls me toward him. "I'm fond of you, Ada. I hope you know that."

It is strange to stand so close to a man, though with Daniel it feels natural and good. But my insides are tumbled up, too, with grief and weariness, and I am afraid to look into his face. I finally manage to lift my eyes to his. I nod, thank him again and, pulling my hand from his, I go back into the house.

༜

I am taking out the slops while the Dickinsons eat their breakfast. The smell of the frying meat and potatoes made me feel sick a while ago, and now the stink from the chamber pots is doing the same. My stomach has been a strange, churning pit since Auntie Mary left us. I sit on the stairs to gather myself. So quickly do I have to leap up when I hear footsteps coming toward me that I nearly spill the contents of the pots down my apron. Mrs. Dickinson is upon me before I am properly standing.

"Begging your pardon, ma'am, I came over a bit queer, that's all."

"No matter, Ada. I was sorry to hear about Mrs. Maher. I trust yesterday's funeral was a success."

"It was, ma'am."

"The years dull the knife of a pain that stabs."

She brushes past me, on up the staircase, and I stand there like an abandoned infant, tears plopping into the chamber pot and the smell from it making my throat close off. I nearly wish they wouldn't be kind and would just let me get on with my work. Every gentle word and sympathetic look from them has me blubbing like a gossoon no matter how hard I push against it.

Miss Emily tells me that I look drawn, and it is no surprise to me, as I am not getting much sleep.

"I'm very tired, miss," I tell her. "My cousin Maggie has turned me out of her bedroom. I couldn't argue, of course, when she has lost her mother, but truly, I'm fit to be tied. I was comfortable there. Maggie marches around Kelley Square like the queen of Sheba, complaining about every small thing. Thankfully, I rise to come here before she gets up. And I'm so fagged out by evening that I take to the bed the minute I'm home, but she certainly lets everyone know that she is back."

Miss Emily is showing me how to make quince jelly, and the apple perfume of the fruit fills the air until I feel I might swoon. "I've only met Maggie Maher once," Miss Emily says. "I thought her ferocious and mighty."

"Huh. Maggie would love that. Every evening she sits around the place, bawling over Auntie Mary. She keens like a crone when she'd be better off staying quiet. Even Uncle Michael is fed up with her carrying on. She ruins every meal he tries to take, with her histrionics."

Miss Emily begins to mash the fruit. "I could write to Mrs.

Boltwood and ask her to summon your cousin back to Connecticut."

"Oh." I look at her. "Would that be fair, miss? She's mourning the same as myself. More so. She has no mother now."

"A little sparrow tells me she is needed. We will say nothing more of it."

Her decision quietens me. I wonder if it is fair on Uncle for Maggie to be sent back to Connecticut. But surely he would not mind so much? Maggie upsets the house, from dawn till dusk. It would most likely be a relief to him to have some peace. Miss Emily hands me the cheesecloth to flatten out and gives me a conspiratorial smile. Together we place two layers of the cloth over a pot and pour the fruit onto them. The way she takes the jelly making in hand reminds me of Mammy. I the pupil, she the teacher.

"I've had no mother to speak a word to this three months, miss. I'm only realizing that Auntie Mary was as good as a mother to me, now that she's gone."

"Yes, a mother is one to whom you go when you have troubles, I suppose, to get them smoothed over. I rarely run to mine." She wipes her hands briskly. "But I am here for you, Ada. You may speak all your sorrows to me." I don't know what to say to this; I am grateful for her care, but does she mean she never talks to her own mother? I have nothing to say, so I say nothing.

❧

The last golden leaf of autumn is hanging from a spider's thread at my bedroom window. I sit on my bed and watch it reel and twirl, as surely as if there is life inside it. I am so entranced by the leaf's mad dance that I am startled to realize there is somebody standing in the room. I turn to see my cousin peering down at me.

"Maggie! There you are—I didn't hear you knock."

"That's because I didn't knock," she says. "This is my father's house. *My* house. I don't have to knock." She gives me her bossiest look. "I'm going back to Connecticut. But before I leave, you'll have to find somewhere else to live."

"I beg your pardon?"

"You heard me, Ada. Daddy is a widower now, and I can't have the two of you alone here together. It's not right. Father Sullivan raised the matter with me after the funeral."

Maggie is not looking at me; rather she glares over my head and out the window. She wears a Florence bonnet trimmed with electric blue ribbon that surely once belonged to Mrs. Boltwood and a smart wool cape. It's far from Slievenamon she is in her rig-out; imagine her tripping down the mountain to Fethard with those ribbons flying.

I stand up to face her. "Your mother would have wanted me to stay and take care of Uncle Michael."

She snorts. "Take care of him? And you kowtowing to that Emily Dickinson with every hour that God sends."

"I work for the Dickinsons, Maggie, the same as you work for the Boltwoods. And I do my bit here."

"That pair of auld ghouls. And their two daughters, with neither chick nor child between them and not a hope of it either."

I don't bother to point out that she is a spinster the same as the Misses Dickinson.

I feel homesick; I want Mammy and the sweet repose of home. I look straight at Maggie. "Where will I go?" I ask.

"How am I to know? You'll not stay under this roof anyway, if I have to turn you out myself." She pulls on the ribbons of her silly bonnet and ties them under her chin. "I'll speak to Daddy.

For now I have an appointment with Father Sullivan before I leave for Connecticut." She waves her hand like departing royalty. "You keep the bedroom nice, I'll say that for you." Maggie turns and goes, and I hear her humming a tune to herself as she walks down the stairs. The strap.

# Miss Emily Welcomes Miss Martha Dickinson to the Family

SUSAN BRINGS THE BABY TO ME, FOR I DO NOT WISH TO LEAVE the house, even for the short jog along the path to the Evergreens. I went to Kelley Square for the waking of Ada's aunt and felt gut-punched for days afterward. But, for Ada, I went.

Baby Martha is a bonny girl, stout and alert, even at eight days old. She was born one day after Thanksgiving, so Sue managed to enjoy her pumpkin pie and turkey before the joyous—and no doubt arduous—event.

Last night I picked white chrysanthemums from the garden for Susan. I peered into their tightly wadded, half-ugly faces and bade them watch over my dear Dollie and her baby daughter.

"Chrysanthemums smell of Thanksgiving, don't you think, Sue?" I say, handing them to her. She smiles and nods, and I help her out of her sealskin cape. She looks wan and tired; guilt plucks at me, but she had assured me in a note that she was strong enough to walk the path to the Homestead.

Before sitting, Susan hands Martha to me, and the baby looks out from under her lace bonnet like an old soul delivered from the heavens. Her weight on my arm, the heavy heat of her head, is wondrous to me. I sit on Mother's chair, opposite Sue, who is settled on the sofa.

"'For you formed my inward parts; you knitted me together in my mother's womb. I praise you, for I am fearfully and wonderfully made.'"

"Is that something you wrote, Emily?" Susan asks.

"For shame—you do not know your Psalms, Mrs. Gilbert-Dickinson!" I dip my head to Martha. "You are both fearfully and wonderfully made, my little one."

The baby feels gangly in my arms—an uncontrollable parcel of limbs, torso and head. But she is soft—so soft—too, and fragrant. She has that sweet, creamy smell that hovers around all babies. I gather her closer to me, and she nuzzles into my chest.

"Greedy, like her father," Susan says, and we giggle at this small betrayal of both Austin and Baby.

Susan unbuttons her bodice, then stretches over and takes Martha. I watch amazed as the baby catches herself expertly onto Sue's breast and begins to suck contentedly. I do not have any recollection of seeing Sue nurse Ned, though of course she must have. The baby makes a bundle of sweet noises as she suckles, little snuffle-clicks and grunts.

"I can hear the milk hitting her throat," I say, and Sue smiles, justly proud that she has succumbed to neither wet nurse nor goat's milk.

I look shyly at Sue's exposed breast, so white and full, and veined, too, with a tracery of blue. I sit beside her on the sofa and link her arm.

"I have missed you, Sue."

"I have not been anywhere lately, Emily, save at home."

"No, but when you carry a baby, you change. You become a remote Madonna, wandering the world slowly with head held high. You're unreachable in that state." I lean in to stroke Martha's cheek while she feeds.

"Really, Emily, you say the most provocative things some-times. A remote Madonna indeed!" Sue smiles and slots her pinkie into Martha's mouth. Her breast falls, heavy but deflated, while the baby bucks, her face collapsing into outrage. Martha wails, and Susan struggles to settle her wriggling daughter. I am about to speak when there is a short rap on the door and Ada comes in with our coffee.

"I brought you some beef tea as well, Miss Susan. Mammy always took it in the weeks after birthing, and she swore it was why she got back to herself so quick."

"How thoughtful," Sue says. "I thank you." She places Martha on her shoulder and rubs her back to soothe her cries.

Ada lingers by the parlor door, and I can see that she is itching to speak again.

"Yes, Ada?"

"Could I lift the baby? It's just that I miss my sisters, and . . . well, I'd like to hold her for a moment, if you didn't mind, Miss Susan."

"Of course, dear."

I have Ada sit in Father's wing chair, and Susan places Martha in her arms. The baby stops whimpering and looks up into Ada's face. As Susan walks back toward me, I see Ada spit on her finger and rub a cross onto the baby's forehead. She lifts Martha close to her face; they stare at each other like two old friends getting reac-quainted after a long separation. Ada puts the baby to her shoulder and strokes her back, up and down, eyes closed; she looks content and whole, every inch the little mother. Martha emits a long, gur-gling belch, and we all three laugh.

"Well now," Ada says, "you have room in there for more, Miss

Martha." She stands up, carries the baby to her mother, then leaves us.

"I am sure that is the happiest I have seen Ada since her aunt died," I say, to fill the silence that she has left in her wake.

"That girl makes me shiver somehow," Susan says, lifting Martha to her other breast. "Does she quite know her place?"

I look at my friend and will myself to defend Ada vigorously. The best I can manage is, "Yes, she does. And she is lovely, truly," to which Susan shrugs.

Sue is a puzzle to me sometimes. We are sisters, and we love each other, but she does not always see the world as I do, and often this takes me aback. Foolishly perhaps, I want those I love the most to be as *I* am, to see everything as *I* do. And, therefore, to like *all* of those who are dear to me, which now must include Ada.

❦

"Martha is a good, solid name," Ada says, lining up our jars of quince jelly, ready for the cellar. The jelly is amber-colored and nicely set, a successful batch.

"Yes, it is. A bequest from the Bible. But I think Ada is the most perfect of names. A palindrome, complex in its very simplicity."

"Miss, you may as well be talking gibberish for all I understand you."

"Your name is the same front and back: A-D-A." I draw a line in the air first forward, then backward. "A-D-A."

"But sure I know that," she says. "Come on, get the basket, and we'll bring these jars below. It gives me the all-overs going down there by myself."

I stack the jars into the big wicker, and we take either side of the handle and shuffle down the back stairs.

"Why were you named Ada?"

"Why is a fly a fly? Why were you named Emily?"

"For my mother, of course."

She stops, and we set down the basket. "Mrs. Dickinson is called Emily, too? Well, my goodness, I never knew that." She shakes her head. "It certainly gives the lie to the name suiting the wearer."

"I can't imagine what you mean," I say, but I elbow her in the side, to let her know that her meaning is very clear to me.

We stack the jars of quince and go back up to the kitchen. Ada moves slowly and stops often to take a moment of reverie. I sit at the table and watch her adding sticks to the stove. She squats, feeding twigs one by one, watching them crackle and flame.

"What is it, Ada?"

She sits back on her hunkers. "Miss Emily, how well you know me. I'm glum in myself."

"It is hard to lose a beloved relative."

"Well, it's not only that, miss. Father Sullivan says I've to leave my uncle's house in Kelley Square, and my cousin Annie says she can't take me in—with her brood of children there isn't the room. And I feel terrible about leaving Uncle Michael alone anyway. He's turned inside out since Auntie Mary died."

"And must you obey this Father Sullivan?"

She looks up at me with moon eyes. "Yes, miss. Him *and* Cousin Maggie, who started this whole palaver, as you know."

"But you will come and live here, Ada. You may occupy Margaret O'Brien's old quarters."

"Mrs. Dickinson won't agree to that, surely? No doubt she likes having her house back to herself and the family."

"Don't worry about her, or Father."

Ada snaps a few more sticks and pushes them into the blaze. "I wasn't looking for that, miss, you know. It never occurred to me."

"I know, my Emerald Ada. I will speak to my parents, and all will be well."

"You're awful good to me, Miss Emily," she says.

"Think nothing of it."

Ada grins, rubs her hands briskly and looks around to see what work to tackle next.

# Miss Ada Walks Out with a Man

MISS EMILY HELPED ME ARRANGE THINGS IN MY BEDROOM AS IF I were a valued guest, furnishing me with enough candles for a year and a brass bedside holder with its own snuffer cap. I didn't like to tell her that Uncle Michael had gifted me an oil lamp of Auntie Mary's; the candles would do if I ran out of oil. She heaped rugs and coverlets on my bed.

"Against the drafts. The windows can be whistly in this room. I don't want cold to bother you." She looked around, satisfied with her help. "Ada, I hope you will be more than comfortable here."

"I will, miss, I feel settled already."

Miss Emily pulls people toward her; that's the type she is—she blankets them in her friendship. She and Miss Susan let me hold Martha, the new baby. The gorgeous feel of the little one seemed to fill me up and open me out. I was surprised to find Miss Susan visiting so soon after the confinement, but it seems the pair of them would do anything for each other. Mr. Austin and his wife may be more burdensome to wait on than the other Dickinsons, but they are certainly fond of Miss Emily and always go out of their way for her. And they produce gorgeous children; Little Ned is a star of a child, and Miss Martha is as placid a babe as any mother could hope for. I held her and allowed my mind to conjure thoughts of babies of my own.

༓

I am seated on a stool that Miss Vinnie gave me from her room for my bedroom—"For lacing your boots," she said. The family have been nothing but kind since I moved here, and the Homestead's bright, familiar rooms seem to welcome me as an old friend. Uncle Michael was upset when I left Kelley Square, and I was, too, but we both knew I had to leave; we couldn't go against Father Sullivan, whatever about Maggie. I miss Uncle's daily company, but there is a privacy in this house that I enjoy. For the first time ever, I am on my own; I do not have the crutch of family to hold me up. And I like the powerful feeling that gives me—it brings a rare contentment.

Boots laced, I go down the front stairs and dip out through the conservatory; I see Daniel Byrne ambling up from the orchard. He stops for a moment, then comes along toward me. I pull my shawl tight around my neck against the cold.

"Hello, Ada," he says, smiling.

"Daniel. There you are." He stands before me and shuffles his feet. "Were you down boxing the fox?" I tease. "Should I search your pockets for Dickinson apples?"

"Sure there isn't an apple left below," he says, grinning. I get a picture of him in my mind, up a tree as a boy, filling his rolled-up shirt with stolen apples and sneaking away somewhere to crunch on them until his stomach groans. Daniel holds up a ragged rug. "I'm going to drape this around the pump, to stop it freezing."

"That would be a help to me. It's a curse when the water goes to ice." The low winter sun makes his hair glow. "Well, I'd better be getting on." I make to go back to the kitchen. "The meat and chestnuts won't roast themselves."

"Ada, would you be at all interested in going to the circus with me? The Van Amburgh will be on the common from Friday, and it's meant to be a spectacle."

"I heard that, all right."

"Have you heard the song?" He pulls himself up straight and begins to chant:

> *"'Van Amburgh is the man, who goes to all the shows,*
> *He goes into the lion's cage, and tells you all he knows;*
> *He sticks his head in the lion's mouth, and keeps it*
> *there awhile,*
> *And when he pulls it out again, he greets you with a*
> *smile.'"*

I giggle and clap, surprised by his boldness, surprised that he knows such a song at all. Daniel bows.

"Does your man really put his head in the lion's mouth?" I ask.

"I have no clue. Why don't we go along and see?"

"I'll have to ask Mrs. Dickinson about finishing early on Friday."

"Well, let me know. I'll be around the yard all this week." Daniel tips his cap and strolls away.

I examine the gait of his long body as he saunters off toward the barn. He is a manly man, no doubt about it. I smile to myself, thinking he must know that I am watching him go, that I am taking him in. I wait until he is inside the barn before I dip back into the house to be welcomed by the kitchen's pleasant heat.

❦

The night is biting. The New England cold is not at all like the cold in Dublin; it is sharper and meaner altogether. Earlier the rags I washed and pinned froze on the clothesline; they hung, stiff little flags, waving dully, the very opposite of summer bunting. How forlorn the rags looked after all my work to make them usable again.

But it is not washing or work of any kind I want to think of now, ambling up Main Street beside Daniel, in the thick of the throng that makes for the common and Van Amburgh's tent. A drone of voices drifts above the crowd; people seem excited, a little anxious, maybe. I have my Navarino bonnet on and some old kid gloves of Miss Emily's—she said my woolen mittens were too coarse for walking out with a man. I look up at Daniel; he is handsome in that Irish way—he has a bit of a jaw on him, but that is balanced out by good, even features and generous hair. It occurs to me that Mammy would like him, and the thought pleases me.

Mrs. Dickinson gave me a talk this morning, summoning me to her bedroom for all two minutes of it. Her room—if possible— is even sparser than my own, with little more than bed and bureau. I stood a long time waiting for her to speak; I wondered if she expected me to divine what was on her mind.

"Rouge spoils the complexion," she said at last. "Don't wear any." She stared at me, and I stared at the tallow of her bedside candle, which was running. I wanted to pinch the wick or blow out the flame, to stem the flow. "Only vulgar women paint themselves," she said. And then, "You may leave."

It wasn't in my plan to wear rouge—it makes girls look wanton, I think—but after she spoke to me I felt like going down to Cutler's to buy a pot. Just for pig iron. But I wasn't sure that Daniel would like to see me painted up, so I didn't.

Daniel puts his hand to my back now to guide me into the circus tent. Truth be told, I am wary, though it takes a bit to scare me. The place is dim, and it stinks of dirty straw and manure. The men are rowdy, shouting to one another; the women are quiet, looking at everything. An Irish lad I recognize from about the town lunges in front of us. He is a tall chap, well made, and he grins a lot.

"There you are, miss," he says to me.

"Hello."

"Don't get caught up in that Danny Byrne's capers, miss," he says. "You'll be sorry."

"I can mind myself."

"I'd say you can, all right. Is it the Dickinsons you do for? I thought I saw you around their place." He offers me his hand. "Patrick Crohan."

"Ada Concannon." I hold out my hand, and he squeezes it warmly. "Yes, I work for the Squire and his family."

Daniel steps forward. "Will you go away out of that, Crohan. Can't you see she's with me? Find a girl for yourself."

"We're only talking, Byrne."

"Well, take your talk elsewhere. Come on, Ada."

"Go on, you go-boy!" Crohan roars, though he is standing right beside us.

"I'll lace you, Crohan, if you don't stop," Daniel says. Then, to me, "Don't mind him, Ada." He steers me up the wooden stairs to take our seats.

"I wasn't minding him. He seems all right. Who is he?"

"Nobody," Daniel says. "Well, I work for his uncle."

I look back, and Crohan is watching us go; the crowd streams around him. He waves and grins, and I smile at him. Daniel and I sit, and a small orchestra starts a rousing beat. A parade of women troops into the ring; they are half dressed in spangles and fur, and some of the men whistle and call to them. The women bend their bodies back like bridges and flick their legs over their heads; they turn cartwheels around the floor. They go on and on with this until I am mesmerized by their elastic grace and by the music; their skin gleams in the light. The women have hard faces and hard bodies. The way they dance makes me wonder about their lives—if they ever do ordinary things, like bake bread or scrub steps, or if their whole day is about tumbling, twirling and putting on costumes.

The music hurtles on—the same lively tune over and over—and the women dance out through the curtains. In trots a tiny pony, a child-size fella who is not much bigger than a lamb.

"My God, look at that pony. What a scut," I say, relieved that the women with their bare, flashing legs have disappeared.

"It's from South America," Daniel says, and there is a giddiness in his voice. He leans up out of his seat to get a better view. "And it's a horse, Ada. Not a pony at all. A horse!"

He ripples with energy, and I enjoy watching his excitement. The curtain opens, and three more teeny horses trip out into the ring. The circus master cracks a whip, and they run around, tossing their long manes from their eyes.

When the horses leave, a troop of clowns trick-act their way through mishaps involving chairs and buckets and water. My cheeks ache from laughing, and we all pound our feet for more when the clowns bounce and roll through the back curtain.

The hard-faced women return; each one lights a torch from a brazier and places it in a circle around a box in the middle of the ring. The box is entirely covered in black cloth. The women dance to the edge and stand there, and in time to a terrific drumbeat a man marches in and goes toward the box. He is draped in what looks like a small white sheet—it barely covers him—and his brown legs glisten in the torchlight. In one huge sweep, he pulls the black cloth away to reveal a cage with a lion inside it. We all gasp. The lion lopes up and down, tossing its head; up and down, back and forth it goes, looking bored and, maybe, annoyed.

Van Amburgh—for it can only be he—lets himself into the cage and faces the lion. He picks up a stout stick and pounces forward, waving it in the lion's face. I can barely look, I am so sure the big cat will wrench off his arm at any moment. Or his head.

"God protect him," I murmur. Daniel reaches over and takes my hand in his.

Van Amburgh holds the stick aloft and snaps the fingers of his other hand over and over above the lion's snout. The animal opens its jaw, gapes it wide and wider, showing its long teeth. Lines of spit swing in its mouth, a dark cave from which, I fear, a mighty sound will escape any second. I sit and cringe, huddled against Daniel's side. The man plunges his arm into the lion's mouth, and, miraculously, the great cat does not close his maw around it. Van Amburgh dips swiftly, keeping up a manic jig, and inserts his head between the lion's jaws. There is not a pip from the audience. We crane forward watching the man hold himself still in the beast's mouth. The torchlight makes everything flickery and slow. Suddenly the lion jumps backward, away from Van Amburgh, and tosses his mane; he roars, but it is a gentle sound, like a throat clearing. Everyone claps; some people pound their feet on the wooden steps, and the din all around is ferocious. Daniel grins at me, and my heart leaps into my throat.

We fix our eyes once more on Van Amburgh. He waves his stick, calling for silence, and approaches the lion again. The big cat seems to have had enough—he sits, then lies down at the back of the cage. Van Amburgh roars, "Rise now!"

The lion doesn't move, and neither does he lift his head to look at his master. Again Van Amburgh shouts at him, and again the lion sits like a cat in front of a fire, refusing to stir. The man begins to beat the lion, and I can hear—and almost feel—the dull thud of the wood against the creature's back. The whole tent goes quiet; the only sound is the wallop of the stick against hide— *fwack, fwack, fwack*. All around me people wince; mothers cover their small children's eyes, but some of them start to bawl anyway. A woman sitting in the front row stands and begins to hiss. Boys and girls take up the hissing, and men start to boo. The lion cowers, and Van Amburgh belts him again and again.

"Oh, this is not right, Daniel," I say, "it's not right at all." My stomach turns to jelly, and I want to leave; I cannot stand to see an animal so poorly treated. Men get to their feet and shout their protests.

Daniel jumps up and shouts, "Leave off!" at Van Amburgh.

Van Amburgh steps from the cage, and the lion rises and returns to pacing, but slower this time. It opens its jaws, and the teeth are like daggers. People are stamping their feet and shouting, "Boo, boo!" Van Amburgh holds up his hands; I don't like the beards of black under his arms, the screeds of coarse hair. It looks horrible to me, and I turn my face away. The crowd goes slowly silent.

"Did not God himself say," Van Amburgh shouts, "in Genesis 1:26, that men should have dominion over every animal on earth?" I look back at him, standing with his hands aloft like a preacher. "And God said, 'Let us make man in our image, after our likeness: and let them have dominion over the fish of the sea, and over the fowl of the air, and over the cattle, and over all the earth, and over every creeping thing that creepeth upon the earth.'"

"You're the creeper!" Daniel shouts. "You're no better than

any animal!" He pulls me by the arm to let me know that we are leaving.

We descend the steps, and all around us people start to get up from their seats, too. A silent sea of people drifts forward, turns its back to Van Amburgh and leaves the tent. We surge out into the cold night and walk away.

# Miss Emily and Miss Ada Celebrate Birthdays

I WANT A BLACK CAKE FOR MY BIRTHDAY, FOR IT BRINGS THE winter season tight to me, it seems. Ada is back from Cutler's with my prunes, apricots and a little nutmeg for shredding. I am ready to begin the brandy syrup when she asks me, rather timidly, if she may help.

"Get some of your exalted butter, Ada, and grease the milk pan for me. Mother vaunted your butter to the skies when our cousins were here from Boston. It would have pleased you to hear her." I line up everything and take stock. "We need nineteen eggs for this."

"That's a powerful lot of eggs, Miss Emily." Ada keeps her head bent while she slips the butter across the pan and rubs it in.

"Is anything the matter?"

She shakes her head, then looks up at me. "I'm not right since I went to that circus. Honest to God, it was like bedlam. Your man—the lion fella—is half mad, I think."

"What happened?"

"He stuck his head in the lion's mouth, but when the lion got fed up and didn't want to do more, he beat the tar out of him.

With a big fat stick. It was desperate, Miss Emily, very violent. The poor thing was terrified out of its wits. We could tell."

"His behavior sounds medieval. Did people object?"

"Most left, though the show was hardly begun. Daniel Byrne hooshed me out of the place before I knew what was what. But I was not sorry to go."

"I am glad to hear that Mr. Byrne took you away from it. The circus whips up such a frenzy when it overtakes the common. I cannot imagine that it is the safest place for animals. Or girls."

Still, I think, it would please me to walk among the tents and hear the *hoy-hoy* of the men, rallying their horses. I would like to see the women in their scant costumes, as they mince and trip, their bodies pliant and strong. Such lives as they have could never be mine.

I blend the sugar and butter, feeling the strain of the effort through my wrist and across my shoulders. Baking will make puffed-up brawn of my arms yet.

"Is this the cake you'll have for Christmas, miss?"

"No, Ada, this is my birthday cake. I like a flavor of the Caribbean to cheer up my Decembers."

"I was born in December, too, miss. The tenth of the month."

"Why, Ada," I say, laying down my spoon, "how wonderful! We share a birthday—*I* was born on the tenth."

"Well, if that doesn't beat all, Miss Emily. We're birthday twins."

"This shall be *our* cake in that case, and we will enjoy fat slices of it together on our birthday. How pleasing this is."

I take dried pears from their jar; they were as pink as plums when picked, with crinoline hips and the flesh of candies. Now they curl—silenced yellow tongues—in my hand. I glance at Ada, and she is smiling roundly, forgetting now her Daniel and his saving of her from the lion. She uses her hands to mix together raisins and citron rind; the smell is glorious.

"Daniel says it will snow before the week is out," she says, making me realize I do not see well into her heart, for it is her Danny who is causing her to smile and not our shared celebration after all.

> *"I stood and watched by the window*
> *The noiseless work of the sky,*
> *And the sudden flurries of snow-birds,*
> *Like brown leaves whirling by.'"*

"Oh, that's lovely, Miss Emily. Did you make that up yourself?"

"Alas, no, Ada—that is the work of Mr. Lowell, the poet. And I have rarely read anything as perfect as it." I am fighting the molasses through the dry ingredients, and, seeing my struggle, Ada takes over. "And yes, I believe that your Daniel is correct—it will snow soon." I pour a half-pint of brandy syrup into the mix and sniff deep on its fire.

> *"It sifts from Leaden Sieves—*
> *It powders all the Wood—*
> *It fills with Alabaster Wool*
> *The Wrinkles of the Road—'*

"There, that is a snow poem *I* composed."

"You are as much a poet as that Mr. Low, or whatever you call him. Snow coming from a sieve—that's perfect. Say it again, Miss Emily."

> *"It sifts from Leaden Sieves—*
> *It powders all the Wood—*
> *It fills with Alabaster Wool*
> *The Wrinkles of the Road—'"*

"It powders all the wood! Well, that is smashing. I can see it, I really can. You should do more of the writing, miss."

"Yes, Ada, I should. It is a matter of carving the time."

☙

I steal up to the cupola to look at a sugared Amherst. The snow is very deep—it reaches up to the wagons' stomachs, and they can move neither forward nor backward. They lie like corpses on a prairie from one end of Main Street to the other, their wheels poking through the top of the snow. With the wagons so abandoned, we will hear the ting of sleigh bells soon, at all hours. I knew that it would snow when the sky lay so huge, gray-yellow and brooding above. It snows slowly and somberly, the flakes scattering down on the town like an anointment. Men in dark cloaks drag themselves through the drifts, their factories and offices too crucial to forsake, it would seem. Father has already been out to scatter grain for the birds; he padded across ice in his slippers, and Mother scolded him. I was pleased that he put our winged friends before Mother's safeguarding of his health. Now he has set himself up in the dining room to peruse papers, but he does not want company, so I confine myself to wandering between my bedroom, the kitchen and my cold eyrie in the cupola. It is a taxing time for fingers and toes, and I am bundled in two shawls over my wrapper.

"You look like a vagrant," Vinnie says, meeting me on my way down from the cupola.

"I am cold. Come, let us do calisthenics, to warm up our blood."

"I prefer to take the broom to the stairs and sweep like a dervish. That is all the exercise I need," she says.

So, alone in my bedroom, I bend, jump, swing, twist and kick, feeling my body's resistance, until I am informed—by Ada—of Mother's resistance to my "thumping."

"You're like the wreck of the *Hesperus*," Ada says, to my panting form. "Now, give me your other dress and I'll get those ink spots out for you."

"You are full of business at all times, Ada."

"My world doesn't stop over a bit of weather," she says, and grunts to show how put-upon she is. I hand her the dress—my best piqué. "White as snow in no time, Miss Emily. But honest to God, why you gave up wearing your good brown is beyond me."

I follow her down to the kitchen. "I am like one of Vinnie's cats behind you," I say as her neat back descends the stairs ahead of me. "Do you notice how they trail her through the Homestead like a posse of devoted children?"

"When you get Miss Vinnie, you get cats, all right. I'm fed up with them and their fur. I dread that one day Mrs. Dickinson will find an island of cat hair floating in her soup."

"But they keep the mice away, and we should be grateful for that."

Ada warms milk in a pan, and I watch her soak the ink-spotted sleeves of my dress in it.

"By whatever miracle, the ink loosens and disappears in the milk," she says. "That Mrs. Child knows everything there is to know about cleaning. And more besides."

Ada's devotion to *The Frugal Housewife* amuses me and Vinnie. Mother, of course, made us read it, too, but our favorite parts were the anecdotes about fallen girls and how to raise children well and so forth. We would say to each other in grave voices, "Do not dress your children in restrictive clothing, if you wish them to be either healthy or pretty." I particularly liked the bit that said hair hanging over their foreheads would turn children's eyes. I would cross my eyes hugely, for Austin and Vinnie's entertainment.

But our most favorite passage was on womanly frivolity. Austin would pretend to read from *The Frugal Housewife* for us while exaggerating its content and tone. He glowered at us and said, "Did anyone admire this woman, this vain and foolish young thing, who served water in Boston and Sandwich crystal tumblers? Or did they exclaim over her placing of Irish linens by their plates? They did not! Ludicrous, conceited woman!"

Mrs. Child likes to make her point with drama, and I am totally in her favor because of that. Who does not want a narrative spun out of every small event? Who doesn't enjoy the richness of a good story? Mother threatened Vinnie and me with the deportment chair when she heard us make fun of *The Frugal Housewife*, but she never had us perch on the awful thing, for she knew we would find mischief to conduct there, too. Austin's renditions only made her smile and scold him mildly.

"Now, Miss Emily," Ada says, "are you going to sit there like a clump of muck, or are you going to do something useful?"

Her goose-blue eyes needle through me, and I know that she will not permit me to write a scrap in her lair today.

❧

The snow is no appreciator of persons; it enters the town extravagantly and distracts us all from the work at hand. All except Ada. I am trying to be very Dickinsonian in order that I may write—I do like to be churlish and muggy and dour—but the snow brings evenness and calm. I lack Austin's natural Dickinson grit, it seems. I have shunted my desk over to the window to watch the flakes descend like swans—here a wing expanded, there a whorling plume—and the beauty of it all consumes me, drags me to earth. That Susan, Austin and the children will spend Christmas at our table—hurrah!—is what occupies my thoughts, not the lines I might write. I hope that Austin will be convivial; he sometimes regains his old ways at feast times.

Vinnie enters my room, softly as a squaw; she stops before me and reads out a letter from our Norcross cousins to say they cannot come for my birthday. I gasp when she says they will stay at home.

"Of course they won't come," Vinnie says. "Nobody ventures forth on these frozen days that does not have to." She goes to my bed and flaps the pillows like a serf, then tucks the eiderdown neatly.

"How sad. For once I feel like having company."

"The Norcrosses will visit when it thaws, my dear."

"They have irritated me by refusing to come. I can't help it. Nay, they have wounded me. I do so wish they would just sit into a sleigh and visit."

Vinnie perches on the side of my bed. "Emily, please don't be ridiculous. Our cousins would put themselves in danger. You cannot wish for that."

"We could send our sleigh—it is superior to theirs."

"Father would not let the horses out, and you know it. The Norcrosses will stay at home."

"I say no a lot, but I cannot bear it from others. Is it not strange that I, who turn from so many, cannot tolerate it when others run from me?"

Vinnie comes to stand behind me; she pets my hair. "Our

cousins are not running from you, Emily. They simply cannot travel. They must not."

"I want to share love, Vinnie. How can I show my love if my closest ones will not spend time with me?"

She drapes her arms around my neck. "You show love in many ways, my dear. Just think of the fun we will have at Christmas, with Austin here to entertain us. And Susan and the babies. There will be ample opportunity for love and joy."

"Yes, of course. We will have sport, if Austin's mood is gay. And if Father permits laughter."

"Oh, Emily, you are being gloomy. I fancy you spend too much time with Ada and her woes. Those Irish drip with melancholy. Try to be pleasant. You know that Mother frets if all is not happy at home."

"I will try." I place my hand over Vinnie's. "But you misunderstand Ada if you see her as gloomy. She is all cheer with me."

"Come. You must lift yourself out of this seat and take the air. Go. I insist."

I rise and hug Vinnie and clamber down the stairs before I can change my mind. I fetch the least cumbersome pair of snowshoes and strap them on. Bundled up like an alpinist, I trudge through the garden. Pleasing suck-and-sump noises rise from my feet. The snow has stopped falling, and winter shines through the trees where mere weeks ago leaves murmured. Air cleaner and sweeter than any air I have tasted for a long time fills my mouth and nose. At the foot of the garden, I find a redpoll on a bush, chirping merrily to the sky.

"You sit here singing, and nobody can hear you. Why do you sing?"

He chirrups and cheeps, as if to say, "I live to sing." And so I am castigated by a red-capped, brown bird, browner— if it is possible—than my cloak.

I catch a movement from the corner of my eye and am alarmed to see a man coming toward me from the orchard. He is nobody I know. I step awkwardly in my snowshoes and pull myself up to accost him. The man tips his cap and plods on, his legs sinking into the snow up to his knees.

"Hallo! What do you want here?" I call to his retreating back. He is a big fellow, wide and tall.

He turns to face me. "Your father needs me to clear paths through the snow."

"And you are?"

"Patrick Crohan."

"Well, Patrick Crohan. Go about it. The shovels are in the barn."

"This is not my first time here." He shrugs and walks on.

"Well then," is all I can think of to say. His casual, insolent manner distracts me from saying anything more useful. I watch him go into the barn and wait for him to come out to begin clearing the snow, but he does not emerge.

# Miss Ada and Mr. Daniel Byrne Are Found Out

THE KITCHEN HAS A VIEW OF THE BARN. MISS EMILY TEASES ME that the builders put the window there especially for me so that I could keep an eye on "a certain someone" while he works. It is true that when I fill the lamps or pluck a chicken, my eyes wander to the window to see what I might see. Daniel is out there this morning with Moody Cook. Moody leads the Squire's favorite horse, Dick, out of the barn to shoe him. Mr. Dickinson prides himself on having the best horse in Amherst, and he is lavish in his care of him. Daniel washes Dick's feet, and because I have the window ajar to stop it from steaming, I can hear him coaxing the horse.

"Come on, sir," he says. "Come on, Dick, you're a belter. Good man. Whoa, now. Good man, Dick."

He goes on like that, relaxing the horse and talking him up at the same time. They're like two old butties having a one-sided chat. The horse's breath and Daniel's mingle in the freezing air. The yard is cleared of snow—the men shoveled it away—but the air is still frost-heavy. I think how cold Daniel's hands must be, and I long to warm them for him. I consider heating soapstones for him to slip into his pockets, but then Moody would know about us.

Daniel glances up and sees me poking my nose at the window. He raises his hand in salute, but I, like an eejit, dip backward. He has seen me and knows I have seen him, and now I feel properly foolish. I look around the kitchen for something to distract me from my blushes and realize that I have spent so much time gawping into the yard that I am late for setting the dining-room table for the family's breakfast. I get going, but I am still arranging delft and cutlery when they come in. I dish up the hash and apple-sauce, pour their coffee.

Mr. Dickinson steps up to the sideboard. "I will take an egg today, Ada. Would you care for eggs, my dears?"

The three women look from him to me and shake their heads. "Boiled, sir?"

"Poached," he says, sitting and lifting the *Springfield Republican* to his face. I am nearly out the door when he calls, "Not too much vinegar, Ada. You almost poisoned me with it last week." He shakes his paper. "'As vinegar to the teeth, and as smoke to the eyes, so is the sluggard to them that send him.' Is that not what Solomon says, Emily?"

"If you say so, Father."

The egg sets me back for finishing the plucking, which sets me back for getting the slops, which sets me back for starting the wash, which in turn means I will have less time to plan the Christmas feast. I can feel bars of annoyance threading through my spine, but I soften them because that way folly lies. I can hear Mammy saying, "God made time, Ada, but man made haste," so I decide I will take everything slowly and get it all done, regardless of the chores piling up.

The kitchen door swings wide and Moody Cook stands there grinning like the newly mad.

"Miss Concannon, a cup of tea and a slice of something delicious, if you please."

"Close that door and sit down. I'll get you a bit of soda bread."

"I'd eat the socks off a dead minister," Moody says.

The door opens again, and Daniel slides through; he stands, saying nothing. Something seems to beat off him and glow; he fills the room. I stop like a statue and stare at him, eventually squeaking, "Daniel," by way of welcome.

"Oh," says Moody, looking between the pair of us. "Oh and oh and oh." He rubs his hands together. "I will say nothing," he says, and chuckles to himself, "nothing at all."

Daniel looks at me, and my insides loosen and tighten in one quick jolt. "Tea, Daniel?"

"If you please, Ada."

I make tea and slice the bread. I roll some butter into a curl with a spoon and place it before the two of them on a tiny dish; I dollop jam onto a saucer. I cannot find it within myself to sit down, so I bustle about, seeing to my cares, and the two men chatter softly while I lift delft from one spot and place it on another, unsure of what to do with myself or how to behave. What I wish is that Moody Cook would vanish and I could take Daniel to my breast and hold him, right here in the kitchen. I would like to press my mouth to his and feel the heat of him. These wild thoughts nearly make me drop Mrs. Dickinson's white teapot, but I catch myself, and, face hot, I place it down carefully. Every bit of Daniel Byrne is pleasing to me, from his scalp to his toes, and I feel silly as a day-old chick when he is near me.

## Miss Emily Welcomes the Tenth of December

THE TENTH OF DECEMBER dawns snow-bright and cold. I find a rough package at my bedroom door. I unwrap the brown paper, and inside is a four-pronged cross made with folded rushes. It can only be from Ada. I place the cross over my bed, ready to defend it from Mother and Vinnie and anyone else who steps into my room.

In the kitchen Ada is wiping brasses with a rag dipped in rum. She rubs and haws, haws and rubs. The sugar-oaky smell of the rum is heady.

She holds up Vinnie's needle case to me. "Look at that, Miss Emily, you can see your face as good as in any mirror."

"Happy birthday, Ada," I say, and the words, to my surprise, emerge shyly.

She leaves down her work and stands. "And many happy returns to you, miss."

"The cross is beautiful."

She knots her fingers in front of her. "I brought it from home. Those are reeds from an Irish river, miss. It's a St. Brigid's cross. It keeps evil from the door, so it does. It has been over my own bed since I came, but I want you to have it."

"And now it is over mine. I thank you." I take out the small box I have been concealing in my pocket and hand it to her.

"There was no need," Ada says, but she is pink with pleasure and fumbles open the lid hastily. "Oh, it would take the sight out of your eye." She lifts the brooch I have given her and mock-pins it to her apron. "I've never owned anything like this. Anything as bright and lovely."

I had sent Vinnie to Cutler's to purchase Ada's gift, with guidelines as to what would be acceptable. She had chosen well.

"The pearls remind me of snow, and . . . well, I thought they would suit your dark hair."

Ada grins at me, reaches over and clasps my hand. "May God bless you, Miss Emily." Gathering herself, she puts the brooch back into its box and slips it into her apron pocket. Sitting again, she polishes the brasses. "St. Brigid performed miracle after miracle, you know. She tricked a king out of land by spreading out her cloak. It grew and grew, sucking up more and more of his fields. Isn't that just marvelous? Tricking a rich man like that!"

She tells it so sincerely, with such belief in her tone, that I can only nod in agreement.

"Shall we try some of our cake?" I ask.

"Let me put the kettle on and cut us a lump each."

Ada brews coffee and slices the cake. We are both aglow, made happy by our shared birthday. We sit at the kitchen table, a pair of avaricious birds, and gorge on wedges of Black Cake, celebrating the day our far-apart mothers gifted us our lives in this world.

# Miss Ada Goes to Mass with Daniel

IN MY DREAMS I HUMOR THE DEAD. I LET MY AUNTIE MARY bake bread in the Dickinson kitchen, as if that were her custom, and I say nothing when she soaks her clothes in the copper basin in the washroom. I watch her silently when she sits on the stool in my bedroom, taking everything in. Then we talk about things—her children and Ireland—and both pretend that she is still alive.

"You're as snug as a cap over the kitchen in here," Auntie Mary says.

"Yes," I say. "My little room keeps the kitchen warm as much as it warms me."

Even in my dream, I realize that I sound like Miss Emily, and I laugh. The dream laughter is real, as it turns out, and I wake to find myself giggling. I also wake expecting to find Auntie Mary in my room, and I am disappointed that she is not sitting by me. But also a little relieved; I have long been frightened of ghosts. In my dream Auntie's cheeks are ruddy and we do not mention illness or funerals or her family or poor, lonely Uncle Michael.

Miss Emily told me that dreams are messages—"couriers," she said—and they try to show us things that we can't see. I lie for a few moments, eyes shut again, trying to reenter the dreamworld, so that I might spend more time with my auntie and find out if she wants to tell me something. But forcing a dream never makes it happen.

I remember another dream I had recently, one where I was harried by lions. They ran to my mammy's door every time I opened it, though it was not actually Mammy's door, because the house sat on Amity Street in Amherst. Lions. Roaming wild in Massachusetts and eager as dogs for notice. The dreamworld is an odd place.

It is Christmas Eve morning, and it is dark; I swish my legs into the cold parts of the bed and swiftly snatch them back. Soon I will have to get up; today will be a long day of preparations. But tonight Daniel and I are going to Mass together at Mr. Slater's home, there being no Catholic church in Amherst. Father Sullivan will travel from Holyoke to celebrate the Mass, and my only hope is that he has a stout sleigh.

❧

I wear my red merino, at my throat the pearl brooch that Miss Emily gave me for my birthday. The ground is cleared of snow, and Daniel stays close by me for the short walk to Mr. Slater's house. His wife welcomes us, taking our coats, and we choose seats in the large parlor and wait for Father Sullivan to arrive. Patrick Crohan and his aunt and uncle sit near us, and Crohan turns in his seat and grins in our direction. Daniel nods a greeting, but Patrick continues to stare at me, like a goat who knows no better than to gawk. I fidget my head this way and that, made uncomfortable by his eyes.

"Ignore him," Daniel says.

"It's all right. He's only being friendly." I wave at Crohan, and he waves back, and I wonder if there isn't something mocking in the slow way he moves his hand.

Uncle Michael comes into the room, and I smile at him; Cousin Annie links him, and she has a pious, put-upon look to her. She seems to revel in the glory of her mourning, in all the attention it gets her. Annie and Maggie were cut from the same cloth, and they couldn't be more different from their parents.

I kneel and pray for Mammy, Daddy and the girls; for Auntie Mary and Uncle Michael; I pray for Miss Emily and all the Dickinsons. I place my face in my hands and close my eyes. I am a little homesick. I imagine Mammy getting the bigger girls to hang stockings on the bed and the mantelpiece, ready for the nuts, fruits and gewgaws she will put in them when all are asleep. It was my custom to help her on Christmas Eve, and we would stay up late stitching the last few dollies that we made from scraps and old clothes. I hope she misses me tonight as I miss her, but I am sure Rose has taken my place and that their two heads are bent by the fire now, sewing button eyes into flour-sack faces.

Daniel kneels beside me, and I wonder if he is thinking of his poor dead mother. Or of his grandparents at home in Ringsend. Being with him here makes it easier to hold up under the yearning that threatens to topple me tonight. I glance at him, and he turns his head sideways and winks. Daddy says that only corner boys wink at women, but Daniel is no corner boy. No, he is not that way at all. I know that Daddy would like Daniel, and that is saying a lot, because Daddy doesn't take easily to anyone.

The lamp oil and tallow make the air in the room thick and comforting. The Slaters have put up a proper crib with plaster statues like you would see in a church. When Father Sullivan gives the final blessing, we all line up to say a prayer in front of the Holy Family.

"No baby yet, of course," I say, looking at the waiting manger and the Blessed Virgin's sweet face.

Daniel reaches down and pulls a piece of straw from the crib. "Keep that with your money, Ada, and you'll have a prosperous year."

I take it and thank him. He puts one finger on the pearl brooch at my throat.

"A birthday present from Miss Emily," I say.

"She's the best of them."

"She is."

Outside, we wish Uncle Michael, Cousin Annie and the Crohans a happy Christmas and they wish us many happy returns. Annie sweeps Uncle away, and Patrick Crohan lingers as if he means to walk with us, but his aunt calls sharply to him and he skulks off. We say good night to the rest of the congregation, and I begin to walk back toward Main Street. People call "Merry Christmas" to one another, and my breath fizzes in the air. Daniel steps in beside me and presses a small pouch into my hand.

"Happy Christmas, Ada."

I look up at him, mortified that I have nothing for him. I did go to Cutler's and touch every pair of wool socks in the store, and I even looked at caps, but nothing felt right to me, and I didn't buy a thing.

"Oh, Daniel, and here's me with one arm as long as the other."

"I don't expect anything from you, Ada. It's only that I saw this and thought of you. And anyway, I missed your birthday somehow."

We follow the lamplighter, who is turning dark to light all along the street with his tall staff. Stopping under one of the lamps, I open the pouch and fish out a tiny mirror with a red rose painted on its back.

"It's beautiful," I say, taking Daniel's gloved hand in my own. He puts his other hand on my cheek.

"Would it be all right if I kissed you?"

I glance up and down the street; the rest of the Mass-goers have scattered, into sleighs and away on foot. "It would."

He leans down and I stretch up, and our lips meet for a few seconds. His mouth is so soft that I feel as if my insides will slither out of me and dance away.

"Can I call you my girl now, Ada?"

"You can of course, Daniel."

He pulls me up into his arms and swings me around, my feet dangling like a doll's above the ground. We both giggle, then compose ourselves and walk on, my paw crooked into his elbow.

❦

Miss Emily is coughing when I go in to light her fire and pour her water on Christmas morning. I expect her to be up, so excited has she been about the day, but she is buried under the covers in her little sleigh bed, with only a tuft of russet hair on show. I set her ewer on the washstand; the steam curls into the cold air. Miss Emily coughs again, and I offer a soothing grunt to comfort her. I get the Franklin stove going with screeds of dry ivy and some sticks.

"I'll have a smart fire here in no time, miss." She doesn't answer, so I slip back to my own room for a bottle of Father John's, then sit on the side of her bed and put my hand to her long back. "Now, Miss Emily. Sit up there and get a couple of swigs of this into you."

"Happy Christmas, Ada," she says, her chest rattling like a clatter of old spoons.

"Many happy returns, miss." I hold up the bottle of Father

John's. "This will have you on your feet before you're twice married and once a widow."

"What is it?"

I prop the pillows behind her and help her to sit; I pull her Indian paisley over her shoulders, and she grabs the edges of the shawl and holds them tight to her neck.

"This is Father John's Medicine—it's like a miracle for coughs, colds and sore arseholes." I slap my hand over my mouth. "Oh, saving your presence, miss, that just slipped out. My daddy always said it. Says it. I'm sorry."

Miss Emily sniggers, but the laugh gets caught in her throat and she has a fit of spluttering; the cough is like a dog's bark, and the more she tries to swallow it, the worse it sounds. I pat her shoulder and tell her to keep going until she can't go anymore. I pick up the bottle of medicine.

"Illness makes desolation, Ada."

"Try not to feel sorry for yourself, miss. See, it says here this works on 'consumption, grip, croup, whooping cough, and other diseases of the throat.' My daddy swears by Father John."

Miss Emily takes the bottle and has a gulp. "It's not so bad. Aniseed." She coughs a little, and I can hear that her throat is softening already. "I cannot be confined to bed today. Susan is coming. And the children and Austin. I cannot miss sitting at table with them. With Sue. I missed her birthday, you know. She is a December baby, too."

"Now," I say, "stop babbling and get into your clothes. You won't have to stay in bed on Christmas Day, miss, not if I have anything to do with it." I take her white piqué from the closet and her blue shawl from the chair. "Your brother and his wife will be brokenhearted for sure if you of all people don't turn up for breakfast. Come on, now. The mantelpiece below is decorated with nuts and leaves. Miss Vinnie was up late hanging garlands and the place looks very lovely." I help her to her feet. "The fire in the stove is taking. Come stand by it, and we'll get you washed and dressed."

❧

The day passes in a fug of roast, mash, slice, season, pour, serve and wash. The family proclaim themselves very pleased with their meal. I take mine alone in the kitchen with my feet propped near the stove, for they are like two blocks of ice from standing so long. The clam soup is not to my taste, but I enjoy the pork and apple dumplings very much. The family ate all the fried parsnips, but I saved a good mound of boiled onions for myself, and they are savory-sweet, exactly as I like them.

A few tears plop onto my plum pudding when I think of Mammy and the girls, snug at home. And Daddy, maybe spinning a yarn about his time at sea and the mermaids who spoke to him from rocks and tried to lure him into the water. But I can't let my thoughts linger there, because it makes me lonely and sad. In the heel of the reel, I am here now, and that is that. Tomorrow I will take some pudding to Uncle Michael, and I will let him talk about his beloved Mary and all that they left behind in Tipperary. He likes to talk about Slievenamon and the neighbors in Killusty and Fethard, and I like to let him; there is a mournful comfort in looking back that we both enjoy.

A sharp rap to the back door startles me. I get up and open it to find Patrick Crohan standing there.

"Patrick. Hello! Is everything all right?" I peer past him into the gloom.

He looks down at me, then drags the cap from his head like an afterthought and twists it through his hands. "I only wanted to wish you a happy Christmas, Ada."

"Well, that's very kind of you. Many happy returns." We stand for a few moments in silence. I wave my hand toward the clutter in the kitchen. "You can see I'm occupied here, so . . ." I go to close the door, and he wedges himself into the space, startling me. "What is it, Patrick? What do you want?"

"I want you, Ada," he says, his mouth hung open in a way that unsettles my heart.

"I'm spoken for, Patrick. I'm walking out with Daniel Byrne. You know that."

"What do you want with that scruffhead?" He comes so close that his coat buttons scratch against my apron; I can smell spirits on him, and I pull back. "I'd be properly good to you, Ada. Sure why wouldn't I? Aren't you a lovely little thing?" Crohan lunges forward as if he means to put his mouth to mine, and I hop sideways so that he staggers instead into the kitchen.

"Are you drunk, Patrick? Get out of here this minute, and leave me alone. Come on, out now."

I push him toward the door and through it, closing it after him; he shouts something, but I can't hear what he says. I stand with my back tight to the door, hoping that he does the decent thing and goes home. When no further sounds come, I tidy my dishes, keeping one ear cocked in case Crohan knocks again. All is quiet, and I clear the leftovers and put them away.

Mrs. Dickinson comes to ask me to rekindle Miss Emily's fire, as she will retire early, owing to her cold.

"Susan will accompany her up the stairs, as she does not wish to go alone," Mrs. Dickinson says. She smooths her skirt with both hands and remarks absently, "My daughter loves to be a child. She does not desire to grow up."

"I'll see to the fire now, ma'am."

She leaves, and I open the back door and look out into the

darkness; Crohan is definitely gone. I get some ivy and dry wood and take my basket up the stairs. The embers still glow in Miss Emily's stove, and they make a pleasing low heat in the room. I stoke them up and manage a fine blaze; the oil lamp I light by the bed warms the air even more. I hear voices outside the door, so I haul my basket and go to leave.

Miss Susan is talking urgently. "But how can you truly understand me, Emily, as you claim to? My arms, my mind, all of me, is glutted with duty: to the children, to my home, to Austin, to our friends. You please no one but yourself."

"But I please you, do I not?" Miss Emily murmurs.

"Of course you do, my dear. But you see me as others don't, as no mortal could. I am flesh, I am bone. You must not idolize me, Emily."

I open the door, and they stand, arms tightly around each other's waist and bodies pressed close, front to front; Miss Emily's head is lying on her sister-in-law's shoulder.

"Forevermore, Sue," she says, lifting her eyes to Miss Susan's face. She startles when she sees me in the doorway and breaks from their embrace. "Ada! Why do you sneak around so?"

"Begging your pardon, miss, I was doing the fire. The stove. Your mother told me to. I wanted to have the room warm for you. I'll go."

"Well, go. Quickly," Miss Emily says. She turns from me and marches into her room, Miss Susan close behind her. I hear their voices high and irritated as I run down the back stairs to the kitchen, afraid my basket will tumble from my hand I am going so fast.

# *Miss Emily Refuses an Invitation*

FROM THE CUPOLA I WATCH MOTHER AND VINNIE STROLL OUT together and turn toward the town. How easily they amble along, unfettered by anything so mundane as the relentless press of words. They talk, probably, of lace and lawn, of whom they might meet in Cutler's or the Amherst House. Part of me envies their ability to crowd their minds with trivia, part of me is glad that I cannot. Words command me—they beg to be courted, danced and bedded and will not leave me alone until I comply. But it is not only words that keep me here, I know that. It is a fact that if I do not leave the house, I cannot lose myself; I am better contained in my home, looking inward. This is where I best function.

Main Street is framed by the view; it is a moving landscape of carriage and pedestrian, squirrel and dog. Sometimes people I know stray into the picture, and I style myself the artist who has painted them in, though inevitably they display their own will. I see Mrs. Sweetser forage in her nose and flick what she has found there to the footpath. I see Moody Cook scratch himself all over and yawn like a man newly broken from the earth—a rough and ragged Adam. I see Patrick Crohan walk up to the Homestead and stand staring at the top windows like a hunter stalking prey. He seems agitated, and he cranes his neck upward until I think it is me he seeks, though I fancy myself well hidden. Has he seen me? I step back from the window and go down to my bedroom, where I sit at my desk. I lean forward to look: Crohan has gone, disappeared back into his own life.

I sit at my desk and think of Mother and Vinnie and myself, about how we differ. I have had a great inner conversation about how I am, for hours and days on end. I ponder over whether I shall ever wish to be as social as I was when young. Or shall I withdraw and become a complete hermit, sociable only with those who know me best and will not think to upbraid me for loving solitude? The former, I thought firstly, should be my lot. But I have come to realize that if I gad about too much, I will write nothing. And if I stay at home, I can easily protect myself. I am in the habit of this house, and it is in the habit of me. We mourn each other when we are apart. And so it is folly to separate often.

Mother has begun to remark frequently on my stopping indoors; Father, too. *She* would not understand the demands of the mind, but Father at least does. And he understands, too, that I was not made right for the world; it does not welcome me or my conversation as it does others. My speech is best done on paper. Paper that I can stash away in this trunk or that nook, for Father could not bear for the world to read my insides. He does not know how much I write, but he would dread my becoming a Woman of Letters, a breed he despises. How far that would sink me, in his view. And dear Father, he would not welcome being dragged—a reluctant anchor—to the seabed with me.

No, I will not send my birds out to nest, save to those who will nurture them alone, in private rooms. My words are best enjoyed by those who know me, and I shall remain happy to sit in the light of my own fire and draw pleasure from its heat.

I say this, and yet and yet. I often wish I were more like dear

Sue—vivacious and able and *outward*. She holds her salons with grace and enthusiasm; she loves to be in large groups, to discuss and debate. What a trial it can be to remain resolutely *inward*, to be always tripping over your own toes for looking downward, toward the heart.

I drag myself from my room and go to the parlor; I set the Aeolian harp that Cousin John made on the windowsill and lift the sash to let the breeze do its work. I watch the strings move and listen awhile to the harp's tingling chant, its crescendos and falls. Needing a melody, I sit at the piano. Up and down the scales I teeter; Messrs. Hallett and Davis, who fashioned the instrument, would button their ears and scold me—I am out of practice. I play some of my invented airs, embellishing them as I go. Vinnie calls these my "ghost tunes." They madden me with their mournfulness and fun, my strange compositions, but they please me, too, and I like to run through them before turning to my Beethoven waltzes and the quicksteps I love so much.

A voice says, "You are a rare spirit."

Thinking it is only Vinnie, I continue to play, but then Susan comes to the side of the piano and stands watching me. I look from her broad cheeks and soft eyes to the piano keys, then back again.

"Have you come to scold me?" I ask.

"For what?"

"For holding you too dear."

"Emily, we are friends. Sisters. It is not possible to hold each other too dear."

I bash my fingers along the keys, then stop. "But you belong to Austin and the children. And I belong to no one. You told me so."

"You are melancholy today, dear Emily. Come to the Evergreens tonight. I am having a small salon, a select few people, nothing overwhelming. We will hold it in the library, not the parlor." She leans in to me. "There is a man I would very much like you to meet."

"Who is this man?"

"A poet. A great poet and a great man."

"What would I have to say to a poet and *great man*?"

"Come, Emily. Now you are choosing to be stubborn."

Susan walks to the pier glass, and I turn on my piano stool to observe her. She stares at her reflection, then licks a finger and runs it over each eyebrow.

"You live only the length of the hemlock away," I say, "but sometimes it feels you are farther from me than the moon."

She turns to face me. "You are the one who does not come out to play, Emily. You cannot find fault with me for distance." She walks over and kneels in front of me, takes both my hands in hers. "Meet the poet. You two would have so much to discuss. I know you would delight him. I have shown him some of your verses already, and they please him. Say you will come."

"I cannot. Mother needs me."

"Lavinia can look after your mother. And the Irish girl—she seems ever-present. Your mother will not want for anything. And as you say, you will be but the length of the hedge from her."

I bend forward to kiss Sue's cheek, but she rises quickly. I am left—mouth puckered—hanging in midair. Her bombazine crackles as she moves across the floor to sit on the horsehair sofa, where there is room only for one. I turn to the piano and begin to play my Rossini aria, hoping its pomp and pageant, mixed with the feline cry of the wind harp, will discompose Susan and send her away. Today I have no use for her.

# Miss Ada Takes a Ride on a Buckboard

❦

"ARE YOU TRYING TO CHARM A SUP OF TEA OUT OF ME, DANIEL Byrne?"

Daniel is back at the Homestead to look over the Squire's horses. He goes from place to place, seeing to animals, and is much in demand if Moody Cook is to be believed.

"I'd murder a drop of tea, Ada," he says, standing in the doorframe in such a way that I cannot see his face for the light behind him.

"Come in." I take the pearwood caddy to the table, then to the stove; from there I start rooting around for a big cup, all aflutter because he is here. "Back from your gallivanting," I say, to cover that my head is addled.

"There's little gallivanting in it. The work is hard, and I have that eejit Crohan hanging out of me night and day. He has my heart broke."

"Patrick Crohan? We saw him at the circus. And at Mass." I do not mention Crohan's Christmas-night visit to me in the kitchen; something holds me in check, for I do not want to alarm Daniel or cause trouble with his employer.

"The very man. He's from the back of Godspeed at home. Tipperary or somewhere like it."

"My mammy is from Tipp. All her people are from Killusty near Fethard."

Daniel wrings his cap in his hands. "Oh, I'm sorry. I didn't mean anything by that. Tipperary is tremendous, I'm sure." He sits suddenly at the table. "Crohan is a consequence, that's all I meant. He trips over himself, does things arseways. Ah, he's bewildered. Half the time I think he's been to Conkey's Tavern before he comes to me. His own uncle knows he's no use."

Daniel drops his head, and neither of us speaks. Placing the milk jug near his hand, I find I want to pet the knuckles and the sprouting of light hairs on them. I would like to run my fingers across the little hillocks and feel their bony strength. I linger for a moment.

"Crohan comes here sometimes to do bits and bobs for Mr. Dickinson. He's a bit of a quare hawk, right enough. There's something off with him. He's pushy, maybe."

"He's as mad as a brush if you ask me." Daniel grins up at me and passes his arm around my waist. "How have you been keeping, Ada?"

I slip away from him, in terror that Miss Emily or, worse, Mrs. Dickinson will come in. Sitting opposite Daniel, I fold my hands around my teacup, then remember myself and take it by the handle with my fingers.

"I'm grand," I say. "I think I upset Miss Emily, though, and I haven't seen hide nor hair of her since. Not alone anyway. She'd normally be under my feet in the kitchen most of the day."

"What happened?"

"It was nothing, really. I interrupted a private scene. A conversation. I don't know. She barked at me." I twiddle the edge of my apron, for I am still trying to fathom why she got so annoyed. "It's not like her to be snappish."

"It'll blow over, I'm sure. No one could be angry with you for long." I look up, and Daniel holds my gaze; he offers me his hand across the table, and I reach over and let him hold mine. His skin is warm and rough, the skin of a hardworking man. "Will I get to see you at all?"

"I have New Year's Eve off. The family are going across to Mr. Austin's house for the day."

"That's marvelous. We'll do something. The snow is melting— we could take a long walk together."

"I'd like that." He lets go of my hand, swigs his tea and rises. "Don't think bad of Miss Emily," I say, feeling guilty for complaining about her. "She's not altogether well this weather."

Daniel settles his cap over his hair, salutes with one hand and is gone out the door as quick as he came in. I clear the table and run my finger across the place where his mouth met the rim of the cup. I put my lips to that same place and drink back the lukewarm dregs of his tea.

❦

It is mild for late December, and the sun hangs low and orange in the sky. Daniel said he would come for me, and I stand outside the Homestead, sweeping my eyes up and down Main Street to try to catch sight of him as he approaches. That way I can settle myself before he sees my face. He makes me giddy. Even thinking about him sends my chest into a spasm. I taste the day's weather on my tongue and feel glad it is not too cold.

There are old leaves on the pathway, and I am wondering if I would have time to get the broom at them when a buckboard pulls up and stops at the bottom of the steps. The horse paws the ground, and I glance at the driver, thinking he has stopped at the wrong place. I look again when I realize it is Daniel himself. He hops down, dragging the cap from his head.

"I'm sorry it's not a buggy with a hood and all, but it was the best I could do."

"Well, it's lovely," I say, going toward the trim carriage and wondering if it is safe.

"I'm glad you like it. I know a wainwright in Holyoke, and he gets me to try out his new gigs and carriages, to make sure they're sound." Daniel slaps the horse. "And this is Betty, the sweetest mare in all of New England."

Daniel rubs her flank, then lifts me by the waist into the seat and gets up beside me. He pulls a blanket over both our legs, clicks at the horse, and we trot on. The mare has hard, sleek withers and a reckless tail; I hope that she will behave.

"Where are we off to?"

"I thought I might take you out to Mount Norwottuck."

"Do you mean to climb it?"

Daniel laughs. "Not at all. It's a couple of miles to the top. We'll just go and look. See what we can see." The buckboard springs under us, and the horse trots gaily along. "You'd think she'd been waiting for this all her life—to take two jackeens out to the sticks to gawk at a hill."

I laugh and slip my arm through his elbow crook. The wind in my face is sharp, and I don't even mind that my cheeks will be as ripe as plums by the time we get to the mountain.

Daniel croons to the horse on the jaunt out, cajoling and mollycoddling her. "Great girl," he says. "Hup, Betty, hup. That's it, hup now. You're a smasher, Betty."

He goes off into another place when he is at that—talking to horses; I hear him with the Squire's horses. It is as if nothing exists but him and the animal. I don't mind; I am happy as a brooding hen sitting next to him, feeling the heat of his long body against mine. And I like to see the countryside unfolding before us, as if it were put there for our pleasure. I ask him if he has ever driven the Dickinsons' cabriolet, and he says he has. I tell him I would love a go in it, to enjoy its creamy insides and peep from its oval windows.

"Maybe someday we'll have a carriage like that," Daniel says, and I am made quiet by this remark.

Mount Norwottuck is a sloped triangle rising out of the valley in a stand of small mountains. Daniel stops the buckboard, and we sit and look across at it.

"It's lower than Slievenamon," I say, "but beautiful all the same."

A lid of cloud hovers over the mountain range. The hills themselves are navy, and white with snow, too, richly dark and bright against the sky and cloud. I think it would be nice to be at the top, breathing the thin air and lording it over the valley. Whenever I climbed Slievenamon with Mammy or Granny Dunn, I felt like a queen looking down over Killusty, Lough-copple and Kiltinan Castle perched on the banks of the Clashawley, and far off to Fethard, closed inside its high walls.

Daniel twists his body toward me. "What do you miss about home, Ada? About Ireland?"

"Apart from my family? I suppose I miss Dublin itself, its dirty din. I miss Tipperary, too. My granny's place, the peace there."

"I miss the Liffey, the stink of it."

"Me, too. I used to swim in it."

"Did you, now?" He scratches his head. "I miss the sea. It makes me itchy or something, not being near the sea."

"I miss the way people *are*, too," I say. "You know, people from Dublin are freer than the people here—they don't fuss as much. Dubliners are open. They talk more."

"They laugh more, too, if you ask me. Some of the ones here are wound very tight."

"But they are good people, too. They live well. We can all learn from that."

"You cannot take on their ways, Ada. It is impossible to become them."

"I know. That's not what I meant."

"They are themselves and we are ourselves, there's no getting around it."

I listen to Betty's slow munch-crunch on grass and watch her toss her mane. I think about Miss Emily and what a conundrum she is. She can be wound tight, like Daniel says, but she is free, too, in many ways. Well, in any case her mind is free. I remember the word I heard her murmur to Miss Susan—"forevermore"— and wonder what she meant by it. Betty whinnies, breaking into my thoughts. I turn to Daniel.

"I didn't know my own restlessness until I got here. I seemed to calm down inside myself once I was settled."

"I know what you mean, though it still feels strange to me. Everything. The air."

"After seven years? Surely not?"

"It does, even after all this time."

"You'd like to go home, then?"

"Maybe. Sometime. If I could."

I look around at the snow-patched grass and the mountains, at the clouds scuttling across the sky. It is lonely here, I think. It feels lonely to not know a place well, to be away from the beauty of your own area. It is green here, green in a way that I do not welcome, because it makes me heartsick for Tigoora and for Mammy's home in Tipperary, Granny Dunn's tiny house above Killusty.

"What is it like, the part of Dublin you're from?" Daniel asks.

"Tigoora? What do you mean, what is it like?"

"Is it a town?"

"No, it's country, but near enough the city. Not like my mammy's first home, in Tipperary, where my aunt and uncle are from, too. They all lived under Slievenamon."

"Slievenamon. It's such a lovely name. Tell me what it means, Ada."

"It means 'women's mountain.' It's very peaceful there. Very safe." I shiver a little and pull my coat snugly around me.

"You're cold," Daniel says.

"The way it is, we're in America now," I say, more to myself than to him. "We have to make the best of it."

"And we have each other."

"We do," I say.

Daniel jumps from the buckboard and helps me down. "Let's walk."

We link arms and stroll a pathway under trees. The grass there is just letting go of frost. The blades stand like white spears, and I toe them with my boot to better see the pearls of frost that still cling to them. Huge trees form a canopy over the path ahead of us, and I wonder if we should turn back, in case we trespass onto someone's land.

"I took the pledge, you know, Ada. Father Mathew's pledge," Daniel says, stopping suddenly and looking down at me. "I tasted wine once and didn't like it. So that was that. I'm for total abstinence, like the good Father said."

"It's a pity there aren't more like you."

"It's Adam's ale for me. That alone."

"Adam's ale?"

"It's what they call water sometimes." He fidgets with his coat button. "I have a bit of money put by, you know, Ada. A nice lump of money."

"It is always wise to save, Daniel. Yes. 'Sow frugality, reap liberty.' Isn't that what they say?" I look up into the bare branches of the trees and wonder at their size. "Everything is bigger here," I murmur.

Daniel stops walking and turns me to him by the shoulders. "Do you know what I'm telling you, Ada?"

"I think so," I say, my neck and chin starting to scald. I look up at him, at his face so serious.

"Grand," he says, and drapes one arm around me so that we can walk on. He seems lighter in himself having spoken, though my heart jigs in my chest.

"It's after getting bitter," I say, hawing on my cold hands.

"It is. We'll go back."

We daunder toward Betty. Daniel lifts me up into the buckboard and gets up himself. When he settles the blanket across us, he leans over and puts his mouth to mine. I feel his soft tongue pressing between my lips, and I open my mouth wider to let him in. We sit and kiss, and all sorts of feelings come over me. Between my legs swells, and I want to mold every part of myself into every part of Daniel. I put my fingers to his face to feel the working of his jaw and to hold his mouth even closer to my own. His tongue is so soft, so fragrant, that I would happily have him swallow me whole. Every move of his mouth only makes me want to kiss him more. He licks my teeth, sliding his tongue over my gums, and I nearly rise out of my seat with the sweetness of it. I forget about the cold, about what he has suggested to me, about Miss Emily and work and the whole lot. I kiss Daniel and he kisses me, and all there is in the world is our two mouths, our two tongues, our closed eyes, our hands holding the other's cheeks. We break away, both panting a little. We smile and turn our faces, then look again. Daniel takes up Betty's reins, clicks his tongue, and says, "Walk on."

❧

I am late getting up; the Lord only knows why. Too much air, maybe. Mammy used to call me her rooster, the way I woke at the same time each morning and could get everyone else up. The fires have to be set still, and so I run down the stairs with my boots in my hand, thinking I will light the stove first and put on my boots once it's blazing. I fling open the door to find Patrick Crohan standing in the kitchen, having a look around by the dim light from the open back door. He is studying everything as if he owns the place.

"What are you doing in here?" I say. "Is Daniel Byrne not with you?" Without thinking I fling my boots onto the table, and then we both stand gawping at them.

"Oh, Miss High-and-Mighty. Shoes on the table—you'll get no luck from that."

Crohan shakes his head and blesses himself, and I want to thump him. I snatch the boots—they seem to pulse with badness all of a sudden—and sit to lace them up. I look at him.

"I asked you what you were doing. This is a private house. You don't waltz in the door when it pleases you."

"Byrne said to meet him here."

"He meant for you to meet him in the yard, by the barn. You know that. Out with you, now."

Crohan goes to the back door and turns. "How did a slither-arse like you get a start here?"

"You pup. Get out of my kitchen."

"*Your* kitchen? Go on, you little witch." He comes in close to me and looks into my face, then lets his eyes slide over my body. "You're no great shakes," he says. "But you wedged your foot in the door nicely here, didn't you, Miss Concannon? Sitting pretty in that top bedroom. Do you sleep well?"

"Go away, get out!" I push at his side, though I do not want to touch him.

He cackles and shoots out, slamming the door behind him. I am full sure Mrs. Dickinson is going to arrive down to scold me over the noise. Crohan has left a peculiar, sweet smell behind him, and it makes my stomach flip over. I get to raking the fire and shove on my boots, the laces done any mad old way. And that is where Aughrim was lost. As I descend the stairs with the slops, the laces on both boots come undone, and I go arse over head, piss and shite all down my front and covering the steps. I sit among it, and I want to weep. The smell seeps into my nose, and I start to gag, but there's no time for pity because there is applesauce to heat for the family's hash. I haul myself up and clean the stairs. I lift the stinking stools with my bare hands and try not to throw up. Whipping off the soiled apron, I give my hands a good scrub, but of course they still feel dirty. I wash the stairs down again with scalding water and pine oil. Then I clean my hands once more, soaking them in the hottest water I can bear.

I bring through the tray to the dining room and feel sorriest for Miss Emily, even though she is out with me. I am glad that she doesn't know the carry-on that has left me with dubious hands, but it grieves me that my fingers might be foul while I serve her food. *They're clean, they're clean,* I say to myself, over and over, as I dish up the breakfast. Each of the family says thank you—Miss Emily with her eyes cast down, as is her habit with me now—and I scuttle back to the kitchen, mortified. I scrub my hands again.

I charge out to the yard once I know that the family are settled with coffee and everything else they need. Daniel smiles his slow, lovely smile when he sees me.

"Where's that go-boy?" I ask.

"Who?"

"Patrick Crohan. He was in the kitchen when I came down this morning, standing in the near dark. And the lip out of him."

Crohan saunters out of the barn. "Do you want me, Miss Concannon?" he says.

"Don't you 'Miss Concannon' me. And never set foot in that house again, unless you're asked. Do you hear me?"

"He won't, Ada," Daniel says, gripping my elbow and rubbing gently at my other arm.

"The cut of yiz," Crohan says. "She'll skedaddle on you, Byrne, before long. Find herself a proper man." He pulls himself up taller.

Daniel turns to him. "Enough," he says, and Crohan slinks back into the barn.

"Can you not get rid of him?" I say.

"He's not mine to get rid of. It's his uncle who pays my wages."

"Ah, sure, I know that. I just can't stand the sight of him. Keep him away from the kitchen or I'll run him." Even as I say it, I know I will see less of Daniel now; he won't come in for a sup of tea and leave Crohan on his own in the yard with the horses. It makes me want to spit. "His mother must have walked on a grave when he was inside her belly, he's that odd."

❦

I'm up to my oxters in croppins and lights, gizzards and giblets when Daniel raps on the door.

"Will you not step in?" I say, wiping chicken guts from my fingers with a cloth.

"I'd better keep an eye on Crohan. God knows what he'll get up to if I leave him too long."

"He's a fidget of a fella, all right." I go to the stove and take two cans from it. "This one's yours. There are extra spuds in it."

Daniel winks and backs out the door. He blows me a kiss with his lips, and I shake my cloth at him. I am smiling like a loony when I look up to see that Miss Emily has glided in without my knowing.

"Ada."

"Miss." I go over to her. "Do you need some more coffee inside? Does Mr. Dickinson want more hash?"

"No, no. I came to see how you are."

"I'm grand, miss. And you? Has Father John cured you yet?"

She smiles and puts her hand to her chest. "I do believe he has, Ada. I have also had my own father keeping watch, so there was little choice but to improve." She goes to the cupboard and takes down her measuring cup and spoon. "Would I be terribly in the way if I made gingerbread this morning? I want to give some to the children."

"Not at all, Miss Emily. I'm boiling up a chicken broth on the stove top. You're welcome to use the oven."

It pleases me that she is here. She is a little stiff, maybe, a small bit bashful with me, but I do believe we are friends again and there's no harm done. Thanks be to God; I couldn't rest easy if this unevenness between us went on for much longer.

"If we could eat gingerbread morning, noon and night, Ada, what a deal of happiness there would be in the world."

"It's true for you, miss. Do you want the rose water, or will you use it this time at all?" I fetch the bottle without waiting for her answer. "I've been keeping the best feathers for you for making the glaze." I grab the neat brown tail feathers from the jar where I have kept them and hold them up for her to see.

"Thank you, Ada." She glances down, then up at me. "And may I apologize—"

I hold up my two hands. "Don't give it another thought, miss. I think Christmas brings out the bear in everyone. I know my daddy used to be like a devil in December, full to the brim with the excess of it all. With everyone being in on top of one another."

I grab a bit of shortening as big as an egg and soften it; Miss Emily takes it from me and mixes it into the cream. I heat a spoon on the stove top to make the molasses come easier from the cup, and together we knock the gingerbread into shape.

"Doesn't it smell intoxicating, Ada?"

"It does, miss," I say, but the chicken broth is wound so tight into my nose that, if I'm honest, I can't really smell the cake. Today, though, I'll agree with whatever she says; with our feet on the same plank again, all will be well.

## Miss Emily Turns to White

TODAY I CANNOT LEAVE MY ROOM, NOT EVEN TO INVESTIGATE the condition of my herb garden, which is surely by now a disgrace of withered leaves. Something strangles me, sits on me like a neck brace, and I dare not venture even as far as the kitchen. There is fog over Amherst, and the insides of my windows weep with condensation while the sun offers its dull light to my room. The outside world will make no demands on me today. Nor any day, perhaps.

I lock my door with its imaginary key to release my freedom, for if the outside cannot be let in, I can still try to unleash my own insides. I sit to my desk and hope to write a few lines—something about the fog—but the words defy me, and I throw down my pencil. I look out: the sun is trying hard to glare its way through the mist. I open the window a little; the robins in Austin's white oak chirp meekly today, afraid—maybe—to break the pearly spell. And yet the sounds of the town are amplified: rolling wheels, men's shouts, factory din, a train. Noise thunders above or through the fog, I am not sure which; it seems to echo back as if in a great hollow.

Yesterday, from this very window, I lowered my basket filled with gingerbread to the children who waited below, a custom I recently began and which the small people delight in. I usually send word to my nephew that I am making gingerbread, and he alerts his playmates. They wait to see the sash go up and the basket teetering on its string. It is a mode of greeting the children that suits me well; I get to stay in the security of my room, but I also get to halloo to them and see their angel faces.

They ran up the steps, through the gate, and took the ginger-bread in greedy handfuls; its dark goodness stained their mouths. The sun shone on their pretty heads, warm and nurturing.

"Many thanks, Miss Dickinson!" they called. "Thank you, Aunt Emily!"

"Go well, little ones." I watched them run off to their world of play in the bright sunlight.

Now the fog shrouds the sun, but I know it will break through eventually; it is stronger than any vapor.

I sit again and try to write. I manage a morsel:

*The Sun took down his Yellow Whip*
*And drove the Fog away—*

Nothing else I conjure coheres with those lines, which are all that want to come down to me through the corridors of my brain. I fold up the piece of paper and put it away with the others in the boxes in my drawer. I peer at them a moment, my sad little scraps and sadder little booklets, the string-bound parcels that I can neither open nor destroy. They are but one more layer in my polar privacy. I place a tray cloth over the bundles, for they seem to leer and mock me. *No more will you write. It has left you, that urgency, that wellspring, that ability to connect things.* I close the drawer and sit by my fireplace to read.

Mrs. Barrett Browning is to be my companion today, she who died smiling, so they say, and whose last word was "beautiful." I go through the book, page by page, soaking in the comfort of her poetry, I look at her words, one by one. Love. Thee. Breath. Smiles. Tears. It pleases me that each word is solitary, a loner. Side by side, their staccato nature blends with others, but in the end they stand alone. Each word is a fence post—upright, demanding, shrill— but each one holds the fence erect and, as such, is indispensable.

❧

Ada comes to my bedroom carrying two sprigged calicoes and my brown wool dress. She brings her spick-and-span aura with her, and I wonder if my room smells stale, if it smells of me. I notice a new confidence around her—the pluck and poise of love, no doubt. I court vicariously through Ada and Daniel Byrne; I watch their shy, sweet glances tossed like luck pennies back and forward in the kitchen. Sometimes a stray penny lands on me, and I pocket it gratefully.

Ada holds up my gowns. "These are clean and aired, miss."

"Yes." I watch absently as she puts them away among my other dresses. Their colors riot in front of my eyes. "From now on I shall only wear white," I say. I do not know where this sentence—this decision—has descended from. It is true that I love white—my favorite dress is a snowy cotton wrapper with mother-of-pearl buttons and a pocket; I feel such ease in it, such freedom. But to forgo all color?

"Miss?" Ada says, her arms aloft, holding the dress she was about to hang.

"I will be Mr. Collins's Woman in White. No, better, I will be Aurora Leigh in her 'clean white morning dresses.'"

"Black is for mourning, miss, surely?"

"No, *morning*, Ada. Morning! The early part of the day. How slippery meaning is."

I feel a flutter in my limbs; I am warming to this notion

now—white has long been of importance to me. This morning's fog, far from being oppressive, made me restful, and that sort of tranquillity always vivifies me somehow. Fog and snow and blank paper—these things seduce me, they energize me. Can calmness and energy be bedfellows? It strikes me that if I am pure in dress, my mind may empty itself of all concerns, and that will make it easier for me to write.

"Well, I suppose the white dresses are easy to keep," Ada says, uncertainly. "They do bleach well."

"All around me is color, Ada. I do not need to add to that. The woodpecker's crimson head shines, the daffodils in the garden dazzle, and the plummetless purple well of words awaits me. That is color. I will wear white!"

"You will need new gowns, then, miss. Will I order yards of cotton from Cutler's? Will I send for Miss Leonard, the seamstress? We should consult your mother."

"I fancy dimity, Ada. And a lace collar. Lace trim, too, in lines on the bodice. There is no need for Miss Leonard to come. Vinnie can go to her and be measured for me. Sizewise we are one and the same. And my sister loves an outing."

"And what's to be done with these other dresses, miss?"

"My Norcross cousins will have them, gladly. And Vinnie and I shall sew at least one new dress ourselves to save the cost of the seamstress." I turn to her. "Leave me now, dear Ada, for I must think."

I stand to the window; the sun has pierced the fog, and it is all but gone, lifted like a veil to reveal Main Street and the town. Now I miss its spectral covering. This decision—to wear white—sings poetry to me: it will speak of my obedience to words, my dedication. It may signify that to me only, perhaps, but to whom else do I need to show my allegiance? I am giddy with excitement and cannot wait to tell Mother that I need new stuff for gowns. Perhaps she and Vinnie will get some good cloth for me when they go to Boston; they surely have the sweetest of dimity in that city.

Even the sewing of a new dress does not daunt me, though I am usually a complaining cat when it comes to needlework. No, I will happily baste, stitch and hem until my fingers bleed. Not onto any new dress, of course. I shall be careful where the drops fall; I will not brook stains on my alabaster future.

From now on I shall be candle-white. Dove-, bread-, swan-, shroud-, ice-, extraordinary-white. I shall be blanched, bleached and bloodless to look at; my very whiteness will be my mark. But inside, of course, I will roar and soar and flash with color.

❧

I write by night now, when nothing thrums but my lamp. It makes a halo around my desk, and its oily stink creates a heady balm. There is no sound save my pencil across the paper and the soft clicks that emanate from the fire in my stove. The house sleeps; Amherst sleeps. Only I endure. And when my pencil tires of flicking word arrows onto the page, there is the moon to admire, full-faced and lovely, a bright coin. I enjoy it at every stage of its passage from plate to curving wedge to sliver to fingernail. I love its pallidity.

I am both exalted and calmed by my farewell to colored clothing; it speaks to me of the way feelings reside in me: I am at once whimsical and wistful. Are these not strange mates? And yet in me they are permanently entwined in love's long embrace.

❧

Mother, being Mother, complains about my decision to wear white.

"Oh, Emily. Must you? It is not practical. And pale colors

drain your face. They make you wan and sickly to look at. Must you really?"

"Yes," I say, already comfortable in my favorite white wrapper as Vinnie and I fashion another. Mother has a headache and has thus far refused to partake in our sewing festival. "Would you wish me different, Mother? Is that what you are saying?"

"Of course not, my dear." She pauses. "But people will think you work here if you dress like a servant."

"People? What people?"

She tuts. "And dimity? It is more suitable as bedcoverings. But at least pin your cameo to your throat if you must wear a wrapper. Or your garnets. Then I will know it is you and not a serving girl crossing my path on the staircase. Or a spirit!"

Vinnie and I bend our heads over our work; we sit either side of the fireplace. Mother is on the love seat, *Godey's Lady's Book* in her lap, but she rises and comes to me, her paisley shawl aloft. She tucks it around my shoulders.

"There. That is better," Mother says. "Now you will not look like a revenant, passing from room to room."

"How very poetical of you, Mother," Vinnie says. "You have been reading verse, I daresay."

I snort, and they both look at me. "My apologies. I only meant that Mother does not care for poetry or books. Usually."

"Be that as it may, Emily, it is rude to make noises with your nose. Quite, quite rude."

I shrug off the shawl and continue with my sewing. Vinnie waves her arm to catch my attention; I look over, and she crosses her eyes in the same comical way we did as children. We suppress our laughter, and I suppress something more, for it pains me to hurt Mother, however trying she may be. She scuttles around us all, trying to please Father and trying to make us right, though it has been clear for a long time that neither Vinnie nor I will ever be right, in her eyes at least. She would have us more like herself: cautious and resigned but willing, the type of young woman who craves to be a bride.

Father wanted a friend for life in Mother, and that he got. He is fond of saying, "There is no place for argumentative women in this world. None at all!" and Mother obeys and does not quarrel. Are they equals? I think not. Poor Mother, she has been saddled with an opinionated husband; odd, independent, single-minded daughters; and a son who drifted from sunny to haughty. But she must take at least part of the blame for all of us.

# *Miss Ada Receives the Gift of a Fish*

I AM WORKING BUTTER, SLOW AND STEADY, WHEN A COMMOTION outside knocks me off my rhythm. I put my paddles in water and slip to the window. Dick, the Squire's horse, is dancing around the yard like a man with a burr in his drawers. Daniel dances with him, but he is all the time talking to the horse and petting his long snout. He keeps with the animal, leaping whichever way the horse leads him. Crohan looks on, holding himself back by the fence in case he might have to lend a hand. Sure what good would a useless yoke like him be anyway? I pity Daniel, saddled with that fella; he's nothing but a worry, a hindrance. Crohan only has work because his uncle gives it to him; no one else would take him on. He has the kind of face I would like to thrash, God forgive me for thinking it.

I go back to my butter and soon get lost in the slip-slap of it again; I watch its color go from primrose to a pale buttercup. I chant in my mind, *Come, butter. Come butter. Come butter, come.* The smell of it brings me home, and though the milk is grand here in America, it is nowhere near as fine as Irish milk. *Come, butter. Come butter. Come butter, come.*

I hear a soft rap on the back door; Daniel opens it and walks in.

"God bless the work," he says. "Did you put a cinder under the churn?"

"The churn is away being fixed," I answer, and I lift my foot to show him the cinder under my boot.

"You're fierce clever, Ada. No fairies will steal *your* butter."

"They won't. Is the horse all right?"

"Something spooked him."

"Or some*one*." He stands close to me, and the January breeze that has caught in his clothes comes off him in waves. "Will I heat a sup of buttermilk for you?"

He gives me a quizzical look. "How did you know I like it warm?"

"Don't men always like their buttermilk warmed up in winter?"

"We do."

I place a jar in a pot of hot water and pour in the buttermilk; I stir it around and around, aware of Daniel near me the whole time, willing him to touch me, even just a hand to my hair. He doesn't come to me, and I stir the milk on and on, then test it with my finger. I lift the jar and hand it to Daniel.

"Now," I say.

He slugs it back and, quick as quick, leans forward and kisses my mouth with his milky mustache. He skips out the door before I can say a thing; I wipe the froth from my lip with my fingers and turn back to my butter, only to find Miss Emily in the doorway.

"Miss! I didn't know you were there." She is looking at the back door. "He was only here a minute, that's all."

She smiles, a tight little smile. "I am come to tell you . . ." She blinks and puts her hand to her head. "I am come to say . . ."

But she does not finish whatever it is she wishes to say, for she swoons sideways, and I jump to her side and hold her up.

"Sit here now, Miss Emily. Sit awhile."

"Oh, Ada. My head swims and my stomach has such pains."

I have lemon brandy out for making an Election Cake, and I pour a jot and make her drink it back.

"Now," I say. "Now, now. Do you want to go up and lie down?"

Miss Emily nods, and I help her to her feet. I move to tuck my arm into hers, but she bats me away and walks ahead. The seat of her dress is streaked crimson—blood on snow. Thanks be to God, I think, it is only that; I feared there was something terrible the matter with her.

"It's your flow, miss," I say as we go up the stairs, and she nods miserably, her face as hoary as her gown.

"It doesn't come often, Ada, and when it does, it flattens me. Every time."

"It's the same with myself. They don't call it the Curse for nothing."

"The Curse? How charming."

And the funny thing is, she means it. Words are treasure to Miss Emily; the most ordinary thing sends her off into one of her reveries about the nature and beauty of words.

I get her settled in bed, and she seems to want me to linger, but I am thinking of my butter, melting in the heat from the stove, and the cake still to be made and now rags to fashion, too. And all this on a day when Daniel is about the Homestead and I will barely get to glimpse him, for I am up to my shoulders in work.

"Your Daniel is a good man," Miss Emily says.

"He is, miss. Kindness is as rich as yolk in him."

"You make a fine pair."

I fidget with my apron. "I'll go and see to the rags, miss. We'll get you comfortable." She nods, and I unclip her snood and let her hair fall free on the pillow. "Now, take your rest."

❧

A lipping fish sits on the table in the kitchen when I come down the stairs. The back door swings wide, sending in a breeze that at least has saved my butter. The poor fish looks like he is trying to say something from his jutting mouth—a plea for mercy, maybe, a last gasp for water. I think Daniel must have left it for me, but no, he wouldn't throw it here and leave. The fish's gills puff and drop; its blood and scales mark the table. I wrap it in a cloth and give it a blow to its head with the back of the ax. When I am sure it is not moving anymore, I cut off its head and put the body into the scullery sink.

One of Miss Vinnie's cats comes sauntering in; she must have smelled the fish from her perch in her mistress's room.

"Well, what can I do for you, madam?" I say, and the cat stares at me with her steady eyes. "Pssshhh, now." I flick my hands at her, but she doesn't move. "I have enough to be doing without entertaining you."

Me and Miss Vinnie disagree over the cats; I don't want them in the kitchen, but she says they do no harm. None except their falling hairs and muddy paws on my clean floor. I take the fish's head and toss it out the back door, and the cat goes haring after it. I linger a moment to see whether Daniel is around the yard. Patrick Crohan steps out of the barn and grins over at me; he waves his two hands and does a little jig, then disappears back inside. He is a broth of a boy. But there is no time to get het up over Crohan. I have to see if Mrs. Dickinson would like fish for tea, with pickled oysters, maybe, and a posset to follow. And there is much to be done besides.

❧

With the rags made and given to Miss Emily and the butter wrapped in burdock leaves, I take my duster to the parlor and run it over the ornaments—the wax flowers under their glass dome always remind me of dead things. There is no one about—I had been hoping to catch Mrs. Dickinson—and the room is as silent as if it has been empty for years. I think, not for the first time, how forsaken the house feels without children to run through its rooms. I miss the rush of small people underfoot—there was always a clatter of them at home, and if they didn't belong to us, they belonged to someone not far away. Miss Vinnie's cats are like silent, spoilt children, but real little ones would liven up this house. Ned comes and goes sometimes, of course, but Miss Susan always keeps him quiet when she brings him, the poor lad. He should be beating a hoop through the yard, not sitting still with a picture book, like a little scholar, under his mother's eye.

I lift the blue-and-white tureens and dust under them; I move Mrs. Dickinson's bandboxes, heavy with trinkets, and wipe them carefully. The pictures on one box show the city of Paris: sand-colored buildings and ladies in skirts like fancy cakes. The paw-feet on the china fruit bowl unsettle me, so I just flick the feathers across them, not wanting to touch; they remind me of Van Amburgh's lion. I finesse the drapes, sweep out the room and ready a speech about dinner for Mrs. Dickinson. It is only when I have the lines rehearsed that I realize I know neither what the fish is nor where it came from. The missus is sure to ask both those things. I scoot back down to the kitchen and go out to the yard in search of Daniel.

Once more Crohan steps from the barn; he appears and disappears like a púca.

"Do you like the fish I brung you?"

"What's that?" I ask, knowing well what he has said.

"I caught that bass myself this morning. It's a largemouth."

"Poached it, more like."

"I brung it for you, Ada," he says, and I dislike the sound of my name on his tongue.

"There was no need to bring it," I snap. "And I thought I told you before not to set foot in that house without an invitation." I turn on my heel and head back to the kitchen.

"You could thank me!" Crohan calls. "You might have manners and say, 'Thank you, Patrick, for that fine fish.' A good word won't rot your teeth. Hah!"

I slam the back door and stand against it. Do I want a fish that Crohan has touched? What harm could he have done it? It's a magnificent bass for sure, and cooking it would certainly save me a trip to the town, for I was going to seek out a nice bit of beef to stew. It occurs to me I could use the liquor from the pickled walnuts as catsup for the fish; Mrs. Child says the two go very well together. I decide the fish will do, Crohan or no Crohan. Once again I go in search of Mrs. Dickinson, this time armed with enough to coax her into having freshwater bass for tea. Either that or Miss Vinnie's cats will have the feast of their lives.

# Miss Emily Takes the Path Between the Houses

THE RAIN FALLS, DRENCHING ALL AROUND US; IT SLAP-PATTERS on the eaves of the house and sounds like a chorus of protesters, wanting some wrong to be righted. Looking at the downpour from my bedroom window, Ada says, with some satisfaction, "It's like Irish rain."

"Longfellow assures us that rain falls into everyone's life. So we must endure it."

"Yes, miss." She sniffs deeply at the open window. "It's scenty, too. Do you get that?"

I go to her and stick my nose up beside hers and breathe. She is right—this rain has a headiness like lavender or jasmine. "So crisp," I say.

"That's the spring on its way, miss, for sure," Ada says, as if she herself has manufactured the season and will shortly lay it out before me.

"Spring comes late in Massachusetts, Ada. We may have to wait another few weeks for its gifts."

Last night I wrote by the light of the moon, and I, too, thought of the end of winter. The moon sailed past in her plated gondola, the stars her gondoliers, and all that sparkling light pushed my mind forward to springlight and sunlight and summerlight. It is hard when you love light so but it does not love you and merely stings your eyes. Tonight I will garden a little by moonlight in the conservatory. I will coax adder's tongue into speech and cause bloodroot to hemorrhage under my hands.

For some reason these thoughts of herbs, brightness and gardening make me long for Mother's honey-sweet figs and their unctuous hearts. They are dry now, of course, so not nearly as luscious, but still I want to eat them.

"May we have some figs with our custard this afternoon, Ada?"

"You can, of course. I'll plump them up in a pan of water. Or better yet in apple juice." She lifts my wrapper over my head and helps me with the sleeves. "But breakfast first, miss. Don't be galloping through the day when it's only started. I have a big egg for you below that I mean to poach as soon as you're ready."

ᵛ

I eat my egg. Ada has poached it to my liking; its vinegar tang and pink sheath put me in mind of oysters. Oysters skip my thoughts to poor Hypatia, her skin pricked and torn open by oyster shells in ancient Egypt and her death from that stabbing. I shake this vision from my mind in favor of Venus borne from the ocean on her clamshell. From Venus I travel to Susan, and I think that this morning I will leave my nook and go to her. Writing a letter to Sue would not be enough for me today; I must sit in the same room as her and hear words fall from her own lips.

I thought of her last night as I potted herbs in the dark. The moon was an opal-bright roundel in the black, a conduit to another world. I fancied that Susan was the moon, the clouds around her a shawl. She was lit up and drifting, the clouds draped around her in gauzy wreaths. Into the clay went my fingers and the delicate stems, out of my mouth came the name of Sue. She makes me think of the biggest things, the best things, and it is my hope that we will lie together in the churchyard at the end. She may be Austin's truly, but she is also mine.

"I will go across to the Evergreens today, Mother," I say.

Mother stops scraping butter onto her toast. "Will you, Emily? I am pleased. Are you not pleased, Edward?" Father grunts from behind his *Republican* and shakes it a little to indicate both his pleasure at my outing and his displeasure at being interrupted while he reads. "I will send a note to keep Susan at home that she might greet you. She has her finger in so many pies about the town that I fear she is rarely in the house. She makes it so awkward for callers."

"Sue is sociable, Mother. It is hardly a crime. A woman of her intelligence needs a variety of companions," Vinnie says. "I will accompany you to the Evergreens, Emily."

"I prefer to go alone."

Vinnie pulls a cat into her lap and dips her face into its neck, to hide her eyes. "As you like."

I now wish I had not mentioned my plan, for Mother is overly excited at my leaving the house and Vinnie is put out that I will not let her come with me. Why can they not be more like Father— somewhat indifferent to my movements?

"I will run a ribbon through your worsted cape to brighten you up, Emily," Mother says. "What color would you like? I do believe I have a floret gauze with pink in it that will do nicely." She rises to go to her workbox.

"Do you have a blue, Mother? I should like a goose-blue ribbon—one the match of Ada's eyes." And with that they all turn to stare at me—even Father lowers his paper—and I smile. "What is it? Yes, Father? I notice things like the color of people's eyes. It cannot be helped." I wave my hand at Father and go to the sideboard to refill the coffee cups.

Mother follows me; she unpins her large buff cameo and fastens it to my breast. "There, now, that will do. You look brighter already, my dear."

The air swoons around my face, sharp and fresh. I love the way air astonishes me every time I take great new gulps of it. It arouses greed in me for even more air—more and more! The air in the house—even when it enters by open windows—never stirs as sweetly as it does in the garden. I stand on the pathway between the Homestead and the Evergreens and hold my face up to the sky and let all the cold, clean Amherst air press down on my eyes, my nose, my mouth. A robin flits from the elm, its belly flaming; *pip-pip-cheerio*, it cries, and looks at me as if it might stop and ask a question, if only it had the time. It is good to be outdoors, though I am glad of the hedge that hides me from the street. I stop a moment to listen to carriage wheels and horse hooves; I wonder who is passing by so busily, but I daren't look in case I am seen. I dash the short stretch between the houses.

Sue is ready for me, knowing I am to come to her. It is so long since we have spent an afternoon and a twilight together, letting a whole day slide to its close without paying any heed. When I am alone, the days have more hours; they like to trick me. Daily I am duped by the clock. But today is a day for Sue, and time will be of no consequence.

Susan meets me at the back door, Martha in one arm and Ned clinging to her skirt. Foolishly, I had imagined it would be Sue and me, the two of us alone. She must read this on my face, for she hastily says that the nurse will shortly take Ned for his nap. I grab her free hand in mine and pump it.

"Happy St. Brigid's Day, Susan."

"Saint who, Emily?" She turns into the kitchen, and I follow.

"Ada says the first of February is St. Brigid's Day in Ireland. A celebration of the new spring there."

"Is winter not still clutching hold of Amherst? Are we in Ireland?" Susan looks around, pretending to be lost. "Can you see emerald grass, Ned? Run to the window! Do you spy a grass-roofed cottage?"

Ned goes to the window, looks out and giggles. "No, Mama. All I see is Papa, marching home to see us."

"Oh, really?" Sue says.

Baby Martha drools a long line of spittle and shows her gums to me in a smile. Susan places her in a bassinet in a corner of the kitchen, and we wait for Austin to come through the door. He stops when he spies me.

"Emily, I did not expect to see you."

"Hello, Austin. I have come to wish you all a happy St. Brigid's Day."

"Indeed," he says. "Well, I shall take my meal here. You ladies should go to the library, much more comfortable. Ned may stop with me."

Feeling we have been dismissed, I follow Sue through the hallway. She wheels Martha before her and invites me to sit by the fireplace. She places the bassinet in the corner and struts back across the room like a dancer.

"You are such a peacock, Sue."

"A peacock?"

"Yes, I mean that. You are no mere peahen or peachick. You are the pouting peacock, complete with tail feathers that wink like eyes."

"From you, Emily, I know this is a compliment. And I shall accept it as one." She bows and takes her seat.

"Beside you I am a mere turkey." I go to her and sit by her feet. "Dollie, is everything well with you?" Austin did not greet her when he came in, and it perturbed me.

Sue sighs. "Austin does not like when I am milk-heavy, Emily. We had a dispute of sorts this morning. I was dressing, and he asked when I mean to tackle my 'silken layer.' I told him I have no desire to reduce my food intake while I am nursing, and he would not speak to me again. He watched every morsel I took at breakfast, until I could eat no more and excused myself early from the table. We have not spoken since."

"Perhaps he has returned now to apologize to you. Do you wish to go to him?"

"No, no. Austin and I will speak later. Come, let us talk of pleasant things. Do you have new poems for me to dissect?"

I look at her and realize I know little of the intimacies and quirks of married couples. I want to cheer her, to make her forget my brother's thoughtlessness.

"I have no poem sufficiently ready for your eyes. But you got yesterday's letter? Did Ned take it safely to you?"

"Yes. Though, as always, it was delightfully obscure. I attacked it like a riddle. I do so enjoy puzzling you out, Emily."

"And did you take its message?"

"I found love there. Etched onto paper in fine phrases."

I lift her sweet, soft hand into my own and rest my head on her lap. "I love you from a distance because I have no choice. But in pen and ink my heart keeps on. Dear Sue. My own Dollie."

She rests her hand on the back of my neck, and though it is cool, it burns my skin. I place my hand over hers.

"Rise now, Emily. The maid might see us. Or Austin."

I stand quickly and press my lips to hers before she can object. She laughs and pushes me away, and I sit opposite her. She is one of those women who look happy even when they are not. Her hair pouts outward over her ears, and her fine eyes are steady always. The lace collar she habitually wears throws light up to her face, making her appear as if she is aglow. I am glad now of Mother's bright cameo and the blue ribbon in my shawl; I might be some match for Sue in gaiety of attire, if never in beauty.

The maid bustles in with tea, and when she leaves, Sue pours for both of us. We eat spice cake, heavy with maple syrup; I let its dark heat tingle my tongue.

"There has been a pleasant quiet at home," I tell her. "I have had time in which to think of you."

Sue sips from her cup. "Shouldn't you fill your hours more productively?"

"I am productive: I bake, I sew, I write, I garden. But I call you to my mind often, for comfort."

"Do you not wish to walk through Amherst, Emily, to see what might be seen?" She sets down her cup. "Do you not wish to go to church once more?" Her look is hesitant, and it pains me a little, for she knows me so well. Why must Susan, above all people, question my need for solitary hours?

"I have seen my fill of Amherst, and I have heard enough at church. The pictures in my mind interest me more."

"I am having a soirée on Saturday," Sue says. "I insist that you come. And Lavinia and your parents, too, if they wish. The poet will be here again."

"'The Poet,' you say. Is there only one poet in the world?"

But Susan does not take my teasing today, and, as always with Sue, I bend to her desire. Her mind is occupied with Austin and with ironing out domestic rucks, which is as it should be. We drink our tea and listen to the clock tick and Baby Martha's fos-sickling noises from her bassinet. If Sue cannot come to me in spirit today, all I can do is endure it; there are days when she cools and retreats, and this is one of them, I fear. We sit on, drink our tea, and the clock's pendulum seems to become drowsy and ponderous, as if the air has grown fat. The ticking sounds sluggish to my ears; it goes slow, slow, slow, then halt.

## Miss Ada Has a Visitor

A COLD, OLD SMELL INVADES MY SLEEP, A CURIOUS, UNWELCOME sweetness. It sickens and frightens me. I thrash my hand over the eiderdown, half in and half out of wakefulness, sure that there is something on my covers or in the room. My eyes are glued together, but I force them open and shoot upright in the bed.

"Lord Almighty!" There is someone in my bedroom, I am certain of it. I am afraid then that it is the ghost of Auntie Mary, here to watch over me. I want to see her and yet I dread to. "Don't come near me," I whisper.

I fumble with the lamp chimney and get the wick lit. There is no one at all. I sit back against my pillow, relieved, and release a short spurt of laughter. Thanks be to God for that. I leave the lamp lighted for my comfort is gone. I lie back and notice that my door is open a crack. I get up to close it, and it opens wider. I do not even have time to exclaim when Patrick Crohan slides into the room and shuts the door behind him.

"Don't open your mouth," he says. His breath comes fast, and though he is stock-still, his whole body appears to twitch.

I cannot speak—a cry gets stuck in my neck and will not emerge. My legs won't move either, but I fling out my arm and push him. He grabs both my elbows and shoves me back to my bed and onto it. He pins me there, his bulk pressing down on me.

"You're a dirty strumpet, Ada Concannon," he hisses. "Making eyes at me, and you already taken. I saw you at Mass. I see you when I come to the kitchen." His breath stinks of whiskey, and his lips are salty with cracks. He pulls at my nightgown, and his cold hand lands on my breast and squeezes. "Do you know what happens to girls like you?" He kneads at my breast, hurting me. "You go to hell."

"Get off me," I say, but my words are a squeak that I can barely hear myself. All the air, all the will, is knocked out of me by fear. Still I try to fight him. "Get off me, get off me!" But he holds me down with his weight and pulls and shoves at every part of me.

❦

I have no wall mirror in my room, so I lift the pocket mirror that Daniel gave me for Christmas. My fingers will not work. It is not just that they are cold—they suddenly don't know how to work. I fumble with the tiny clasp on the mirror until it clicks. I hold it up to my face: my eyebrow has a welt—a purple ridge—my top lip is swollen, and a pearl of blood trickles from one side of my mouth. I am shaking, and I ache through to my bones: in my arms, my thighs and, most of all, between my legs.

The smell of him is everywhere: ammonia mixed with dirt and something worse, a sort of sweetness that makes my throat close off. My mind fights with my nose, trying to lock down what it is, and then it hits me: it is the smell of almond. He carries the bittersweet aroma of almonds around him. It revolts me.

# Miss Emily Sits for a New Daguerreotype

❧

I DO NOT LIKE THE CAMERA. I DARESAY THAT THE CAMERA DOES not like me either. And I do not like photographic studios. I do not relish sitting like a stone while a man peers at me through his lens. I curse Monsieur Louis-Jacques-Mandé Daguerre. I curse his mother for birthing an innovator.

The last time I sat for a picture, I was but sixteen. Sixteen and bold-faced. Velvet-chokered and hopeful, twirling a blossom in my fingers. That there has been no likeness made of me in twenty years or more alarms Father.

"You might die, Emily," he says. "How would I remember you?"

"With ease, Father," I say. "Remember that I was small like a pipit and my hair was chestnut bright and my eyes were like the brandy left in the glass when the party ends. Remember that I was a kangaroo beside the beauty of my sister and the handsomeness of my brother. Won't that do?"

"Goodness, Emily, I refuse to remember any of that. Now, look here, I have recent molds of your mother, Lavinia and Austin, but none of you. Must you be so singular? So stubborn?"

"The essence of the person drains from daguerreotypes after

a few days, Father. Would you have me fizzle away before your very eyes?"

He rattles his arms in annoyance. "I will have Mr. Spooner, the photographer, come here, Emily. You will not need to leave the house." He draws himself up to settle the matter. "Spooner has not embraced this new ambrotype nonsense. He will produce a fine portrait of you, my dear."

❦

Mr. Spooner comes, a compact person with a beard that wishes to defy gravity—it pokes from his chin, a horizontal bush. Mother has forbidden me to wear white. I wear Vinnie's old blue check; it sits lumpily around my chest, a curious match for the image of my sixteen-year-old self. I squint at that picture; I remember the day my likeness was taken. I was shortly to go to Boston to visit with my aunt's family. Father insisted that before I leave he must have a daguerreotype of me, to keep him company. I was chock-full of youthful bounce: eager and excited in my planning for school the following year and in happy anticipation of acquainting myself with Boston. There I would visit the graves at Mount Auburn and contemplate the souls snug beneath the cypresses; I would marvel over the wax figures in the Chinese Museum; I would enjoy a horticultural exhibition. But all that was ahead of the girl in the daguerreotype.

When I compare her—button-lipped and erect—to the image that looks from the mirror now, I feel lachrymose. My young self looks giddy but contained, as if some strange but welcome news has lately been imparted to me. I am heavier now, of course; my drooping eye droops even further, and my chin flops a little lower; I am, perhaps, a touch vinegar-lipped. Such are the vagaries of age. But there is something else: a resignation of spirit, maybe, a lack of wonderment at what might yet come to my door. There is no primrose path I wish to wander anymore; there are few infelicities to tempt me now.

Vinnie says I have not changed one whit, but of course I *am* changed. I have been immeasurably altered by every person I have met and by every word I commit to paper. In any case, I am sure I read somewhere that the plain woman can never be satisfied with her reflection or with a daguerreotype, for neither the mirror nor the sunbeam art of the photographer can ever be as forgiving as the sleight-handed portrait painter.

Mother still marvels at Otis Bullard's portrait of Austin, Vinnie and me when I was but nine years old. She stands in front of it often and sighs, the nostalgic exhale of someone who is content but a little sad. Such a trio of sweetlings we are in that painting, with our cropped hair and bud lips. But surely Mr. Bullard was being economical—we each have the same unblemished, identical face. Perhaps we were very alike back then and it is only in later years that our features have parted ways, so to speak. I held a pink moss rose that day and a botanical book that I was, at that time, in love with—it was my constant companion. Vinnie wanted to hold her cat, but Mr. Bullard gently suggested she hold a sketch of a cat instead—"less inclined to jump"—and to everyone's amazement she agreed. She was, I think, afraid of Mr. Otis Bullard.

We wore dresses with gigot sleeves—mine in green velvet, Vinnie's in silver-blue—and Austin looked every inch the Squire-in-waiting in his starched collar and black jacket. It was January, I remember, and cold, and that may account for the blush to all our noses and cheeks. Or perhaps again the artist took liberties and gifted us the healthy flush that winter had stolen. Whatever the truth of the matter, Mother treasures this painting as no other in her possession; I think she likes that our extreme youth is bound into that canvas and that it is untouchable there, a static, innocent hoard. It is as well she likes it, for no one—including me—is fond of the daguerreotype captured a few years later, and doubtless none of us will fancy the current one either.

❦

Mr. Spooner is a flapper. His hands flap, his lips flap, even his coattails flap.

"Come, come, Miss Dickinson," he says, waggling his arms at me like a demented schoolteacher with a brazen child. He does not touch me, but he maneuvers me with his whomping hands until I am seated in such a way that pleases him.

Ada has dusted and swept the room so that it sparkles, but Mr. Spooner wants no furniture and no "trimmings" in the background.

"I detest baubles. We must remain clutter-free, clutter-free," he intones, erecting a white backdrop behind me.

Mother and Vinnie stand by—a Greek chorus of encouragers—all smiles and nods, so that I will not get up and refuse to take part in the charade.

"Emily," Vinnie says, "you look wonderful. Does she not, Mother?"

"Very handsome," Mother says.

I fiddle with my sleeve buttons, glancing at the tiny cameo of the blindfolded woman on one. I wonder if she has the right idea—to go blindly in the world, neither see nor be seen. Spooner urges me not to move and slips the copper plate into his black box.

"Hold still, hold still," he says over and over, until I notice that even Mother is irritated by his constant repetition. "Mustn't breathe the vapors, mustn't breathe the vapors," he chants, and

Mother puts her hand over her mouth and steps back. "Hold still, hold still." It takes all my powers not to smile, for I must *hold still*.

I concentrate on keeping a death face, my features fixed like those of a person mortally frightened, or so it feels to me. I allow my mind to go here and there, up into clouds and above oceans. Westward across Massachusetts, over Mount Norwottuck, as if I were a wheatear returning from Africa. But it is difficult to imagine well with an audience present, urging you to inertia. I fix my stare on the brass peg below the lens and feel my eyes will soon water, which will be the undoing of it all. My breath backs up in my throat, and I long to breathe deeply, but there would be too much movement in that. Tick-tock goes the clock, tick-tock goes my heart. My mind soars upward, and my body tells me it will not stay stagnant much longer; I have almost reached patience's end when I am released: "And . . . *done*," Spooner calls, and I come back to earth.

I let my torso crumple, and then I stretch my arms and waggle my neck. Mother shakes her head, and I compose myself.

"Thank you, Mr. Spooner," I say.

"What is a photograph but a mirror with a memory, madam?" Spooner says, glancing at Mother with a smug smile. He is so pleased with his phrase he repeats it. "A mirror with a memory, yes."

"Indeed, sir."

"Madam, be so good as to line up my next victim," he says, a quip he surely trots out—along with the rest—at every sitting. We dutifully laugh, and Vinnie takes her place before the black box.

Mother is sitting for Mr. Spooner when Ada bustles in with rum and rags, intending to clean brasses, it would appear.

"Begging your pardon, ma'am," she squawks, backing out of the room. I go after her. "I forgot it was this morning," she says flatly.

"That is quite all right, Ada." Her skin is mottled and strange, and she is curiously quiet. She fell lately, on the stairs, and bruised her face, but the marks have healed a little.

"I'll go back to the kitchen, miss."

"Mr. Spooner is quite the enthusiast, Ada. Constantly seeking new prey."

"Miss?" she says.

"He likes to photograph so much that we are afraid he is going to line up Vinnie's cats for a portrait next." She keeps her eyes to the floor and does not smile. "Who is out the back today, Ada?"

"Out the back?"

"In the yard. Who have we got?"

"Daniel is there, Daniel Byrne. And Moody Cook. Mrs. Sweetser's girl—Nancy—will be here shortly to help me with the bleaching." She wrings her hands. "And Crohan is there. At least I think he is."

"I see." I pause for a moment, wondering what Mother will say to my plan, but the opportunity is too ripe to let wither. "Go and tell them to gather by the barn, Ada."

"All of them?" she asks, her eyes round as plates.

"As many of them as you can find."

⅌

Mr. Spooner sets up his box in the yard.

"Superior light in the outdoors," he says, to no one in particular.

He lines up Daniel Byrne and Moody Cooke and Mrs. Sweetser's girl. He calls for chairs and puts Ada sitting at the end of the row, then drags her by the arm to the middle, as she is the smallest. "We need one more for balance," Spooner says. "Isn't there one more?"

Daniel Byrne whistles through his teeth—a clear, melodic blast—and Patrick Crohan slinks from the barn. Ada keeps her eyes forward, but I see that she goes rigid when Crohan slopes in front of her to take his place at the end of the line. Ada has forgotten to remove her apron. I scurry forward, and she unties it hastily, knocking her hair askew in her hurry to pull it over her head. I pat down the stray hairs for her and smile, but she gives me a grim look in return. Perhaps it is wrong of me to ask her to be photographed along with the man she loves, but I think she will thank me for it when she sees the daguerreotype. She is a vain little thing, and it will suit her nicely to see how pretty she looks when Spooner returns with a cabinet card for her to display or to send home to her family. And when she takes in how handsome her Daniel is, too.

"My hair parting is like the map of Ireland, miss," she hisses. "I look a fright. I think I should step away into the washroom. I'm in the middle of sorting the clothes anyway."

"No, no, Ada. Stay. The laundry will wait." I squeeze her shoulder and move to the side.

"Hold still, hold still," Spooner calls, one arm aloft to keep the group from moving. "Hold still, hold still."

No one moves, save for Ada, whose hands worry in her lap. I think to run and pluck a blossom for her, to stay her fingers, but it is too late. So I watch her agitate and realize that her hands—her hardworking, tiny hands—will be nothing but a blur in the photograph.

By and by Spooner says, "And . . . *done*. You may all relax now."

A dove breaks from a tree in a sputter of wing beats, and Ada leaps from her chair and runs indoors. Daniel Byrne stands in the yard looking after her.

# Miss Ada Keeps a Secret from Daniel

THE DICKINSONS ARE SEWN TOGETHER LIKE MOST FAMILIES are—in uneven patches and scraps—but they go together well in spite of that. Miss Emily is the cause of a certain part of the up-and-down nature of the family, but Mr. Austin makes waves, too. No one else would say that of him, perhaps, but I see it. He has the worst of both his parents: the Squire's distance, Mrs. Dickinson's moroseness. But he also has a peculiar spark of his own—a sort of rumbling anger that bubbles under everything he is and does. That anger dances across his face and into his limbs, making a restless creature of him. He is fine-looking, too, of course—all wild hair and brooding eyes—and that brings its own troubles. Something about Mr. Austin exhausts me. I can always sense when he is in the Homestead, because tiredness threatens to keel me over. The tense way he carries himself leaks into the atmosphere around him and the very rooms he occupies.

It is to Mr. Austin that Miss Emily turns when I tell her what Crohan has done. Well, I half tell her, because I cannot bring myself to say what happened in its entirety; I am too ashamed, and I don't want to upset her.

"Ada," she says, coming to me as I labor over the linens, "did Patrick Crohan do something to you? Something untoward?"

My heart lodges in my throat; I do not want to talk about what happened to me. My haunted nights are bad enough without having to speak of it to Miss Emily. I step away from the copper and dry my hands on my apron. I look at her, anxiously twisting her slender fingers and frowning at me. How can I make her my confessor? She is too delicate in herself; I don't wish to trouble her with the awfulness of what occurred. So I choose to say little.

"Ada, speak to me. Did that man assault you?"

"Yes, miss, it was Crohan who bruised me. I did not fall on the stairs as I first said."

"My poor Ada." She holds her hand out to me, and I take it. "Go on. Tell me what happened."

"Crohan hit me, miss, with his fist, because I would not agree to kiss him. He found his way to my bedroom and accosted me there."

"But that is terrible, Ada. Appalling! I shall go to Father at once." She drops my hand and makes to leave.

"No, miss, please don't." I grab her fingers in mine. "I fear that your father will turn me out. Where would I go then?"

"But, Ada, that man is violent. He should not be allowed to walk away."

"Leave it go, miss. I don't want any more bother. Please. For me. I'm asking you."

"As you wish," Miss Emily says, but she looks wholly unsettled, and I know that the matter is not at an end.

Sure enough, she goes to her brother and it is Mr. Austin who comes to my bedroom late one evening—alone—to talk to me.

"Are you positive," he says, "that you did not entice him, that you did not invite him in?"

"Yes, sir."

"Is he someone you know well?"

"Yes, sir. No, sir. I only mean he works for your father from time to time and he comes to the kitchen. With Daniel Byrne. The Irish all know one another around here, sir."

"He comes to the kitchen? You ask him in?"

"No, sir. He comes uninvited. He left a fish."

Mr. Austin pushes his hand through his hair, exasperated, it seems, with me. "Is Emily the only other person who knows?"

"She is."

"What does she know?"

"That he came unasked to my room. That he hit me." I am too shamed to tell him of Crohan's threats when I warned him away from the Homestead. I feel a yawn breaking from my throat, and I try to tamp it down, but up and out it comes.

"I am tiring you."

"Yes, sir. No! I'm only yawning. It's not to say I am weary."

He turns to the fireplace and puts his hands on the mantelpiece, his back to me. "Did the man force himself on you, Miss Concannon?"

I am afraid to lie. "Yes, sir."

"And do you bleed?"

"A little."

He turns quickly. "Not now. Not after what you say happened. On a monthly basis, I mean."

"Oh." My face burns. "Not every month, sir. My flow is irregular, as they'd say."

He clicks his tongue and chews his lip. "I see. I shall ask the apothecary for tansy or Spanish fly or whatever concoction they use these days for such things. I know not what they prescribe anymore." He leans in close to me. "You will take it, and we will say no more of this indiscretion."

"Thank you, sir. Many thanks." I look at the floor, and Mr. Austin turns away and leaves.

My bones feel broken with tiredness. The bruises that Crohan left on my thighs are faded, but he may as well have inked them on me, for the skin seems to throb under my petticoat. I sit on the stool, put my head in my hands and weep.

I take the tincture every couple of hours and wait for the flood that will surely follow. Even in the night, I get up every two hours or so and sneak to the kitchen to warm water and take it. The tansy tastes of grass and oil; its awfulness fills my mouth. At night I soak brown paper in warm water and paste it over the yellow bruises on my arms and legs. I have been bathing balm of Gilead buds in a tot of rum and painting that onto my cuts. All of this because of what Crohan did to me. The hurt he caused to my body is one thing, but he has disordered my mind in a way that I cannot make peace with. I don't trust my own thoughts, for the terrible memory of him comes unbidden and chokes me at all times of the day and night. I swallow cups of tansy, and with the horrible taste of it, I try to douse him out of me.

And, at last, I bleed. Heavy, clotted blood spills out of me so fast I am afraid to move. I have had to fashion big fat rags to stop the red streaming down my legs. All my innards hurt—from the top of my stomach down, it feels as if something drags through me and means to force itself out, one way or another.

I sit to peel the spuds. I sit to pluck a chicken. I sit to knead dough. All the things I normally do standing at the table, I must sit for. If I don't sit, the ache and pull between my legs threatens to make me collapse in a heap on the kitchen floor. This must be what birthing feels like, or near enough to it.

Everything has been torn asunder—my mind rattles along trying to forget what happened, but my body screams it to me. The sight of my own blood turns my stomach, the smell of it even more so. It has a high, tinny stench; it smells old and bad. Even bleeding the chicken out into a bowl gets me thinking again; I push away the thoughts and turn my mind to work.

It is awkward to pull feathers from sitting, but after dunking it in a bucket of hot water, I take the bird in my lap like a pet. Mammy always strung up a chicken to pluck it—a rope from the rafter tied to one chicken leg—but I like to stand over the bird. Today I sit and go at the tail feathers and wings. The grab and tear settles me a bit; there is a violence to it that soothes me somehow. I barely even notice the prick of the quills, the tickle of the after-feathers or the bird changing from decorated to bald. I am not with myself at all; I am somewhere far away. I try to pray, but the words won't come to me in any order.

By the second wing, I am weary and all I can think of is lying down; the feathers in a cloud on the floor around my chair look inviting. But I will not lie down, because I cannot. I can't prostrate myself on the floor any more than I can go to my bed. Apart from the work I must do here, my bedroom is no sanctuary for me now. I enter it with fear each night, and I am sure the air is tainted with his almond stink no matter how long I leave the window open or how much attar of rose I drip onto the mat and bedspread. The room seems to crowd around me; it breathes its wooden breath, hawing all over me, the way Crohan did.

And the heat of the bed worsens the itchiness between my legs. I kick off the covers and slap at myself—a trick Daddy taught me for solving an itch—and it lessens for a few minutes, but back it comes to torment me. It hurts me to pee, too, and so I wander through the day with a bladder fit to burst to delay the moment when I will have to sit on the pot and feel the scald of it coming out of me. I wish my mammy was here, or Auntie Mary. Someone who would comfort me and tell me what to do. For I cannot speak to Daniel. Mr. Austin warned me not to tell him or anyone, and apart from his warning I simply would not know what to say. What words could I put on what Crohan did to me? And what would Daniel think of me at all?

Miss Emily comes to the kitchen to bake a cake for her nephew, who is in bed with one of his ailments.

"Will you take the cake to him?" I ask, and Miss Emily stands and stares at me as if I have said something altogether mad.

"No. I will send it by Father. And I will send flowers, too, for Sue. Shall we go to the conservatory and see what attractive blooms grow? Or we could make a garland with pine branches from the garden."

I don't want to go out into the yard; Crohan might be there, and I cannot stand to look at his leering face.

"If it's all the same to you, miss, I'll stop here. What cake are you after? Give me the recipe, and I'll get the bits ready."

"Perhaps I should send something more ambrosial to Ned, for building his strength?" She looks at me, but I do not know what to suggest. "No, I won't. He loves sweet things. I shall make my coconut cake."

"Grand so, miss. I know that one by heart."

She goes to the conservatory. I avoid looking out the window into the yard, as I have for days, for fear of who might be there. I sit for a few minutes to gather myself, and when I sense that Miss Emily might be coming back, I go to the cupboard for sugar, grated coconut and flour. We dried the coconut the last time we made the cake, and I am glad we did, for it swallows time to prepare it from fresh. I am starting to cream the butter and sugar when she comes back with a clutch of blue and white hyacinths.

"Look, Ada. Are they not embarrassing in their loveliness? And to think Hyacinth was a graceful Grecian man."

"They are gorgeous, miss." I take the flowers and put them in water, stopping to stick my nose into their open bells; their perfume is pungent and sweet. "Don't leave them too many days in water, miss. Tell Miss Susan the stems go to mush in water. Tell her that."

I don't mention that my mammy always told me that the recently dead smell of hyacinths, as it seems a morbid thing to say when little Ned is not well. Mammy washed every corpse in Tigoora for waking, and she told me that as each soul lifted, it left that hyacinth smell after it. I leave the flowers by the sink; Miss Emily will wrap them later in paper and ribbon. I soak the dried coconut in warm water to soften it, and Miss Emily sifts the flour. She is in a gay mood, and it lightens me to be around her.

> "I wonder how the Rich—may feel—
> An Indiaman—An Earl—
> I deem that I—with but a Crumb—
> Am Sovreign of them all—"

"Is that one of your own rhymes?" I ask, and she nods.

She is shy about her verses, but I like it when she recites snatches of them to me. It makes me glad to know that the nights she spends writing by lamplight come to something.

I hear a gentle knock-knock at the back door, and there is only one person it can be. It is not Moody Cook, for he strides into the kitchen. And that other yoke sneaks in. I ignore the knocks, hoping that Daniel might peek in the window, see that Miss Emily is with me, and go away. But he raps again, louder this time, and Miss Emily leaves down her flour sifter and goes to the door. I sit on a chair, for my legs have begun to wobble, and if I do not sit, I will crumple to the floor.

"Miss Dickinson," Daniel says, pulling his cap from his head. "May I have a swift word with Ada?"

"Of course, Mr. Byrne."

"My name is Daniel, miss. You might call me that."

"Yes, yes," she says, and steps aside to let him in.

"I'm awful busy," I say to him, so that he will leave, but he looks at me with such pained expectation that I get up and hoosh him ahead of me to the scullery. "What is it?" I whisper.

He looms over me, and I do not like his closeness; it seems to threaten me. I shrink against the sink. He sees me do it and steps back.

"You have fallen away from me, Ada. Have I done something to upset you?"

"No, Daniel." I look at the floor. "I haven't been well in myself, that's all."

"Might you need a doctor?"

"No!" The word snaps in the air between us. "No, I have a remedy from the apothecary. Mr. Austin got it for me. . . ." I trail off, because I feel I am saying too much. "I'm grand. I'm as good as mended."

"All right, then," he says, twisting his cap in his hands. He looks down at me, and I can see that he does not know what to make of what I am saying. I long to tell him the truth, but how would I say it?

"I'm grand," I mutter.

"I will be up-country for a week or so with Old Man Crohan.

I will call on you when I return." He nods and leaves me. I hear him say good-bye to Miss Emily, and then he is gone.

I upturn a bucket and sit on it. I am far from mended, far from grand. My rags are soiled with a stinking green, and I shiver without control at odd moments. There is a rash working its way over my back and arms like clouds across the sky. Every day when I take off my clothes to look, there is more of it creeping down my neck and along my wrists to my palms. And I am hot. I swoon with heat so badly at times that I have to pull the collar from my throat and fan myself. My muscles ache so that I don't know if I am coming or going. In my apron pocket, I keep a lavender bag; I pulverize it between my fingers and lift it to my nose to drown the smell of Crohan, the smell of myself.

Miss Emily clangs shut the oven door. It is a signal to me. I stand and go into the kitchen, patching a smile to my face for her.

# Miss Emily Ponders Her Brother

"It is like a pearl, isn't it?" I hold up the shelled almond for Ada to see. "A tear-shaped pearl." I eat the almond, and the fragrant desert of California seems to flow over my tongue. "Mr. Cutler ordered them in for us. Have one, taste one." I hold out an almond to her.

"I'm not baking with any bloody almonds," Ada says, and tosses the cloth she has been wiping with onto the table.

"I don't want you to bake with them. Mother is bilious, and the apothecary said almonds would help. I mean to blanch these and beat them into an emulsion with barley water. Will you help, Ada?"

"The very smell of them makes me want to throw up. I will *not* help. I have a thousand other things to be getting on with. A million."

She grabs the broom and heads for the stairs, and I do not dare to call after her to say that Father is still waiting for his morning coffee. I brew it myself and take it to the dining room, where he is ensconced with his deeds and whatnot.

"Emily?" Father's eyes are as glazed as a cow's, and his hand is out for the coffee. I think to speak with him of Ada and her attacker, though she pleaded with me not to, but Father is heavily occupied and does not wish to be disturbed, so I leave him be.

Sweet April light at last, and the frost will soon be lapped up by the sun. The trees are newly bursting with buds—some even have leaves—and the syringa by the barn offers her purple fragrance for all to swoon on. There is a memorial today at the church for all those killed at Fort Sumter during the early days of the war. Those long-lost, lovely boys must make do with a prayer from me, tossed from my spy hole into the Amherst wind. I never go to church anymore; apart from the dreadful crowds, there is, for me, a lack of meat in its teachings. The godly men rely too much on belief in the ethereal—that which is wanted and hoped for but unseen. I prefer to bow to the flesh and gristle of what lies before me, things I can see. But for the boys who fell in the war, I will send forth words of comfort in the hope that someone out there hears them and puts them to use as a spiritual poultice.

All of the Homestead and Evergreens are gone to the service, and it is at times like these that I miss my old Carlo the most—his warm, wet muzzle in my hand, his silly, faithful dogness. Mother always styled him a model hound, but I knew all of his secrets: avarice, laziness, a hot temper at times and too much fondness for a quiet life. Now, who does that call to mind except myself? Carlo and I were duplicates in temperament, I think. Father has suggested that I get a new dog, but I have not the heart. More than a year without my canine companion has taught me to be alone more fully.

I peep from my eyrie today. With the frost melted, the mud churns up, and tardy ladies on their way to the service hold the ends of their skirts aloft like dancers in a muted ballet. Pink arbutus waves above the street and makes everything look utterly alive. And then Mr. Kellogg's wife, heavy with child (again), comes rolling down the road like a sainted marble on her way to the church. I disdain her yearly birth-giving. What time does the woman ever have to think, or sit alone, or just *be*?

Spittle loosens on my tongue; I am in need of something toothsome. Vinnie jokes that I eat so many sugary things that it is a wonder I do not have a sweeter disposition. It may be that my sister sucked up all the sweetness of the family and kept it for herself. I leave the cupola and pad down to the kitchen, where the stove blazes and Ada chants prayers and sings in the scullery while she scrubs crockery. I hear her call to one of the cats, whom she pretends that she dislikes, but I see her gentleness with them often.

"Sheba-sheba-sheba," she says, "come on, old pet, come here."

But the cat must not come to her, for Ada starts to sing again. Today it is a plaintive song, and I stand to listen. She sings about Slievenamon, her mother's home, and says she will never forget one she met there.

Ada stops her scrubbing when she finishes her song, and there is nothing but a taut silence. I do not want her to know that I have been listening—an intruder—so I slip down to the cellar with the butt of a candle for light and go to the cupboard. There I have stowed an oval of gingerbread which I mean to share with the children later. But first I shall sate myself on its gummy mass. I break a piece—I have failed to procure a knife from Ada's store— and, like the low thief that I am, I steal it into my mouth in one huge bite. It is crisp outside and makes a pleasing crunch against my teeth; its insides yield to me, and ginger hops on my tongue. I giggle to myself and wonder if my reason is gone from me entirely.

"The bat thinks the fox cannot see," says a voice in the near dark, and I jump, almost dropping cake, candlestick and all. Ada steps into the light; she is holding an ax. She looks a little deranged, and I am sure I look somewhat crazed also, huddled in the cellar, my mouth filthy with crumbs.

"Ada, you startled me. And you have found me out in my greed."

"I heard scuttling down here and thought we might have a rat."

"And you would slaughter it with an ax? Brave girl!"

She looks at the ax and lowers it. "I didn't mean to frighten you, miss. I had to come and see what was scuffling about." She sets the ax against the wall. "I'll get the brandied peach leaves while I am here. They'll spice your mother's custard nicely."

I break another chunk off the gingerbread and hold it out to her. She grins shyly but takes it, and we stand there, two underground ghouls, scoffing cake.

I belch softly. "Excuse me."

"That gingerbread would bring you back if you were too far gone," Ada says, and she sighs. "Now, miss. Work, work."

I close the cupboard. Ada retrieves a jar of peach leaves from the wine cellar and bundles me up the steps. The cheery kitchen walls are succor to my eyes after the dark below. I sit at the table, near the stove's heat, while Ada heats milk for custard and scrapes long vanilla pods onto a plate, their seeds an army of immobile insects.

"Are matters improved with you, Ada? You know, since that which happened. Do you feel well?"

She doesn't raise her eyes from her work. "As well as can be expected."

"I heard you sing, before. In the scullery. You came across as wounded. Lonely."

She looks up at me, and I cannot read her eyes. "It's a song, Miss Emily, that's all. It's only a song."

# Miss Ada Goes to Boston and Chicopee

I must go to Boston, and I must travel there alone. Mr. Austin has decreed it, and he says it is for the good of my health, not to mention his family's well-being. I felt the itch of contradiction rising on my tongue when he talked of the family, but I softened it. He, of all people, does not take kindly to answering back.

He came across me in the dining room, dusting the ornaments. I stopped what I was doing and greeted him; he stood and looked at me for a time, then came close.

"You have a venereal disease, Miss Concannon. The French disease or the clap, one of the two. I am sure of it."

That is what he said to me, and he was angry, and I disliked his anger because there was blame in it. Even still, I felt I deserved the blame, for I am choked with guilt. I pray in my mind to the Holy Mother to help me.

I tried to tell Mr. Austin that I was feeling fine. "My symptoms are few, honest to God, sir."

He grabbed my hands and held them by the wrists. "*This* is a symptom, these horrible blotches," he said, blatting out the words. "I have seen it before. Many times. And if you do not wish to succumb to this disease completely, you will go to Boston to consult a physician." He tossed my hands from him and glared at me.

"Of course I will go, sir."

"I will make provisions for you, travel and the hospital and so forth. My sister is exceedingly fond of you, and I do this for her."

"Thank you, sir. I am grateful."

❦

I was arranging flowers with Miss Emily when she spotted the rash; I had covered my hands with powder, but it had worn off.

"What is this, Ada?"

I pulled my hands to my sides, but she prised one from my skirts and held it before her. She bent her head and squinted. The rash is all along my palms, and it looks like a splatter of pink berries. The patches are unsightly to be sure, but the rash is not itchy, and for that reason I have not been too worried about it.

"It doesn't bother me, miss."

"That may very well be the case, Ada, but Mother might not have you prepare food if she knew of it."

"I am vigilant, Miss Emily. And Mr. Austin is taking care of me. He says I must see a doctor in Boston, and so I am going there."

"Very well. That is to the good." She put her arm across my shoulder. "You know you can speak with me, Ada, of anything that troubles you."

"Yes, miss," I said, but I would not like to darken her heart with things she does not need to know.

❦

Boston City Hospital is brand-new. It looks like the Four Courts in Dublin with its high green dome. Broad steps lead up to the hospital's entrance; I stand at the bottom of them and consider not climbing them at all. Then I remember the wad of Mr. Austin's letter to the doctor in my bag and know that I must. Mrs. Dickinson thinks I am visiting cousins in Boston; Mr. Austin and Miss Emily thought it wiser to keep the truth of my trip from their parents.

The air in Boston is different to the air in Amherst. It has that wideness that city air holds—it must gather so much to itself: huge buildings, the river, all of its people and, beyond the bay, the whole of the Atlantic Ocean. I stand and breathe in the city, both afraid of and exalted by it. I wish that Daniel were here to see it; I had hoped for a few lines from him on his travels, but he has been gone two weeks now and there is no word yet. It may be that he is in the wilderness and does not get to any town.

I start up the steps and present myself at the hospital's counter. The clerk takes my letter and reads it. He looks at me, and his mouth creases into a sneer. I follow his directions down corridors and up staircases to the place I am to wait to see the doctor.

I sit for a long time. I feel I will go gray with the waiting. There is a peculiar smell like clean on top of dirty. There are two other women seated with eyes cast down to the floor. It is not a place for chatter. I look around, but there is nothing to see; I am sorry that I did not bring Mrs. Child's book with me for company. I think about what Mr. Austin said: the French disease. I always thought that things that came from France were good, like the Alençon lace that trimmed Mammy's wedding veil. Or Bernadette Soubirous, the French girl who had visions of Our Lady when she was gathering firewood. Even the priests' vestments at home in Dublin came from France, and they had "the approbation of the archbishop of Paris" according to our parish priest. But to have a disease from France—*the* disease—is no good thing. And what of the other thing he mentioned—the clap? What can that mean?

I push the thoughts away and try to clear my head. But while I am stuck and idle, my mind wanders of its own accord. There is only one place it ends up these days—it is the same when I am on the edge of sleep—and I fight to pull myself away. But my thoughts have their own will, it seems, and I am back in my bed, with Crohan grunting over me, pushing himself inside me and muttering obscenities. When I try to shove him off, he slaps me hard in the face and bites my lip with his teeth. I shut my eyes and ears to him as best I can and drag myself away from the pain and the high, horrible stink of him. But when he spills himself into me with a strangulated cry, my eyes fly open, and I see his eyes swivel in their sockets and a wayward, stunned look come upon his face.

I slap my hands to my ears and shake my head, as if this might remove the pictures from my brain once and for all.

"Miss Ada *Con*-cannon!" The voice stumbles over my surname. "Miss Ada Concann-*on*. For Diseases of Women!"

I stand and hold up one hand. "Yes, I am here."

"This way," the nurse says, and I follow her into a cool, white room. "Undress to your petticoat, behind that screen."

My cheeks roar with heat as I unpeel my clothes, then come to stand before the doctor. The room is huge, bright and cold, and I feel small and lost. The doctor reads Mr. Austin's letter and bids me to lie on the examining table. I shiver at the touch of his hands. He opens my legs and holds me open with his fingers; he pokes at me with a steel implement. It doesn't hurt much, but I feel bad to think of his eyes on me down there.

"Venereal. From the Latin *venereus*, which concerns sexual

desire. 'One night with Venus, a lifetime with Mercury.' Are you familiar with this phrase, Miss Concannon?"

"No, sir," I whisper.

He pushes my legs together, and I keep my knees tight. "You have contracted gonorrhea, Miss Concannon. A common disease of the immoral. You probably know it only as 'the clap.' I will prescribe calomel—a mercury salve—and you will take Daly's Sarsaparilla and Nerve Tonic. The great Mr. Daly assures us that his tonic permanently cures the disease you carry. I am not as confident as he, but you will take it anyway. It will help."

"Thank you, sir." I sit up, and the doctor studies me.

"Quicksilver and sarsaparilla. Have you not got the most tuneful of remedies, Miss Concannon?" He points to the screen, and I get up to dress.

❧

I have no Bible. Only the one book sits by my bed, Mrs. Dickinson's *Frugal Housewife*. It is to that book that I turn each night to ward off bad thoughts, as much as to lower myself toward sleep. I am weary after the din of Boston, and Mrs. Child's words settle me. I read her remedies and advice and recipes until my eyelids feel like purses that are forcing themselves shut. She tells me that the buds of the elder bush, simmered with new butter, make a soothing and healing balm. She says that night sweats may be helped by fasting early and late and drinking cold sage tea. I read in her pages about earwax making a useful lip balm and that pearls are best cleaned with torn paper. It is not until the word "almond" leaps from the page that I realize I have been nodding off. That word—and its stink of Crohan—wakes me again and harrows up all my pain. I could cry with tiredness and frustration. Is he, and what he did to me, ever going to leave me be? Will my mind be forever agitated?

I put aside the book and go to my chest of drawers. I unwrap the calomel and sarsaparilla and stand them on the chest. Mrs. Child says not to tamper with quack medicines, but surely if the city doctor recommended these things, they cannot be the work of quacks? I take the tonic first, a long swig from the bottle. Then I stand with my back wedged to my door and paint on the balm. It is thick and silvery, and it stings my flesh, but my hope is that that means it is healing me.

I am getting better. I will get better. I will *be* better. When I put on my apron each morning, I feel a little whole again. I am getting better. I will get better. I will *be* better.

᪥

There is no confessional in Amherst, for there is no Catholic church. I go to my cousin Annie's house at Kelley Square to talk with Uncle Michael. He lives with her now, sharing a room with Annie's boys. He got fed up rattling around his place, all alone, like a specter. He let his house, and now strangers occupy its rooms and sleep in its beds and eat off its tables. I cannot bear to think of them there, shedding their dirt into corners and making scruffy what Auntie Mary always kept so beautiful.

"That's an awful grand coat, Ada," Cousin Annie says, knowing full well it was her father who bought it for me but preferring a sly compliment to saying what she wants to say. Which is that—in her opinion—he wasted his money on a fine coat for me.

"Thank you, Annie."

She puts her hands out for my gloves.

"I'll keep them on, if it's all the same to you. I have a bit of a chill."

"Please yourself," Annie says. "You will anyway." She always treats me like an elbow relation, rather than her mother's niece and her own cousin.

Annie leaves me standing in the hall while she goes off, shouting to her father to come down to his guest. She says "guest" as if I am a stranger to her and all of them; it stings me every time. I look at the pictures hung in the hall—cheap landscapes bought at Cutler's. Nothing like the beautiful oils of winter scenes and the watercolors of the sea that the Dickinsons have in their hallway. I look out the side windows at the rain but only see myself in the glass, staring back. Miss Emily could stand at a window for a week, gazing, quiet as a cadaver. I hear footsteps and turn to see Uncle Michael come down the stairs, looking like a cabin of bones holding up scraps of flesh. I am shocked by how bad he appears; it is only a few weeks since I saw him last. I wonder if Annie is feeding him at all.

"Ada, you've come to see me." He holds out his arms, and I go to him; he feels brittle and small, an imitation of the man he was.

"I have, Uncle Michael. But I am looking for something off you, you won't be surprised to hear."

He doesn't invite me in, and we sit on the stairs together, a sorry huddle to look at, I am sure.

"What is it, *a leana*? If I can help at all, I will."

"I need to make my confession, Uncle." I wind my gloved hands together in my lap.

"You are in luck. Father Sullivan is coming from Holyoke to Mr. Slater's home this next Sunday."

"I know that, Uncle, but the thing is, I don't want Father Sullivan as my confessor."

"I see. Well, maybe we could get you over to Chicopee to see a priest in the church there. They have a plan to build a basilica, you know, eventually." Telling me this animates him; he was always a man for churches and grand buildings. "I will take you myself."

"Thank you, Uncle Michael." I hold his hand in my own, and it is rivered with purple veins like the hand of an old, old man. "Are you strong enough, do you think?"

"There's not a bother on me, Ada. Sitting in a carriage won't knock any wind from me, will it? It's a day out for us. We'll take a lunch in Chicopee. How's that for fancy?"

Uncle Michael chuckles to himself, and I am glad that it is to him I turned. I could have waited for Daniel to get back from his travels and gone to him, but I would have had to explain why I didn't want Father Sullivan to hear my confession. I would have to admit to not liking the man—another sin to add to my list of sins—and to why I could not tell that priest about what I had done. No, I cannot let Daniel know I want a blank-faced confessor, a stranger to me and to Amherst. I cannot tell Daniel a thing.

ॐ

I sit in the church in Chicopee and toss around the words "the clap" in my mind and think of the way Mr. Austin spit them. To clap is normally a nice thing, something good at the end of a performance. Why is it used for this? The other way of saying it is worse. Gonorrhea. It sounds like a lumbering thing, a thing that would crush and kill you. Though the doctor in Boston said it was not a death sentence; he said it clearly. I cannot decide which way to tell it to the priest in the confessional. I don't think that telling him I have "a bad disease" will be enough. And what type of sin am I guilty of anyway? Venial? Mortal? Have I sinned against the Sixth Commandment even though myself and Daniel are not married? Am I really an adulterer? The word is horrible to me.

Uncle Michael waits outside the church, taking a bit of sunshine on his face. I sit in the pew and slip off my gloves. I examine my hands in the gloom, and they look a little better, I think. I am missing a day's pay to be here; Mrs. Dickinson was outraged that I wanted another day off. I told her I had to bring Uncle Michael to Chicopee, but I left her to guess the nature of the trip. She shook her head until it looked as if her curls would collapse and at last said I could have the day, but she was not one bit happy about it.

"Mind you catch up properly with all that you neglect," she said, and I answered that of course I would.

The church smells like the church in Tigoora, of varnish and censer smoke. It is vast, though, as big as a barn. The Stations of the Cross are carved from marble, which makes them less brutal than the painted ones at home. The wounds on Christ's skin don't look so angry; they are white bulges instead of bloody sores. I put my gloves back on and mumble the words of a hymn to keep myself occupied: *"Ubi caritas et amor, Deus ibi est. Ubi caritas et amor, Deus ibi est."* I know it means "Where charity and love are, God is there" because my last schoolteacher said so. The hymn comforts me now—the thought that God is more than likely charitable to women such as me.

The priest comes at a clip down the aisle and disappears into the confessional in a flurry of skirts. I wait a moment, then enter the box and am immediately fearful of the pounding of my own breath and of what I will say. The confession box is airless and smells of melted wax. I wonder if this is what a coffin feels like, the tight, wooden stuffiness of it; the thought makes panic rush up into my throat. The priest slides back the door and waves his hand in blessing. I feel dismayed and wonder if his *Manual of Confessors* will list such a thing as the clap, or if I am the first person ever to come before him with it.

The priest mutters his opening prayer and then is silent. I shift on my knees; the prie-dieu I am kneeling on is hard, and I wait for him to continue, but he appears to be waiting for me.

"Confess," he says, and I see the side of his face in the flicker from his candle.

"I . . . I . . . I have been fornicated against, Father," I say, and I have no idea where the words spring from.

"By whom?"

"A man." He tuts loudly, and I swallow. "A man who works for the house I work for, Father."

"Did it occasion the loss of virginity?"

"It did, Father."

"Will a child be the result?"

"No, Father."

The priest sighs and puts his hand to his forehead. "Henceforth protect your chastity strongly. Say the rosary each morning and night for a year. *In nomine Patris et Filii et Spiritus Sancti.*" His hand flutters again, and he bangs shut the small door between us. I stay where I am for a moment, then steal from the box and out of the church.

❧

After all the fuss and palaver of Boston—its clanging bustle— Chicopee is a mercifully quiet place. And it has gentled Uncle Michael, coaxed him back to some sort of joy. He smiles hugely when I walk toward him, and I feel doubly blessed: to have the priest's absolution and to have my uncle's company. He holds his hand out to me and says we must do something while we are here. I perch on the wall beside him.

"Do something? Like what?"

"Whatever it is people do on a day out, Ada. We'll look at buildings. We'll eat large and walk long. See what's to be seen."

He is a little giddy, more himself than he has been in the six months or so since Auntie Mary died. I look at the sun stippling the path through the branches of the trees. I treasure the silence of the street we are on; it has a lackadaisical air despite all that takes place in the nearby textile mills and iron foundry and along the busy canal.

"They call Chicopee 'the crossroads of New England.'"

"Do they indeed?" he says. "How do you know that?"

"Miss Dickinson told me. Miss Emily. She has a headful of knowledge."

"Tell me, now, is she always gliding about? They say she walks the house at night like a púca."

"Not at all, Uncle. She's no ghost. She is in the kitchen with me as often as not and is as good at baking bread as any cook. And her sister sweeps the stairs morning, noon and night and manages much else besides. Their mother doesn't tolerate idleness."

"Oh," he says, sounding disappointed.

"But she's always writing things," I tell him. "Even while she bakes, she can be composing a verse. And she writes into the night in her bedroom."

This seems to please him, and he nods. "Why does she hermit herself away, do you think? She used to stroll the streets the same as Miss Lavinia. She was always visiting, they say."

"She prefers her own company, that's all. And the writing takes up her time. She goes out to the garden and conservatory. She's mad for growing things—flowers and all that."

"She was well liked always. People took to her."

"Miss Emily's not gone anywhere, Uncle. She's right there in the Homestead, the same as she ever was."

"But, hiding behind windows and lowering baskets of cake from them is not right. She should be out gallivanting with her kind. With men!" He lets out a strange giggle that ends in a gasp.

"It would do her no good," I snap. "Men are never what they appear to be."

Uncle Michael turns to look at me. He puts his hand on mine. "Have yourself and young Byrne had a falling-out?"

"No." I snatch my hand from his.

"He's a solid young fella, that Daniel Byrne. Every girl in Amherst had her cap set at him, you know. Then you waltzed into town. Hang on tight to him, Ada. He's a good one."

"What are we doing sitting here? We need to go and find an inn where we can eat."

I get up and start to march ahead of him down the road that leads to the river. I don't want to hear about how good Daniel is; don't I know it already? Amn't I in pain with the thoughts of his goodness? All I want of a sudden is to stand and look into the river. I miss the Liffey that passed so near my home in Dublin. I miss its swirling, secretive hurry as it rushed on to get to the sea. I miss the weed stink that wrapped itself around me. I come to the covered bridge that connects both sides of the Chicopee River and I stand at the fence looking down into the water, waiting for my uncle to catch up. The river doesn't have the clay smell of the Liffey, but its brown, busy movement comforts me nonetheless. The sun warms my back. I watch ducks paddle furiously against the current, then let themselves drift. Paddle, drift, paddle, drift. Is it a game, or are they really trying to get somewhere? Back to their nests, perhaps, where eggs or chicks wait for care.

Uncle Michael slides up beside me, puffing gently from the walk. He puts his hand on my shoulder. "Don't let any man ever take anything that's yours, Ada," he says.

I nod; I think of telling him it is already too late for that, but I don't wish to vex him. "I won't, Uncle Michael," I say. "Let's go. The sun is turning me to butter."

"Lead on," he says, holding out an arm toward the bridge, and we walk it together, our boots making a pleasing, rhythmic echo through the bridge's high chamber.

# Miss Emily Grieves Her Brother

FATHER WORKS. MOTHER SLEEPS. ADA TOILS. VINNIE TALKS TO her cats. The mice keep up their clicking dance in rooms where no puss is present, but they will not last long. Across the garden Susan tends to my brother and his children; she entertains guests. Amherst burbles on. And I sit here with my little halter, trying to secure time and lead it along. It is not that I have nothing to do— there is a myriad of tasks that call to me urgently—but I am on a slow day and I cannot seem to lift my hands to anything. I think of Longfellow, who says that there are days where darkness and dreariness must reign. But he also says the sun shines behind the clouds; that makes me applaud his poetic optimism.

I rise from my desk and open my bedroom door; I leave it ajar to hear the sounds of the house. Ada recites her prayers and sings hymns as she works—her new custom. The beat of the song she chants today sets off a rhythm in my chest: ba-*ba*-ba-*ba*-ba, *de*-de-*de*-de-*de*. Vinnie is reading aloud a letter from our Norcross cousins: no doubt the cats purr, lick their coats and ignore her while she does so, but they are audience enough for my sister. Mother coughs in her sleep, though perhaps she is awake? I am selfish in my aloneness and choose not to go to her, but she hacks once more and I am roused enough to flitter down the corridor and open her door. Her breathing is steady, and I leave again. Her bouts of repressed spirits and illness worry us all.

There is a certain guilt that wraps itself into me because I choose to travel my own road. My travels, of course, do not take me far, but I know that I grieve Mother, Vinnie and, especially, Austin. Even Father, my great ally, looks at me sometimes with uncomprehending eyes. But it is Austin who finds me the most alarming. Dear Austin; when we were children, how close we were. Anytime I was allowed to school—Father often considered me too delicate to go—I would write to Austin. From Mount Holyoke my letters buzzed like honey-heavy bees, full of youthful skittishness, which he returned in his own missives. He wrote to me from Easthampton, and we would poke fun at everything from Father's gravity to Moody Cook's plainness to whatever slattern Mother had hired to help with the washing. And I begged Austin often to give up his schooling and come home to me; I was lonely, and Father hovered over my health like a nervy physician, making me timorous in return. I was often housebound, receiving Dr. Brewster regularly and being condoled with by all the elderly spinsters in Amherst. When Austin did come home, Mother and I made special pies in his honor—ones heaving with apples and plums—and all was light in the house. Father loved to see him about the Homestead. He would look at Austin with relief and satisfaction and make singular pronouncements.

"You are a trout rescued from the Sahara's heat," Father said on one occasion, setting Austin, Vinnie and me off into giggles over Father's gravity, his ticklish analogies, his constant worrying as to our well-being and our whereabouts besides.

But since Harvard, and since Sue and the babies, Austin has hardened; levity has been leached from his very blood, it seems. We rarely banter anymore, for my brother takes the world very seriously now. Being in his company sobers me. Still, I love him with all my heart, but I know, too, that I vex him keenly.

Just yesterday he sought me out to speak with me about Ada. He came upon me in the library, where I had gone to choose a literary companion for the afternoon. Austin stood by the window and addressed it instead of me.

"Are you aware of Miss Concannon's ailment?" he said.

"I am aware that Patrick Crohan hurt her."

"Yes, but do you know what this might mean?"

I looked at Austin, waiting for him to tell me. "Is she ill?"

My brother turned to me and clicked his fingers like a man taming a dog. "You exasperate me, Emily," he said. "Can you be so *not* of this world that you fail to grasp my meaning?"

"If you explained your meaning, perhaps I might understand."

"You know nothing of anything," he spit, "cooped up here in your gilded cage."

"It is hardly gilded," I said, but either he did not hear or he chose to ignore me.

"I am not sure that Miss Concannon belongs in this house. In any respectable house. She has loose morals."

"For shame, Austin. There is nothing wrong with Ada's morals. She is eighteen years old, far from home and bereaved, besides. Have you forgotten that her aunt is so recently committed to the soil?" I smoothed my skirt. "Ada has a steady young man— Daniel Byrne. And she works harder and more cheerfully than any other help we have had."

"She is from Ireland, and one sure thing about the Irish is that they disdain the truth. They have two, nay, *three* faces apiece. Do not be fooled by her mellifluousness—all Irish people lie." The subject was heating him, and he began to expand his thoughts. "You have to understand that there is a certain island madness about the Irish, Emily. They are unhinged and vicious. Oddly, one could say that they display generosity and viciousness in equal measure. But a cataract of lies is all you can expect from them. Truly."

I waved my hand at him. "We are all capable of flowers of speech, Austin. Even us New Englanders. But Ada? I do not think she would make a gifted liar. She is good, she prays a lot and sings hymns. She is devout."

"All Roman Catholics are devout, Emily. It doesn't mean that they are not devious sinners also."

"Austin, Ada went with her uncle to the church in Chicopee. She wished to visit a church. Amherst lacks one of her faith, and she misses it."

My brother tossed his head. His hair—always a big, devilish halo—bounced and shook. "She is steeped in Romanism, Emily. She misses the pomp of her Holy Mass, that is all."

"It is my belief that she wished to speak to a priest."

"Does she converse frankly with you? Of intimate things?"

"Yes. No. I do not know. Is Ada compromised in some way, Austin? You must tell me if she is. I count her a friend, and I wish to help if she is troubled."

"A friend?" he snarled. "That girl is less than you. She was raised on swill milk, no doubt, in a Dublin tenement. She is not your friend, she is your servant."

"My friends are my domain," I murmured.

Austin stared at me for a few moments, then took his leave. Yet again he was grieved with me, and yet again there was little I could do about it. But what could he mean about Ada? Had Crohan done more to her than she had told me? And under my father's roof?

A thunder shower offers itself to the town; I run up to the

cupola to welcome it. Cardinals and chickadees start to sing faster, and there is frenzy to their music. Soon a scorched smell wends in through the window, and I know it is about to pour. The rain drops like honey at first, big, slow drips but soon there is a raucous din and all four windows are thrashed as if the weather is angry with us and cannot decide which part of the house to beat first. I revel in the storm, my turbulence about Austin—and about Ada— a match for it. The rain stops, swift as it began, and the town is as golden as someone newly bathed, glistening and clean. In the relaxed aftermath of the thunder shower, I resolve to speak plainly with my brother and get him to speak candidly with me. And I will also do my best to love him anew.

# *Miss Ada Makes a Decision*

❧

I THOUGHT I WAS MADE WITH MY POSITION HERE. THE DICKINSONS are a good family to be sure, and the house is comfortable. My room is small but pleasant, or at least it was once. Now it is a burden, for its walls seem to scream my sin to me, night and day. I whisper to myself after my rosary, "You have been absolved. You have been absolved." But it doesn't help.

When Miss Emily produced almonds in the kitchen, the smell of Crohan wound like wraiths around my head. It was as if he were in the room with us. I cannot explain how that happened, for I couldn't even smell the almonds, but the sight of them conjured him and his stink as sure as flames engulf paper.

Everything is smells with me these days. The caramel scent of old blood assails me when I undress. The whiff of alcohol—any sort of alcohol—makes a blur of stars appear before my eyes, because it brings back his breath, heavy with whiskey. I—normally as tough as teak—am bending under the weight of a few smells.

I lie into my bed earlier each night, for I know that sleep will not come easy. I close my eyes and dread the musical burr of the train as it passes beyond the house, for it sang its lonesome note when Crohan left my room that night and the two have become a match in my head. Sure enough the train's blare begins, and it brings back the look of brutish wonder on Crohan's face after he had done with me. But I must not let him conquer my thoughts, so I milk my mind for memories of home; I force myself to remember days under the eye of Slievenamon with Mammy, when we would go to stay with Granny Dunn in Killusty.

As I got older, the state of Granny's house distressed me—it was little more than a shack in my eyes. I slept on a shakedown bed of straw there, close to the fire, and I woke one morning with a crow sitting on my heart, its head waggling from side to side as it inspected me. I leapt up, and the bird flew into the rafters, where it primped its feathers. It wouldn't come down despite all of Granny's and Mammy's coaxing with the broom.

"It will bring her nothing but bad luck," Granny said. "The crow on the cradle, as they say."

"Shhh," Mammy said. She grabbed the cooking fork and lunged at the crow; he just peered down at her.

"The black on the white," Granny said. "Oh, I rue the day Ada came here."

"Well, so do I," I said. "The place is that cold and stinking the crow thought it was a byre. That's why he came in."

"I'll give you a clout if you talk like that again," Mammy said, glancing at her mother. I could see from Granny's face that she was injured. She loved her little cabin, damp and smoky as it was.

When I was younger, I liked nothing more than to go there, just Mammy and me on a jaunt from Dublin; we would leave my sister Rose sulking in Tigoora, looking after Daddy and the others. It took a long time to get to Tipperary, by mail coach, by cart and on foot, but we were always cheery on the journey, and we talked and talked. We would knock off landmarks happily: the motte at Naas, the fever hospital in Athy, Castlecomer's coal mine and, as we got nearer to Granny's, the avenue up to Knockinclash

Farm and the big gates at Kiltinan Castle. By the time we crossed the last humpback bridge and could see the mountain, we were nearly galloping. Granny Dunn was always waiting outside, as if she could smell us on the wind. She opened her arms, and we ran to her and let her hold each of us for as long as it pleased her.

"Mam, ah, Mam," Mammy would say, over and over.

"Shhhh, *a leana*, shhhh, Ellen." Granny Dunn held tight to Mammy because she was always her favorite. At last she would let Mammy go and take me in her arms; I sucked up her tobacco smell and enjoyed her firm, lingering hug.

I used to chase Granny's fowl and eat a big blue duck egg for my dinner. I would go and visit the farmer's bull, who had a back so broad you could sleep on it. I remember the bull standing in a field of dandelion clocks that looked like a gathering of moons; he was huge, a statue of an animal. The bull startled if I shouted or jumped, and I did that purely to scare myself. At harvest time I would lie in the aftergrass of other fields and let the sweetness gather me in.

Granny Dunn always set me to work: hulling loganberries, gathering wild garlic or plucking gooseberries—I hated the look of those snotty, bitter globes. We would sit outside her house, Granny under a cabbage leaf to shade her from the sun, me with my head bent over a bowl of fruit, and, if it was gooseberries, picking off their tops and tails with my fingernails. When she boiled them up with sugar, they made a tart red jam that I loved; it always amazed me that the berries changed from green to russet as they cooked.

Granny would fuss over me and fuss over her peat fire and fuss over Mammy besides. Auntie Mary would come from her nearby house, and she was as kind then as she was later. She liked to plop spoonfuls of honey into my mouth and giggle about the neighbors with Mammy, like a girl. She and Uncle Michael always got along well—a love match, Mammy said—but times were hard after the Hunger, and eventually they would make the decision to take off for America.

After Granny died, her little house was shut, and that was that; it was as if she never lived and breathed. The fire was blacked out, the fowl were sold, and the door was locked. And we never went back again, for all belonging to us were gone off the mountain.

Tonight I think of Tigoora, too, and the river rushing through the valley and the particular earthy smell of the woods. I miss the sound of the Liffey at night. The way it burbles away like a friendly animal, always there, always reminding us of its constancy by gurgling past.

Here my ears are assailed by Amherst sounds: the clop of horse hooves, the factory whistle, rolling wagons, men shouting in New England voices—all of it strange to me and welcome in its strangeness, but it is not the sound of home, and it rings hollow for that.

I reel my mind back to my own little part of Dublin. I remember the hazelnuts my sisters and I gathered, and the blackberries. I conjure the pigeon with his open-ended song, left on an up note always, as if he had to ponder what he wanted to say next. I fix in my mind the babby house we made in a bush and how we hid there long after Mammy got fed up looking for us and calling our names in one long stream:

"Ada-Rose-Mary-Kitty-Bridget-Peggy-Annie-Deeel-i-aaa." Sometimes she would just shout, "Concannons! Concannons!" Then, again: "Ada-Rose-Mary-Kitty-Bridget-Peggy-Annie-Deeel-i-aaa. Come home this minute!"

But all this thinking gets me nowhere. Crohan still looms in my head, and Daniel is there with him, a part of the problem, though truly all I long for is his sheltering arms. I haul myself up and lift the bottle of sarsaparilla. Its label is a soothing blue. I read it off in my mind, as I do every night, for the solace it brings: "Daly's Sarsaparilla and Nerve Tonic, Belfast, Maine. Temporarily cures cancers, tonsillitis, permanently cures gonorrhea, syphilis and stomach aches, and is an excellent antidote for poisons." Permanently cures gonorrhea. A *permanent* cure. An antidote to poisons. Patrick Crohan is poison.

I paint on the calomel; it is like a cold tongue licking my skin, and it makes me feel a little faint, which I welcome. It can only mean it is working well, getting all the way inside me. Between them the sarsaparilla and the calomel must be the reason for my sick-smelling shit that looks like boiled spinach in the pot. Though at least the rash is all but invisible now, and day by day I feel a little more gathered together. I decide that I will have a much better day tomorrow, and finally I slide into sleep.

ॐ

"I won't put up with laxadaisy hens," I say, chasing the little madams back to their coop. They poke their heads forward and backward when they run. They are comical, but they gall me, so I shoo them across the yard quickly, to get them inside. "Mr. Dickinson expects a morning egg, and you are not obliging him at all." The hens raise their shiny, apple-pip eyes to me as if defending themselves. "Don't look at me like that," I tell them, and I wag one finger to be sure they get my meaning. "Now, lay!"

I close the door and click the hasp on the coop and wait for them to settle. I listen outside, hoping to hear the satisfied noise they let out when they lay. I wait for the low yelp, that noise that makes me think that carrying the egg has been too much for the hen and she feels lighter for letting it go. No sound—not even a cluck or a yap.

"Silly little strumpets," I say, "I should give you your walking papers." I overheard Mr. Austin say that the other day, when he was in the dining room to discuss business with his father. I liked the sound of it so much I asked Miss Emily its meaning. "Yes, I'll show you your walking papers," I say again, into a crack in the coop, feeling satisfied to have a new threat for the hens—they ignore everything else I tell them.

The spring sun bakes my hair, making me feel better in myself, so I grab the yard broom and sweep all around. I stand for a few minutes and let the sunshine heat me front and back. It is glorious to feel warm, and I say a small prayer thanking God for the sun. I check on the hens once more, and their fusty smell assaults my nose when I open the coop. They all sit like returned queens, each waiting for her subjects. I ruffle under them, but not an egg do I find.

"The Squire will not be pleased," I tell them, "and you can stay in there until you mend your ways."

I slam the door and hear them fuss their feathers, but I resolve to feel no pity. I might take one hen for the pot tomorrow, and that will shake the rest of them. Mammy always said that fowl follow their mistress's mood, and she would coddle and mind her hens as much as she minded us, her daughters. I realize I have been too distracted lately to pound up bones for them; that sort of pulverizing is a great boon to the energies. And if I mix bone with oats instead of corn, it will have them laying again in no time.

I soften toward the hens and decide to change the sops; maybe they are sodden and uncomfortable. I go to the barn for straw and a fork and am relieved to find that there is no one there. I use the yard broom to sweep out the henhouse, then scatter some gravelly earth to keep the lice away. The hens are settled in their nests and refuse to move while I clean.

"You are the most contrary lot I ever met," I say. *Sweep, sweep, scatter, scatter.* "I would be much obliged if you would lay." *Sweep, sweep, scatter, scatter.* I think of my mood and sing a little, to jolly them. *Sweep, sweep, scatter, scatter.* The hens struggle and squawk when I lift them to scoop out the old straw and put in the new bedding. Under Agatha, the bossiest hen, I find a small egg, and I congratulate her. I grab it and slip it into the pocket of my apron. I lift her high to look at her claws to check for bumblefoot, which lately had her tripping over herself, but she has healed nicely since I drained the sores. I put her back in her nest, say, "Good girl, Agatha," and close the door.

In the kitchen I take down the smallest pot. As there is only one egg, I will have it for myself, an early Easter treat. I lift the egg from my pocket and am surprised to find that it is soft. I look at it closely—it has no shell. I place it carefully in my palm. The egg is honey-colored, and when I hold it to the light, I can see the yolk hanging inside, a perfect golden blob. Whenever Granny Dunn got a shell-less egg from one of her birds, she would say, "That may be the last egg she'll ever lay." She called them witch eggs and wouldn't eat them in case of bad luck. Granny also liked to say if you didn't crush the shells after eating a boiled egg, a witch would make a boat of the broken bits and raise storms at sea. I suppose she was trying to frighten me; Mammy always smiled at these stories and told Granny to leave off.

I smell my witch egg; it smells of nothing but the usual—straw and hen dirt. I roll it like a ball on my hand, being careful to contain it so that it doesn't fall. It seems a waste to throw it out. Surely it will do no harm to eat it? An egg is an egg.

I take the sharpest knife; the skin is tough, and I have to pierce it, then pull it away. The innards slither out into the pot like something alive, but all looks well—the glair is unclouded. I beat the egg with a little milk and butter and place the pot on the stove; when it has gathered together, I fork it into my mouth straight from the pot. Witch egg or no witch egg, it tastes delicious.

✌

Mrs. Dickinson calls out to me as I go to leave the dining room. I cannot think what she wants, for I have everything served and done. She rises at her place at the table, and I step nearer.

"This meal is unseemly," she says, waving her hand at her plate.

I look at the dinner: boiled chicken, mashed potato and roast sunchoke. I cannot see what it is she disapproves of; I raise my eyes to hers.

"I apologize, ma'am," I say.

"It is a badly put-together meal, by any measure. Where are the greens? Could you not have made a little gravy?"

I glance again at her dinner; the plate holds nothing but three pale mounds. It does not look appetizing, because everything in the meal is the same color. "I could shell some peas and steam them quickly."

"It is too late for that, Ada." Mrs. Dickinson sits and takes up her cutlery. "You are growing careless, Miss Concannon, and I will not tolerate it. Consider turning over a new leaf, or we shall have to see."

She forks some chicken into her mouth, and I go to the door. As I pass her, Miss Emily half smiles, and I know it is meant as encouragement, but I do not feel encouraged at all. My witch egg curdles in my stomach; I fear there will be ructions before long.

Mr. Dickinson's medical book lies open on the library table. I drag my feather duster over the picture rails, fiddle with the green curtains, then dally by the table to look at it. The book is open at a well-used page, the one of concern to Mrs. Dickinson these days—rheumatic diseases. I put down my duster and rag and make sure that no one is coming. I drag the book nearer to me and search for the clap. Nothing. I turn to the "G" pages and finger my way over the thin paper to find gonorrhea and locate it at last.

There are pictures, lots of ugly pictures of lumpen bodies decorated in welts. I wince but run my finger over them. There is a girl with her back to the viewer, naked from crown to rump. Her long hair is tied with a ribbon, which makes me think she must be very young; she is slender, too—she doesn't have a woman's hips. Her whole skin is dappled with sores, like the knobbles on a raspberry, and her neck in particular is heavily spotted. I thank Mary in heaven that my rash was never that bad and that it has receded to almost nothing. I want to put my arms into the picture and hold the girl; I want to turn her and see her face. I want to know if she is frightened.

I read the words underneath the pictures. It says that gonorrhea is acute and infectious and that men and women are affected differently. It says the treatment is mercury, in the form of calomel, and that side effects might include tooth loss. Tooth loss? I put my hand to my mouth and try to wiggle my teeth. They are all in place, rooted. It also says that gonorrhea can affect a woman's ability to have children if left untreated. For one moment I feel I have been clapperclawed. The doctor in Boston mentioned no such thing. He said between the sarsaparilla and the calomel I would be right as right. He did say that, I am sure of it. I read more. But no, I must not get upset. I take a deep breath and thank God for my treatments. They are working, I will be all right. Daly's Sarsaparilla and Nerve Tonic, after all, *permanently* cures gonorrhea; it's written on the bottle! I read on and see that the book says that sufferers should avoid oral and intimate contact with other people. No contact. No kisses. The page swoons in front of my eyes, and I slap shut the book. I know now that it is time I went to speak with Daniel Byrne.

# Miss Emily Confronts Mr. Austin

❧

I HAUL MY BASKET UP ON ITS KNOTTY ROPE AND PEER INSIDE. The children have, of course, devoured the gingerbread. In its place one of the little dears has left a sprig of apple blossom for me. I hold its delicate petals to my face and inhale its springness.

Out on the street, there is the slow rumble of cart wheels and the pacier clip of hooves. I leave down my basket and lean out the window. The air is so clean it makes me determined to take a turn around the garden later to breathe lungfuls of it. As I turn away from the window, I see Ada march up the street. I go to call and wave, but then I see that Patrick Crohan is behind her, talking determinedly, his head dipping forward, the better to be heard. She ignores him and stomps ahead. He catches up to her at the steps and pulls her arm; it is a violent yank, and I raise my hand as if I might stop him. Ada reels around and pushes him away. She runs up and comes inside the gate, closes it against him and storms up the path. He stands staring after her, a fierce and impatient set to his face. He looks as if he might jump the fence or shout after her, but his gaze travels upward and finds me at the window. A normal man would doff his cap, but he spits on the ground and walks quickly away. He is a brazen jackanapes, that fellow, and no mistake.

I run down the stairs and wait for Ada in the kitchen, but she does not appear. Pulling my shawl tight, I slip out into the yard, past the barn and its animal stench, on down through the garden to the orchard. The man whom Mother employs to tend the plants is staking and tying delphiniums, and he stops as I approach, takes off his cap and stands.

"Has Miss Concannon passed this way?" I ask. He nods and points. I skip by a bed of bearded irises, which also seem to nod, chanting, *Yes, yes, yes, this is the way she came.*

I find Ada standing in a puddle of blossom, looking out into space like a sailor surveying the sea. Her hands are bunched into the sleeves of her coat, and she does not turn to look at me. I wait for her to speak, pulling my shawl ever closer, for there is a cut to the wind. It seems Ada does not mean to say a thing. I venture closer, and a pair of jaybirds scatter from the branches above us, their blue bodies flashing like sapphires.

"Did he do more than hurt you?" I say.

Ada's eyes meet mine. "What do you mean, miss?"

"Patrick Crohan. Did he attack you in a profounder way than you have told me, Ada?"

"He about broke me, miss," she says, and tears rush down her cheeks. She swipes at them with the back of her hand.

"Come with me around the orchard, Ada, and tell me what happened. All of it."

"I need to make lye for soap, miss. I have spuds to peel." Her voice is flat. Dogs raise a cacophony of barks nearby, making us both jump.

"Walk with me. Your work can wait a little."

"Your mother said I need to turn over a new leaf."

"Vinnie and I call that 'the foliage rebuke.' Mother throws it around a lot. Do not dwell on it." I link her and lead her to the orchard pathway and off it, in amongst the trees. "I saw Crohan follow you. I saw him grab your arm."

"He is a bad man, miss," Ada says. "The things he says are shocking. The things he does are worse. I hate him. God forgive me, but I do. I hate Patrick Crohan."

"He need not ever come here again. Let me tell Father now. He can have him prosecuted for trespassing. He would be very unhappy if he knew Crohan had come into our house uninvited. That he slapped you."

Ada snorts. "He's done worse than that." She stops and looks up at me. "But leave it be, Miss Emily. There is no good to be gained in going after him. It will only make things worse."

"What happened that night? Did he injure you in deeper ways than I know?"

Ada sucks air into her mouth and sighs; she holds her face up toward the canopy of branches above us. She looks at me as if testing me.

"He took my virtue, miss."

ॐ

I knock on the door of the Evergreens until my knuckles are sore, and still no one comes. I curse Susan for her shopping flits to Boston and Springfield; I curse Austin for his attachment to his town office. I peer in the windows of the front parlor—I am grateful to be hidden from the street by the hemlock hedge—and then I go to the back of the house. I knock madly, and their girl answers at last; she looks at me as if I am the worst kind of intruder on her day. If President Johnson himself had arrived at the door, she could not appear more irritated. I push past her.

"I will wait within for my brother's return," I tell her, and she, slack-jawed, merely nods.

In the parlor I pace the floor, my steps clicking, then muffled as I pass from wood to carpet. There is a fire smouldering in the marble fireplace, but still I shiver and hope the maid will come and make it blaze. My poor, poor Ada. How could this have happened to her, and in *our* home? What anxieties she must have been suffering since. Feeling cold with rage against Crohan, I go nearer the fire; the mantel is adorned with Canova's Cupid and Psyche sculpture. Psyche is waking from the sleep that Proserpina tricked her into; Cupid has performed the kiss that woke her, purging Psyche of the spell. There is huge tenderness between them, it strikes me, such a delicate passion. I run my fingers over Cupid's hand, the one that cups Psyche's breast; I relish the cold skin under my own. How well man and woman can come together at times, and how badly they meet at others. I agitate my hands and sit, then stand again. Crohan must be expelled; Ada must be seen by Dr. Brewster.

I look around the parlor: its gilt and autumnal silks annoy me of a sudden, and I flop into Sue's green chair. But my heart is giddy and unconcentrated, and I rise again, needing movement to soothe me. I walk the edges of the room and come upon a doll on the floor. It is a sailor doll of Ned's that Mother gifted him at birth; it has an angry little face and lamb-fleece hair. I have never liked this doll—his ill temper alarms me—but looking into his blue glass eyes now, I see Ada's eyes. I kiss the doll's cold porcelain skin and set him on a chair to wait for Ned.

Surrounded by her things, her taste, I think about Susan, about her elegance and her learning. Some, I know, find her haughty and frivolous, but they have her wrong. She is sensitive and cosmopolitan; she is imagination itself. Sue is luminous, a living Psyche. Though I would never style Austin as Cupid—her match.

I hear voices and go into the hallway; its pulsing reds seem to beat down on me. I look up at the painting of Abram and Sara—he ancient and swarthy, she young and virginal. I had not noticed before that her breast peeks from her white robe and that she looks coy, almost flirtatious. The scene makes me shudder, and I wonder why Susan has hung it in the hallway of all places.

Sue is out of sight in the passageway; I can hear her talking to the maid. Like me, she has come into the house through the back. She pushes the curtain aside and steps toward me, removing her cape; little Ned is behind her.

"Emily," she says, kissing my cheek, "how pleasant to find you here."

Ned runs to me and pulls at my skirts; I bend to hug him. I go forward and look into Martha's baby carriage, to enjoy her sweet face; she is swaddled and sleeping.

"I have come to see Austin. I must speak with him as soon as possible."

Sue looks at me. "Are you all right, Emily?"

"Not really. I am dismayed over something that has occurred under my roof, and I wish to gain Austin's counsel."

Sue unpins her bonnet and tosses it onto the hall table; she turns the handle on the call button to summon the nurse, who appears quickly.

"Ma'am. Miss Dickinson."

"Take the children upstairs."

Susan leads me into the parlor and sits into her velvet throne; I take the slipper chair opposite. Baby Martha whimpers as she is lifted up and spirited with Ned to the nursery; then it is silent save for the *crick-crack* of the wood settling in the grate. All is quiet between us, but my silence is agitated, while Susan's is contained.

"Can I be of assistance, Emily?" she says after a spell. "You seem much grieved."

"No, Sue. It is my brother I need. It is a delicate matter."

"Are you well? Is everyone well at the Homestead? Your mother?"

"We are fine, all of us. It concerns Ada."

Susan tuts and looks into the fireplace; she pushes a snort through her nose. "Ada!" she says, and the word is bitter on her tongue.

"Yes, *Ada*. Why do you say her name as if it pains you to do so?"

"I warned you about being too free with her, and look where it has ended. Austin spoke to me of what occurred."

I stand and go to her. "Susan, a young girl has been harmed. Surely you do not condone that?"

"Emily, I am just saying that you are too friendly with the help. I told you not to encourage that girl."

"But you cannot blame her for that Crohan man's sin?"

"Indeed I do not. What happened is despicable. Miss Concannon seems a capable, hardworking girl. But can you keep her in your home now? My concern is for you, for your family."

"Well, my concern is for Ada, first and foremost."

"And I commend you for that, Emily. It speaks well of you."

I pull my shawl together and knot it. "I will go now, Sue. Tell my brother I need to talk to him. Today. Tell him it is vitally important."

I leave her.

# Miss Ada Has an Encounter in Cutler's Store

I WAS IN CUTLER'S, BROWSING CANNED PEACHES AND WONDERING if Mrs. Dickinson might enjoy them. Her stomach was at her again, and I wanted to make digestible dishes to please her. I can feel her ire with me these days; it rises off her like steam. But canned fruit costs, and Mrs. Dickinson is one grouse who likes to spare the heather, so I hesitated. Perhaps, I thought, if she saw the price of the cling peaches listed in the account book, she would not be pleased. But then again, maybe their silky goodness would trump the cost and she would applaud my thoughtfulness.

I held the can and studied its label: it showed peach wedges floating in a sea of syrup in a glass bowl. The curved slices made me remember a recent dream. I had tipped peaches into a dish and was beginning to eat them with a fork when the slices turned into swimming, golden fish. The dream disturbed me greatly when I had it, but by the time I stood in Cutler's, spit loosening on my tongue at the thought of the fruit and its thick juice, I found it funny. Peach fish. Fish peaches. I gazed at the peach can, smiling, when I felt a waft of wrongness come from near me. I did not need to look over my shoulder to know that Crohan was there. I couldn't smell him, but my whole body stiffened against him; my skin and my scalp knew he was nearby, as sure as eggs. I put the can back on the shelf and began to walk toward the door.

"You're nothing but slum lice," he hissed, and his mouth was so near my ear I felt the heat of his breath.

My heart beat like a windmill, but I kept moving. He poked me in the small of my back, and I stumbled. The thought of him touching my coat made me sick, for it brought back the rough feel of his hands on my skin. I trotted faster, bumping in my haste against a woman who was buying ribbon at the glass counter near the door.

"Mind your manners, miss," Mr. Cutler called out.

"I'm sorry," I said, getting out the door and away. I looked wildly up Merchants Row, hoping to find one of the Dickinsons or Kelleys coming out of Kendrick's or Burt's, that I might walk back to Main Street with them. I willed my Uncle Michael to come shambling toward me. I saw no one that I knew.

Crohan was upon me quickly, but I would not look at him. I did not want to see his eyes or his awful mouth. I did not want to smell him. He said things in a low, mean voice.

"You jackeens are all the same. Scum. High-and-mighty scum. I've seen you in your glory. Don't forget *that*, Ada Concannon."

I walked quickly across the common, toward Main Street. He would not leave me alone, and he tried to dance in front of me to continue his taunts, but I broke into a run. Crohan followed and lunged before me; I had to stop so as not to bang into his chest. I stared at him. He was truly like one of the horribles from a parade, but his own face was the ugly mask and his clothes the tattered costume.

"Leave me be," I said.

"I will not. Where is your lovely Daniel now, hah?"

"Get out of my way. The Dickinsons know what you've done."

He grabbed my wrist and twisted it. "What have I done? I've done nothing at all, save what you begged me to do."

"Get off me!" I shouted, hoping to get someone's notice but there was no one to be seen in any direction.

When I roared, he dropped my arm, and I launched across the grass and down the street toward the Homestead. He caught up and kept behind me, whispering vile things about my body, about what he planned to do to me next. When I gained the steps of the house, he pulled my arm, hurting me.

"If you tell Byrne anything, I'll kill you," he said. "I'll strangle the fucking life out of you. Do you hear me?"

I turned and pushed him away, though I did not want to touch him at all. I ran up and stepped inside the gate, closed it against him and jogged up the path. He stood there, for I glanced back, and when he saw me look, he spit on the ground and walked away.

Miss Emily was watching from the window and witnessed it all; she came to me in the garden and questioned me about the truth of what I had told her before. I did not want her to guess the nature of the attack, and I do not know that she had; despite her age she is sheltered, innocent. But I was rattled after Crohan's chasing me home like a dog, and in the end I told Miss Emily what he had done. And in telling her I released a beast that will not be caged. She will go to her father now, or her brother, and all will be lost.

❧

Daniel comes to his door in shirtsleeves; his face is creased with sleep. He looks both more boyish and more manly, with his tired eyes and trouser braces on show.

"Ada," he says, and then he asks me to wait a moment.

I stand on the steps of his boardinghouse, and his landlady stands inside her window, watching me. She is turned sideways, as if to hide herself, but she stares at me, both brazen and sly. I turn my back to her and look down into the heart of Amherst, where the railroad carries men and goods to and fro all day long. Daniel returns with his coat on and his hair combed; he gestures for me to accompany him to the side of the house, out of the window's sight.

"I heard you were back," I say.

"We traveled by night most nights, so I am worn out. I was going to come up to the Homestead today to see you. I'm sorry I didn't send a letter. There was no opportunity for that."

"No matter, Daniel."

"I missed you, Ada."

We step into a grassy alley that runs along the gable wall. He reaches for my hand, but I slide it behind my back so he cannot take it. My face is healed—there is no trace of anything on me—but I do not want him to touch me. He looms over me, and I want to let him take my body close to his and hold me there, but I cannot.

"Daniel, I have come to tell you that we won't be walking out together anymore."

He winces and drags his two hands through his hair. As he lifts his arms, I smell sweat and earth and smoke.

"I didn't mean to be away so long, Ada. Old Crohan kept wanting to go further upstate to look at different horses. He knew I wasn't happy about being gone so much time. The weeks were a curse for me, too."

"It isn't because you went away, Daniel, it isn't that. I think, maybe, we are not a good match. My Uncle Michael says it. I'm sorry."

He hitches his jacket close around him and purrs through his throat; it is a sound meant to tamp down annoyance or stray words. "We get along well, Ada. We are decent to each other. You are dear to my heart, you know that. Your uncle knows it, too."

"Well, he's changed his mind, it seems." I look at my boots, then back up into his face. "He has forbidden me to see you." I turn away from Daniel, afraid he will catch the lies falling from my mouth. "I'm sorry."

"Maybe I should go to Kelley Square and talk to Michael Maher, to see what he has to say for himself."

"No," I say, alarmed at the thought of my uncle's being dragged into it. "You're not the be-all and end-all of my life, Daniel Byrne." I turn away again. "I have to get back."

"What will be will be, Ada," Daniel calls.

I walk away and urge myself on toward Main Street. There is hope, not resignation, in his voice. He is telling me he will not give up so easily. My feet feel as if they are wading through molasses. I think of Daniel's confused face and the beautiful heft of him and allow myself a handful of scalding tears. I dab at my cheeks with my handkerchief and quicken my step to put distance between us. He may have hope, but I have none, for I cannot let him make the mistake of pursuing me.

❦

I sit on the end of my bed and grease my boots with butter, my hand acting as a last. They were Mammy's boots before they were mine, and the furrow of her toes still occupies the leather. It is asking for ill fortune to wear another person's clothes, I know, but boots are different, surely. I love that the ghost of Mammy's foot walks with me wherever I go. When I slip my feet into the boots, I feel her wrap herself around me and give me strength. Even the smell of the butter brings her near to me; it was she who taught me to churn, and it was Granny Dunn who taught her before that. The butter I make is the daughter of Mammy's butter just as I am hers.

There is a rap to my door, and I leave down my rag and boot to open it. Miss Emily stands before me, her eyes searching my face. I hold the door and look up at her. Her brown eyes are lively and quick as a squirrel's, but they can be slow and lingering, too, like the eyes of a cow. Today they have a heavy, liquid look.

"May I come in, Ada?"

I stand out of the way, and she walks in. "Sit, miss," I say, gesturing to the bed, and she sweeps her skirt with one hand and perches on the eiderdown, a dove on snow. What is it Granny always said about dove eggs? If you eat one, you will have no luck.

"I was buttering my boots."

"Yes," Miss Emily says, and she is still regarding me with unasked questions.

"You look like you want to say something, miss. To ask something, maybe?"

She fidgets with the ribbon at her throat; her long fingers are like skeleton bones. Miss Emily stands. "Ada, are you with child?"

"I am not, miss."

"Very well," she says. "Forgive me for asking, but after the attack it was a possibility, you do realize that?"

"I did realize that."

"And you are sure, Ada?"

"Yes, miss. I have bled since."

"Well then, I am glad that *that* is not part of your predicament at least." She goes to the mantelpiece and picks through my things: the mirror that Daniel gave me, the pearl brooch in its box that she gifted me herself, the small pile of letters from home. "You are happy here, Ada, am I right? We treat you well?"

"You have been more than good to me, miss, all of you."

"And your health, Ada, how is your health? I would like to call Dr. Brewster to the house."

"There is no need, miss. I am feeling strong. I had a small ailment, after what happened, but your brother procured a remedy for me and I am fully well now. And the hospital in Boston saw me right."

"That settles it," she says. I am not sure what is settled, but Miss Emily smiles a tight, cheerless smile. It is like she is talking to herself and trying hard to wheedle the right meaning into her words. "Carry on." She waves her hand at my boots and butter, and off she goes, closing the door behind her.

I stand looking at the back of the door, wondering what it was she was trying to convince herself of and if it means anything at all for me.

# *Miss Emily Defends a Friend*

AUSTIN WANTED SUSAN TO BE THE HOUSEHOLD ANGEL OF PAT-more's poem—she was to be his pleaser as wives are destined to be—but, Sue being Sue, she pleases herself before any husband. And I fear, as Patmore further says, that she may have married an iceman and, in doing so, has frozen herself. My brother has shown a coldness today that I was not fully aware he possessed. Yes, I know Austin for a stern man, but with me he has retained at least a touch of his old self, that lighter fellow whom I love so dear. He has not kept as much as I would like, but I can coax buoyancy from him at times. Yet today I am feeling the lash of his detached, legal mind, and I do not much care for it.

He has told Father to turn Ada out. Worse, he has told Mother. Now a great confabulation is taking place, and I have had to leave the room for fear of what I will say if I stay. My nerves judder so when people are heated, especially Austin. But I am no good to Ada out here in the yard, gulping great breaths to settle myself. I must go in to them and wear a head of reason on my shoulders while I fight for her. I walk back through the hallway.

"Like so many young women, she suffers from hysteria," Austin is saying, and I wonder if he refers to Ada or to me. Though he hardly considers me young. "She is like all of her race—they are naturally indigent and find it hard to rise above that. It leaks out in their moral framework." He spies me in the doorway. "Ah, Emily. Are you restored?"

I look at Austin—at his haughty mien, his arrogant head— and I want to shout poetry at him: *Amputate my freckled Bosom! / Make me bearded like a man!* Because if I were a man, I could battle him well and make him listen to me. I sit on the sofa beside Vinnie, Father and Mother flank the fireplace, and Austin commands the floor. Father has his spectacles on, which means things are serious indeed—he wears them only for business matters.

"You cannot make Ada leave," I say. "We need her. *I* need her. She is tireless, better than any help we have ever had. And she is a good person."

"She is not scrupulous in the company she keeps, Emily," Vinnie says.

"How can you say that, Vinnie? You do not know what has happened. You know nothing of the ills that she has suffered."

"She has brought this upon herself," Mother says, patting and repatting her chest as if her heart might leap out and land at her feet.

"No, Mother, she has *not* brought this on herself. Ada was attacked by that Crohan person. She has done nothing wrong." I look at Father. "Surely you know that Ada is innocent, Father?"

"I do not know what I know, Emily. Your brother tells me that Miss Concannon has questionable morals, and I have no reason to disbelieve him."

"Let me be your reason." I rise and go to him. "Believe *me*, Father. Patrick Crohan attacked Ada in her bedroom. He was violent, he was drunk, and she suffers deeply because of it, in mind and body."

"It is peculiar that nobody heard this ruckus. This attack," Mother says. "Not one of us heard a thing."

"Do you imply that it did not happen? Are you calling me a liar, Mother? Ada and me both? You saw the bruises she was left with. She may have tried to conceal their true nature, but everyone here saw them. All because of that abhorrent man!"

"Do not rage, Emily," she says. "It upsets your health."

"I am not raging. I am defending a friend."

"You persist in styling her your friend!" Austin says. "Really, Emily, the girl knows her place. It is a pity that you do not know yours."

"And you yours, Austin," I say. "Is it really necessary for you to swagger over from the Evergreens to make mischief in this household? Is there not discord enough at home to keep you occupied?"

"Emily," he says, "if you cast your mind back, you will recall that you came to me to sort out Ada's problem. I am merely trying to close the case."

"But this is *not* one of your cases, Austin. This is the very real distress of a very real young woman. Ada is in our care. She relies on us."

Father stands up and tucks the newspaper under his arm. "Shall we adjourn the matter and speak of it again anon? I have urgent business in town."

Mother rises and smooths her hair. "Yes. Let us wait until tempers have moderated. I shall pray, and, in prayer I will find an answer. We should all retire and look to God."

"I believe more in Darwin than God," I say, but no one answers me.

I look from one to the other of my family, and all I see are closed, righteous faces; I cannot quite believe that these are the same people who ate breakfast from Ada's hands this morning. We troop out of the room like a chastened congregation. I take the front stairs two steps at a time to get away from them. At the top Ada stands rigid, an unreadable look on her face.

❧

I go to my room. I sit and lay my hands on my desk; a wedge of light cascades across them. My skin is shirred and white; my nails wear neat crescents at bed and tip. These are my mother's hands, and it has only occurred to me that I have inherited something of hers after all. The sunlight warms my skin, and I think to move my hands, lift paper and ink from the drawer and release myself into a poem. After the tumult of my family's chatter, I need a recess, a place to slip into that is mine alone. The wood of my desk—its fine cherry top—seems to seep into my fingers. The tree it grew inside, the woodsman's ax, the carpenter's lathe—all sing to me through my hands. I close my eyes and think of Ada, of her distress. My breast aches when I think of how she has been violated. No matter what happens, I will help and comfort her; that is my resolution.

For now I need the solace of words. Words bracket silence. That quiet gives propulsion to the words and all that they say. Words smolder, they catch fire, they are volcanic eruptions, waiting to explode. I like to start small. With the fewest words I can manage. If the words run away, I trip them up and pull them back. If they do not cooperate, I obliterate them. Each word is a candidate, sized up and interviewed and given its role only when it has proved its superiority to all other words. The best words—the most suitable candidates—come, most often, unsummoned. They are gifts from who knows what universe.

I may have too much to say, though I say things silently. Can that be so? Silence and words are bedfellows in my world. And with words I address the outer world honestly, for I address Nobody.

> *A word is dead, when it is said*
> *Some say—*
> *I say it just begins to live*
> *That day*

A chain of bobolinks fly past my window, and I jump up to watch them; they are like a coven of witches sweeping by, and I wonder if they are on their way to the deep forests of Brazil. How I would like them to take me by the wings up over New England and away. We would sail together above seas and purple mountains, and all care would be lost in the fine air that lies nearest the clouds. The bobolink is a joyful bird; today I wish I could drink from his beak and capture some of his noisy joy for my own.

"Bobolink, go well to the south and think of me when you are there."

I step back from the window and am glad of the blocks of light that flood my room; they ease my heart. And if I cannot be outside, at least I may welcome the outside in and I may try at least to capture it in words.

❦

Ada comes to my bedroom with a trio of Indian pipes in her hand. She gives the stems to me and stands in the doorway; I bring them to my nose.

"*Monotropa uniflora*," I say. "Did you know these are my favorite of all the flowers in the world?"

"I saw you plucking one for your herbarium, miss. I thought

any flower that has you sit on mud under a tree, in your white dress, must be worth something to you."

"I thank you, Ada. Come in." I pour water from my ewer into a vase and put the flowers into it. I look under their waxy skirts to see their flesh-pink innards. "Indian pipes don't need sunlight to grow, Ada. That's why they are sometimes called the corpse plant."

"That seems morbid, miss, for a thing so delicate and beautiful."

"They own beauty now, Ada, but they take revenge on us for picking them. Shortly, they will turn black."

Her look of horror is almost comical. "Oh, I didn't know that, Miss Emily, or I wouldn't have brought them."

"How could you know? Sit, sit." She sits on my bed, and I turn my chair toward her.

"I wanted to say thanks, miss. I wasn't listening in to what went on below, really I wasn't, but I heard you defend me to the others, Mr. Austin and the rest of the family. You have been more than a mistress to me." Her Nebraska-agate eyes look lighter than ever, and there is worry in them. "You have been a friend, and it has been my pleasure to serve you."

"Ada, this is beginning to sound like a farewell."

She wrings her hands. "It is my feeling that I should go, miss, before I am told to leave. I have cousins in California, Uncle Michael's boys. I can go to them."

I lean forward and take her hands in mine. "You will do no such thing. There isn't any question of your having to leave. There has been a misunderstanding, and I am putting it to rights. Trust me."

"I was probably only ever the dirt before the broom anyway, miss. You'll find someone good to replace me, a girl who will make Mr. Austin happy. I can't do that."

"My brother is not master of this house."

"And you are not mistress of it, Miss Emily," she says quietly.

I kneel before her on the rug and place my hands on her lap. "Listen to me, Ada. I do not want to be without you. I will speak to Father, and all will be well." I lift one hand and caress her cheek; she has the peach-soft skin of the young. "All *will* be well."

# *Miss Ada Makes a Confession*

My bed spoke to me all night; every time I moved, it answered me back in a voice measured out in sighs and groans. Now I stand at the back door, blear-eyed, trying to get the dawn air to stir me into wakefulness. The water for the family's wash cans is heating, and I have dyspepsia crackers in the oven—I found a grand recipe for them in the *American Farmer*—and there are fiddleheads ready to steam, to go with the morning hash. These days I always have a bit of green on Mrs. Dickinson's plate; the fern tops have a delicate grassiness to them that I am hoping will please her. The crackers, too, are for her, to aid her biliousness.

When I put on my shift and pantalettes this morning, I noticed that both felt loose. Peering at myself in my pocket mirror, I could see that my face looks scrawny; I set my hands on my hip bones and felt their jut. I have not been eating properly, and I must right that; my appetite has been poor, and I see now that if I am to be fully strong again, I will have to eat more heartily. I still paint on the calomel, and I bought a new bottle of sarsaparilla, telling the boy at the drugstore that it was to liven up my complexion. I thought he could see through me, see straight to the heart of my sin, but he wrapped the bottle with no comment.

There is mist hanging over the property, and my breath makes cloudy puffs on the air. I can hear the *trup-trup* of the horses in the barn, eager for their oats, no doubt. I leap like I have been scalded when someone walks out of the barn and moves toward me across the yard. I slip back into the kitchen but keep my face to the door, for if it is Crohan, I will not let him come up behind me.

There sounds a soft rap on the back door; Daniel opens it and walks in.

"Good morning, Ada."

"Hello, Daniel."

"I saw you taking the air."

"Trying to wake myself up, that's all." I turn to the stove to move the water pot nearer to the edge, to stop it bubbling over.

Daniel comes behind me and, with his arms around my arms, helps me lift the pot.

"There," he says. He turns me to look at him. "I have not been to visit your uncle, Ada, to test the truth of what you told me—that he forbids you to see me. I think it would be a waste of his time and my own."

"As you wish." I move away from him and stand with my back to the table.

"Patrick Crohan mentions you often, Ada. Already I have flattened him to the floor twice for things he has said."

"Crohan's a pup, and you know it. He would say anything."

"He is, and that is why I have come to you, because I want to hear what you might say. It struck me that I can't keep thumping the shit out of Crohan if I don't know what you have to say about the things he spouts."

"What has he said?" I step up to Daniel, and instead of backing away from me, he comes even closer.

"He was able to tell me that you have a small mirror in your bedroom, a mirror with a red rose painted on it. He was able to tell me that there is a smell of lavender about your nightclothes."

My legs jellify, and I sit. "Oh, Daniel. I never wanted you to know."

His mouth seems to disappear. "Know what, Ada?"

"What difference does it make? He ruined everything, is that not enough?"

"Tell me, Ada. I want to hear." His voice is coaxing now, the tone he uses with horses to get them to do his bidding, to soothe them. "If something happened, we can fix it. *I* can."

"You cannot fix anything, Daniel. Leave it go."

"No, no. I won't be leaving it go, Ada." He takes my arm. "I'll murder him if he touched you."

"Patrick Crohan attacked Ada, Mr. Byrne. He injured her and forced himself on her." Miss Emily is standing in the inner doorway, a chamber stick in her hand that makes her face glow. "He came to this house—*my* house—and he violated her."

We both stare at Miss Emily. Daniel turns to look at me. All the soft lines of his face have flattened out; he has an ugly look that I have never seen before. I don't understand this look, and it frightens me. He drags out a chair and sits, solidly, and then he spits tears like a baby and tries to fight them back at the same time, but they come hard and free. He lurches forward, and I hold him. Daniel sobs onto my shoulder, and his body jerks; I hug him tightly and say nothing, for I do not know what to say. He rubs up and down my back, as if trying to wipe away the stain of what he has heard.

"He forced me, Daniel. He was drunk, and he came to my room, and if I could have stopped him, I would have. I'm sorry, Daniel, I'm so sorry. I was frightened."

He doesn't answer me, just keeps moving his hands over my

back. I look up at Miss Emily, and she stands there, triumphant, as if she has resolved things.

"You had no right to tell him that," I say.

"This needs to be finished, Ada." Her voice is even but grim. "The truth makes us free."

I loosen my arms around Daniel; he is no longer crying. I bend my head to his to try to see his eyes. He pushes back his chair and stands. He pulls on his cap and tips it at Miss Emily and then is gone out the door, quick as a hare.

Miss Emily rushes across the kitchen. "Mr. Byrne! Mr. Byrne! Daniel!"

I run to join her, and we see him disappear into the barn. He is out again in a moment, slipping something inside his jacket; he is swallowed up by the mist after he strides through the back gate.

"Oh, my God. Oh, Jesus, Mary and Joseph, what will he do?"

Miss Emily grabs my arm. "Run, Ada. Get my shoes."

I tear up the stairs and into Miss Emily's bedroom, and I have to scuttle under her bed to find a pair of outdoor shoes. Back in the kitchen, I shove them onto her feet, and I bless Miss Vinnie for choosing shoes with elastic sides, that I don't have to be fiddling with laces. Miss Emily takes my hand, and we rush out the back door. She gasps when we get to the gate, pauses and gulps, like a child entering the sea for the first time.

"Are you all right, miss?" She looks scared, but she nods, and we plunge on. "Where are we going?"

"Does Crohan reside with his aunt and uncle?"

"They evicted him. I heard he's in the shanties now by the mills in Cushman, with some other men."

"Well then," Miss Emily says, "that is where we must go."

# Miss Emily Leaves the House

❧

WE HALF RUN, HALF WALK UP EAST PLEASANT STREET TOWARD Cushman. Everything is gray-mottled, and buildings hulk around us like shades. The mist hovers in a cloud over the streets; it seeps downward and keeps everything fixed. I wish the fog would lift that we might have some sun to brighten our way. Trees are swagged with white. We are the only creatures abroad, Ada and I, and our scurry and scamper seems to disturb the very air. We cannot see Daniel Byrne up ahead, though I am sure he is making a long tunnel through the fog that will lead straight to Patrick Crohan. It is very strange to be out, to rush through Amherst like this; I feel as if my legs are directed by a mighty force. It is as if my actions are being decided by a mind more unwavering than my own.

We pass large and small houses, their residents still abed, no doubt, shuttered in and safe. We come up on the common school where as a five-year-old I learned to spell and chant verses. One by one the mills loom in front of us, and I fancy I can feel around me their cotton, paper, wool and grist. Each of them spills an amount of its wares into the yards in front of it; I see patches of grain and curls of wood, stray scraps of paper and a broken spinning jack. I sniff deeply, but I cannot smell anything of them, though I long to. Men are ghost figures in the yards of the mills, started already on the day's toil. They pay us no heed as we hurry past. Both Ada and I pant after short spurts of running, so we walk a little before we run again. She blesses herself when we pass the edge of West Cemetery—a rapid flit of one hand that ends in a thumping to her chest.

I remain sequestered at home by my own choice or by some reason that is mine but lives outside me. But oh, the morning air fills the lungs with such vigor when you move through it at a pace. The street air holds Ada and me, and it passes us along with a high energy, handing us from one step to the next. It does not feel the same as when I run through the Homestead's garden. I have forgotten the exotic, expanding nature of simple town air.

Ada mutters a prayer as she jogs along: *"Ubi caritas et amor, Deus ibi est. Ubi caritas et amor, Deus ibi est."* Over and over she chants it, keeping herself moving forward with the rhythm of the words. The mills melt away, and we come to the swampy hem of Cushman; the air is sour, fecal, and ahead we see the sorry tumble of shanties that grew up beside the Mill Brook. Though it is early, the place feels alive: a thrush pipes its liquid song to the morning; dogs bark their annoyance back and forth to one another, and somewhere a fiddle is playing, its reedy, melancholic voice traveling toward us. Figures slope through the fog ahead; they thread around the shanties as if looking for a place to rest. Only one of them moves fast. I point, and Ada nods. We run together, past the general store, which is little more than a porched shack, and through the mean lanes lined with cabins, one atop another. A woman sits on the threshold of a house, her skirts hoiked to her thighs, and she laughs like a maniac as we pass.

"Are yiz lost?" she shouts, then laughs again, a chilling,

mirthless bark. "Come here! Come here and talk to me!" she calls. Ada grabs my hand, and we rush along. "Ah, go on so! Pair of bitches!" the woman bawls.

The man ahead stops and looks around, then bounds forward. We follow him, our breath ragged from exertion. My shoes pinch; though they are four years old, I have worn them but once before. We move along and get closer to the running figure.

"It's him," Ada says. "It's Daniel."

Daniel slows now, and at a gap between two shanties he stops. He shouts something, both fists rigid at his sides. We come up behind him in time to see Patrick Crohan stagger to his feet from a campfire he has been lying beside. His eyes are half closed, and his limbs unbend slowly, giving him a quasimodical gait. Daniel leaps forward, and he thrusts and thrusts again at Crohan. I think he is beating him, but when Crohan staggers backward holding his stomach, I see a garnet of blood drip from his fingers, then another and another until the blood washes over his hands like wine.

Quiet reigns horribly; we all stand and gape in the suspended silence.

"Oh, God Almighty. Oh, Daniel." Ada hurls herself at her man and drags him back toward the way we came. "Away now. Come on. Come on, Daniel."

Daniel breaks free of her and stands in front of Crohan. The injured man is not making a sound, but he winces and clutches at his stomach and bends his head to try to see his wounds. Daniel pushes Crohan, and he falls over and lies in the dirt, curled like a baby. He gurgles—a wet, distressed cry.

"Die there, you filthy fuck," Daniel says, and he spits at Crohan's head.

Ada pulls at Daniel's arm. "Come on, we have to get out of

here." She takes the knife from his grip, and the three of us stand and look at it. Ada wipes the blood from it with her apron, and she hands the knife to me. I tear off my shawl, wrap the knife in it and bundle it under my arm. I take Daniel's other hand in mine and we drag him away.

"This way," I say, not wanting to pass again the ruined woman who so recently saw us. We track a different route through Cushman and turn toward East Pleasant Street and home.

Daniel stumbles forward between us. He stops and looks at Ada. "I have no one under God to look to now," he says.

"Hush, Daniel. Miss Emily will help you. She'll see you right. Won't you, miss?"

I nod my assent, though I do not see what aid I can give if the worst has happened to Crohan. "Ada, remove your apron."

She tugs it off and rolls it up. "What will I do?" She looks wildly around, then runs to a hedge and stuffs the apron deep into it and comes back to where we stand.

Dawn spills downward on us, for the sun, risen already, is beginning to break through the fog. There are buckboards and horses on the streets, and I am suddenly aware that we may be seen by anyone who knows one—or all three—of us. We make our way down East Pleasant, each of us silent, Ada and me holding Daniel, to drag and coax him on, as one would a child. He walks forward with difficulty, the magnet of Patrick Crohan, and what Daniel has done to him, luring him backward to Cushman.

On Main Street I look up to see Austin's buggy leave the front of the Evergreens and come toward us. I glance from side to side, but there is no gateway into which we might steer Daniel and conceal ourselves. I huddle into him, and Ada does the same, and she barks at him to lower his head. We shuffle along the side of a fence like some misshapen hexapod, but it is too late; I hear my name called, and the buggy stops.

"Emily Dickinson! Is that you? Confound the gods, it *is* you. And you are out!"

"Austin, I beg you to drive on."

I have uttered the wrong thing; at once I realize it, and at once my brother is alert. He jumps from the buggy and stands in front of us.

"Emily, what is going on here? Mr. Byrne?"

Austin lunges forward and grabs Ada's bloodied hands. He steps in front of Daniel then and stares at him; he lifts Daniel's hands and studies them. Lastly he takes mine in his. As he examines my soiled fingers, the bundle slips from under my arm and falls to the ground. My shawl unravels, and the knife rolls out and lies in the dirt at our feet. Ada groans. Austin kneels and picks up the knife; he hurries it back into the folds of wool and gestures for me to bend down to him.

"What has happened, Emily?" he hisses. I recount the morning's events to him in a whispered torrent. Austin stands and helps me to my feet.

"Daniel Byrne," he says, "come with me."

"Where are you bringing him?" Ada says, stepping up to Austin.

"I am taking him, Miss Concannon, to a place where he will be safe." His tone is all chivalry and disgust.

"Don't go, Daniel," Ada pleads, dragging on his arm. "He's a law man. He'll bang you up in a cell. He'll have you hung before the end of the week." She starts to cry, a whimper that seems to rise and lodge in the leaves of the tree above us. Daniel Byrne stares ahead as if in a trance, but his lips move, perhaps in prayer.

"Austin," I say. "Where will you take Mr. Byrne?"

"Have you no faith in me, Emily? Are you now as suspicious and mistrustful as these Irish you love so well?"

"I want to know what you mean to do with him, that is all."

"I will conceal him at my office. You take Miss Concannon back to the Homestead to gather her things. Meet me at my rooms in town as soon as you can." I look deep into Austin's eyes and see nothing there but the brother I have loved since a child. "Go now, quickly."

Austin shoves Daniel toward his buggy, helps him up into the seat and sits beside him; he tosses the snapper to make the horse drive on. He looks like Father at that moment—somber and determined in his broadcloth; all that is missing is the cane and the beaver hat. We watch the buggy slip away; Ada looks up at me, her eyes teary.

"What have you done?" she says. "How could you let Daniel go with that man?"

"Listen to me now, Ada. We must be stealthy. Nobody can see or hear us when we step inside the Homestead. Do you understand me?"

Her head lolls back, and she wails. "Everything has fallen asunder!" she cries. "It's all fallen to bits!" She throws her head this way and that, and spools of spittle come from her mouth. "Look what you've done!" she cries. The street is filling with carriages now, and she calls attention to us in a way that I cannot have. I grasp her upper arm, pincering my fingers around her soft skin until it surely hurts. She stops short and looks up at me, her eyes glassy as marbles.

"Hush, Ada. We must go. Pull yourself together."

I link her and pull-push her toward the house; she is an unwieldy puppet beside me. At the back door, I tell her that if Mother is within, we must act normally. I open the door, and all is quiet.

I haul Ada up the back stairs and into her bedroom. I sit her on the bed and shove things into her bag. She does not have much: her good dress, some undergarments and stockings, a money pouch, her hairbrush, a bottle of sarsaparilla and a pot of calomel, a small mirror and the pearl brooch I gave her for her birthday, a bundle of letters. I spy Mother's copy of *The Frugal Housewife* beside her bed and throw that in, too. I tie the lanyards on the bag and pull her coat from its hook.

"You'll have to wear this, Ada. It won't fit in here."

Obediently she shoves her arms into the sleeves. I tie her bonnet strings; she looks young and forlorn, and I wonder if I am doing the right thing by her at all. I hear a noise on the landing and peer out to see a pair of Vinnie's cats haunchwise, slapping at each other's face. I go to scatter them, and Vinnie comes from her room and stands to look at the cats. She raises her gaze to me, her eyes sleep-puffy slits.

"Emily," she says, yawning, "look at the silly pusses. They are like sparring hares."

"Yes," I say, hoping that she is sleepy enough not to notice that I have come from Ada's doorway and not my own.

"What are you doing?" my sister asks.

"Ada is late to rise this morning, and I am trying to rouse her." The lie falls from my lips with no help from me, an astonishing wasp that hums in the air between us.

Vinnie bends to her warring cats and flicks her hands at them; they stop their clawing at once and, when she turns, follow her into her bedroom. She shuts the door.

I go back to Ada. "My sister's tongue was quiet in her head this morning, Ada, and her wits soft as blancmange. Thank the stars. Now, let us go."

I take her bag, and we descend the stairs to the kitchen. At the back door, I balk at going outside again. It is full, bright morning now, the sun a dazzling globe over the pines. Words begin to burble in my throat; I mean to tell Ada that she will have to go alone to Austin's office, but it is too late to back away from her now. I clasp her small, rough hand in my own, and we march through Amherst together as if it is our daily custom.

## Miss Ada Accepts
## Mr. Austin's Help

❧

MR. AUSTIN'S OFFICE IS DARK AND WOODY; IT SMELLS BOTH clean and unclean, of beeswax and men's scalps. Daniel rises when he sees us, but he doesn't come to me, and I dare not go to him. Miss Emily and her brother go into a corner to confer, but we can hear all they say, for they make no attempt to talk quietly. Daniel and I stand across the room from each other, and there is succor between us, though we cannot touch.

"I will see to it that they get away."

"They must go soon, Austin."

"We cannot risk the daylight," he says. "At nightfall I will take them to a man I know in the Quabbin Valley. He will see them safe to Boston."

Miss Emily stands before her brother and takes his elbows in her hands. "I am thankful to you, Austin, for all you are doing for Ada and Daniel."

"Thank me when they are safely away, Emily." He pulls back from her. "And I do not do it for them but for you. Your name shall not be wrapped into this affair."

"I need to get back to my lodgings," Daniel says. "My money is there."

"Money?" Mr. Austin asks.

"All my savings. I won't go without them."

Mr. Austin walks up to Daniel; they are the same size, but still Daniel pulls himself tall to face the other man. "Are you aware that you may have killed someone, Mr. Byrne?"

"I am."

"Do you think it wise to show your face today on the streets of Amherst?"

"I'll go nowhere without my money. I earned it."

"And you will earn a murder charge and the rope if you go after that money."

I go to Daniel's side. "I have a bit put by, Daniel. It will get us away."

"Away where, Ada? Amherst is not ready to spit me out yet."

"Well, you'll have to spit *it* out, Daniel. You can't stay here now. And wherever you go, I'll go."

All of me feels like lead, but I have to keep my heart out, to help Daniel along. He has not yet taken hold of what he has done, and he is more scarecrow than man standing here in Mr. Austin's chambers.

"It's a lot of money. I want to get it." Daniel looks to Miss Emily, hoping she will back him.

"How much?" Mr. Austin says.

"Seven hundred dollars or so."

Mr. Austin whistles. "You have been industrious, Mr. Byrne. And penny-wise. I trust that Miss Concannon knows what a prudent man she has snagged." He glances at me and runs his fingers through his rough hair. "I will give you five hundred dollars, to compensate you for the money you are leaving behind."

"Oh, Austin," Miss Emily says, and she takes her brother in her arms.

I am sure she will weep for gratitude, but I do not feel as thankful as she does. Yes, Mr. Austin has been helpful to me always, but his manner—the way he looks at me as if I were mud on his shoe—cuts into me. My face hurts when I am around him as I try to compose it into an expression that will not betray me. I try not to frown, and I try not to smile or yawn, and my skin and jaw ache from the effort. He brings out a watchfulness in me that I cannot suppress.

Daniel has not replied to Mr. Austin's offer, and I see now that he is shuffling his feet as if he means to leave the room.

"Well?" Mr. Austin says. "What say you, Mr. Byrne?"

"It is kind, sir, that you wish to aid me, but I would prefer not to be indebted."

"Nonsense. I will retrieve the money from your lodgings when you are gone, and that will be the end of it."

"So, you will give me five hundred yet take seven."

Mr. Austin whacks the side of his desk with his buggy snapper, and the rest of us leap like scorched rats. "I am giving you your freedom, man. I am breaking the law for you."

"You are fond of unusual financial transactions," Daniel says. I try to catch his eye to warn him to stop.

"What do you mean?" Mr. Austin says.

"You paid a man to go to war for you, they say."

"I hired a substitute. A perfectly legitimate arrangement."

Daniel snorts, and I fear that Mr. Austin will hand him in if he does not temper himself.

"We gladly accept your offer, Mr. Austin," I say, "and we thank you." I look to Daniel for his agreement. He nods and sits slowly into a chair by the wall. I go to him and take the seat beside him.

## *Miss Emily Says Farewell*

🌿

TWILIGHT FINGERS AMHERST WITH HIS TAWNY GLOVE, AND I wait, first for night, then dawn and, lastly, morning and my brother's return. Slowly, slowly, the Pelham Hills drag the evening dark down like a cloak. I sit at my desk, my hands across it, immobile. I listen to a whip-poor-will send out its obsessive call and remember that it can sense a soul departing and capture it as it flees. And what then? I wonder. What does the whip-poor-will do with its soul prisoner?

Patrick Crohan is no more. Word flew throughout Amherst in the late evening, and Father brought it home from town, where he met Mr. Bowles the newspaper man, who knew that Crohan sometimes worked here. Now that it is certain that Crohan is dead, the stars slip from their orbit and spin awry. And, alas, all of great Neptune's ocean cannot wash his killer clean. I almost hear the hiss of the tattlers as they pass the news, and the manner of death, back and forward between them. The gossips do not know who the culprit might be, and long may it remain so. My hope is that our family name does not get snared in their prattle. Then Ada will be safe. There is no better secret keeper than a Dickinson; we are able to close around our skeletons as snug as a shroud.

⸙

Before the news of Crohan came, I bade farewell to Ada at the chaise-house as she and Daniel hurried into Father's carriage with Austin.

"Be sure to live life completely, my little Emerald Ada," I said. "I wish I had." I gave her two heated soapstones for their hands. "Continue to think well of me though we will be apart."

"Tell my uncle I am sorry," Ada said quietly. "Tell him I will write."

We embraced, and Austin bundled her into the carriage before anyone might see. Ada's face looked smaller than ever, and weary, at the carriage's oval window. She raised her hand to me, then put her fingers to her lips and let fly a kiss. I caught it in my fingers and put it to my mouth.

So they are gone, fugitives both. And until I see my brother, I will not know if they are out of danger. For myself, I mean never to go outside again. Out in the world, there is tragedy; it is safer for me to write about catastrophe rather than live it.

My mind cannot surrender the vision of Crohan staggering backward, holding his punctured stomach and lowering his head to try to fathom his wounds. And then, when Daniel pushed him and he hit the ground, Crohan lay so forlorn in the dirt, letting out soft, inhuman whines of pain. I am frantic to rid myself of these scenes.

To switch my thoughts, I turn my gaze around my bedroom; it lands on the pictures over my bureau of Elizabeth Barrett Browning and George Eliot. I remember a far-off conversation with Ada; she stood before the pictures and studied them, as if trying to discern why they were there.

"They must be some of your Norcross relatives, are they?" she said. "Neither of them is a Dickinson anyway—I've seen all of them, and they are handsome people." She peered closer at Mrs. Browning and Miss Eliot.

When I laughed at her remark, she was injured. I told her who the ladies were and that they were heroines of mine, and she accepted that and seemed to warm to them from then on, dusting their frames carefully. I look now at the pair of writers on my wall—are they *so* plain?—and wonder how they coped when their hearts were sodden. But of course I know the answer to that already. They turned to words, and so must I.

I rise and take Emily Brontë from her perch beside my bed. I leaf through the pages, hoping for lines that will hand me consolation. My eyes alight on:

> *No coward soul is mine*
> *No trembler in the world's storm-troubled sphere*
> *I see Heaven's glories shine*
> *And Faith shines equal arming me from Fear.*

Would that I had my namesake's faith in a heavenly God; would that I had her courage.

Inky night folds down over Main Street. I go to Mother to say good night. She is propped in her bed, looking jejune and tiny in her cap and nightgown. It not being the Dickinson custom to make inquiries where they are not invited, she does not question me about being out of doors today. I offer it to her anyway. She is a Norcross truly, and I can see that she would like to ask but is restraining herself.

"I went to Austin's office, Mother, merely to help him with something. Nothing of concern."

"Oh, yes, dear?" she says, as if she does not know I was absent for most of the day. "Vinnie might have aided him. Your brother knows you prefer to stop at home."

"He asked for my assistance. He needed *me* specifically."

"And did Austin's need connect to the fact that we no longer have a servant?"

I look at Mother, her gentle eyes, her innocent face; I am shy of upsetting her. "No, Mother, it did not. Ada has had to return to Ireland, for her mother requires her. And is she not right to heed that call?" I wonder if I have dashed fast enough in and out of the lie. "She sends her deepest apologies to you."

Mother sniffs and pulls her sheet up to her neck. "I will sleep now, Emily dear. Blow out my candle."

ॐ

The night is large and looming; to keep from slumber, I wander the house from eyrie to cellar. In my conservatory the cape jasmine is as luminous as my dress and the calla lily trumpets in silence, its tongue poking obscenely at me. I run my fingers over its succulent petals and will Father Time to slash mightily with his scythe. Up to the cupola I climb, seeking Mother Moon, but she is under wraps tonight, as are the planets. If only I could see Polaris, a lodestar to guide Ada's way. I will miss her about the house; her talk was like music to me, easing my aloneness and affording me a peek into her alien world. I will miss her companionship and the light she brought to the kitchen. I leave my covert and descend to the dining room; the clock shows that it is not yet midnight. My candle throws a monstrous shadow onto the wall before me.

"How will I hurry the hours along?" I ask my penumbral self. She, of course, does not answer.

I go to the kitchen and search for a sweetmeat to liven me up. There is a box of caramel somewhere, if Mother and Vinnie have not unearthed it and scoffed their way through it all. Ada and I made it but days ago; I melted chocolate, she poured molasses, and we took turns stirring as it boiled, both of us damp-faced and tropical from the fragrant steam. No more will we make caramel together or charlotte russe; no more will we fashion potato scones or soda bread. No more will we walk the garden side by side, talking of Ireland and of America, each learning from the other. It grieves me sorely, though I know that Ada had to go, for her own safety and that of her man. Austin has been politic, and it is good that he was.

But what will Sue make of it? Will she feel righteous now that Ada is gone? Will Austin tell her *all* that happened? I think not, for there is danger in spreading the news around, even within the family. There are secrets already between Austin and Sue; both of them have shared intimacies with me about former lovers that the other does not know of; both of them harbor romantic thoughts that dwell outside their marriage. But they are only thoughts, and Austin and Sue are each so proud and so eager to appear *right* that, for now, neither will budge from where they are, no matter what unhappiness ensues.

The box of caramel sits on a shelf in the scullery, and when I snap its lid, sweetness engulfs me. I sit on the stool that Ada used to stand on and hold the box in my lap while eating piece after piece. The first candies I devour, chewing until my jaw smarts, but once the craving for a sweet rush has been sated, I suck, letting them melt to naught on my tongue. Sugar-full at last, I sigh, feeling both enlivened and dull. I wonder if I should have one more piece and put the box back but then decide to take it, for who knows of its existence now but me?

I carry the caramels to the library and sit in Father's Windsor chair; the blinds are up and the curtains open, but I make no move to close them. I shut my eyes and run my tongue over my teeth to undo the molasses fuzz. And it is thus Austin finds me at dawn: snoozing in the book room with a box of candy in my arms for comfort.

I feel a hand on my shoulder, and I rise, still half in sloom. "They are safe?"

Austin nods. "You waited all night, Emily."

I blink to waken myself; through the library window I see that morning bruises the sky. "How were they, Austin? How was Ada?"

"Neither spoke on the journey. I drove hard. The moon was fully round and bright, a great pearl rolling across the sky. It seemed to overtake us, and I followed it all the way to the town of Dana. It was the damnedest thing."

"I saw no moon last night. Are you sure?"

"It shone bright as a lamp, Emily."

"And Ada, where is she? Will she fare well?"

"I left them with a Quabbin man, a good fellow from Dana. He set off with Ada and Byrne while I was there. I watched them go. I instructed him to leave them in the North End. They are no doubt with their own people by now." Austin shakes his head. "I must sleep, Emily."

"Thank you, Austin. For helping them." I choose not to tell him that Patrick Crohan is dead; he will find that out soon enough.

"Good night," my brother says. "But I should say 'good morning,' I suppose." He turns to me. "Think no more on Miss Concannon and Mr. Byrne, Emily. They are gone from us and, at last, are none of our concern."

"I suppose you are right. I will sleep now, too."

I let Austin walk before me through the library. His back is erect; his lofty head holds itself above the world as if he does not quite live in it. My brother leaves by the front door and is gone.

I climb the stairs and lie on my bed; light fidgets across the floor through the windows. My eyes sting from weariness, and I close them and beg for peace. Ada is gone, and her absence turns my thoughts inevitably to Susan. Later today I will ask her to come to me; surely she will oblige and find it in herself to listen well and give me cheer. Though she did not approve of Ada, for reasons of her own, she will understand that there is a gap in my life now that Ada is here no more.

My body hums less noisily, and my legs jerk of their own volition, letting me know that sleep will soon come. All has changed, I think; the bird never resumes its egg, and nothing can be done to undo the terrible thing that has happened. As I fall further into repose, it strikes me that Ada does not know a soul in North End nor in the whole of Boston. I can only hope that her Daniel does. And I further hope that Boston will not ensnare them but that somehow they will end up in a green, leafy spot that will give them succor. I see Ada in my mind, fluttering loosely above the world but at last cocooned in a verdant place. Nature will, I pray, save her.

# *Miss Ada Concannon Returns*

My foot lifts and does not land where it ought to, for the swells make the boat have an uneven rhythm; I move crabways and have trouble correcting my gait. I walk to try to quell the heaving in my stomach. I blame the sea bread we have been given; it ferments inside me like cider, though it is hard and dry as wood. Our sea store is meager, for we did not have time to gather many supplies before we set sail.

We sat silent in Mr. Austin's carriage but talked softly when the man from Quabbin drove us. I spoke mostly, for Daniel was rigid with remorse and could not seem to form his thoughts.

"Where will we go, Daniel?" I clutched his hand in mine and rubbed it.

"I know not, Ada."

"We have money. We could go west. Or north, to Canada."

"They'd catch up with me." He gasped as if only at that moment realizing that he might have killed Crohan.

"Well then, there is but one thing for it. Home."

He whipped his head around to look at me. "Dublin?"

"Ireland, for sure. It's where we belong. But we need a clean start, Daniel, so not Dublin. I know a place we can go, where we'll be happy and safe. Where we can have a quiet life, us and our children."

He put his head to my shoulder, and I held his cheek with my hand. The carriage jogged along, and we both fell into a rough sleep. When I woke, I asked the driver to bring us to the Port of Boston.

I take my walks while Daniel sits on deck, unmoving and silent, his face west to America. He does not seem to notice the beating sails above his head or the plunge of the ship through the water. His thoughts are not mine to know, but I guess that he is wondering about Crohan and whether he is alive or dead.

I watch the sun fall into the sea each night; it dips slowly first, and then, quicker than quick, it plummets into the water, leaving the sky bleached at the top, sooty at the bottom. Tonight the up-surge in my belly gets so bad that I go to the cook to ask for some ginger—Mrs. Child says it will calm the churning.

"The only cure for seasickness, miss, is to sit on the shady side of an old brick church in the country," the cook says, and lets loose with a raucous laugh. I leave his galley hastily; he, and the milk stench of his lair, only make my bile rise more.

I stay below deck and check on my stowed belongings before heading for the steps to go up again so that I might sit with Daniel. As I reach the far end of the hold, I am amazed to spy the woman with the oranges who had traveled on the same boat as me last year. Sure enough it is her, and she is sitting alone at one of the long tables, peeling an orange. She digs her nails into the skin and breaks the fruit into pieces; she pops the slices onto her tongue, and the juice dribbles from her lips. My mouth fills with spit. She sees me watching and holds out half the orange to me.

"It will settle you," she says. "You'll see."

I take it and nod my thanks; the woman turns her face away and continues to eat. I bite into a piece of the orange and chew it up; it tastes bittersweet. I cradle the rest of it in my hand and bring it to Daniel. He smiles when I hold the orange out to him and puts it in his mouth, not even asking where I got it. I am happy as I watch him enjoy its juices; I see pleasure on his face, and I have not seen that for a long time, it seems.

By night on the ship, I dream of Amherst, not the bad that happened there but the good. I hear the midnight click of Miss Emily's door as she goes below to the conservatory to pot plants or to the kitchen for something sugared and cheering. I hear the wind in the pines and the gurgle of the barn's doves. I hear the endless *chip-chip* of the crickets in the garden and the scratch of squirrel claws on bark. I am comfortable in my Homestead bed, with a clean white eiderdown over me. The factory whistle blows, and I rise to go to the yellow kitchen. Miss Emily stands before me and says, "You do not need to brave it out, Ada. I am here."

In my dreams Patrick Crohan walks up to me, then passes, no sign of injury on him. Crohan does not threaten or speak but looks over his shoulder at me and wanders away. I do not tell Daniel about these night thoughts, for he might take a wrong meaning from them; he would maybe think that I want to be back in Amherst and not with him at all. I, who count myself lucky that he wants to be with me when I am a spoiled woman.

I wake to the heaving sea and the slap of sail and rope and bone ache from the hard bench under me. The smells of salt and tar, grease and sweat, assail my nose. I hear the coughs of the other women, their vomiting and whispered conversations. Babies yowl, and mothers shush them; those who are ailing moan and cry out. I wish for the voyage to end, for I am impatient to start our new life. I wish that Daniel could lie alongside me at night and that he did not have to go to his own bunk. But I am glad to have his long body stretched beside me by day as we walk the decks and sit to look at the churning sea. That is one very fine feeling, and I thank God for it. I am strong and determined; my mind is rushing forward to the future and to all that might happen, all the pleasing things that are yet to come.

꒐

The first thing is the rain, of course. We stand at the rail on the ship from Liverpool and watch rain sheet across the sea from Kingstown; it moves toward us like a great travail, the sorrows of the country and our own sorrows made into weather. I take my hands from the railing, and they are grained with salt, reminding me of the day I set off less than a year ago. Sea spray has soaked the ends of my skirts and the cuffs of Daniel's trousers; it has made our cheeks slick. I slip my arm through his and hug him to me.

Daniel knows all about me now. Up on the quiet of the deck one dusk, I told him of that terrible night and everything that happened afterward. The stars came out one by one above us, and the cold was mighty, but we were wrapped well against it. We sat side by side in our steamer chairs, and I got it all out. The words were hard to find, but I managed as best I could, and he listened with bowed head. I told him about the calomel and the sarsaparilla and what they were for. I told him of my growing feelings of health and had him feel the curve of my hips, which are rounding out nicely this last while. We spoke about what Crohan had done to us.

"We were both cursed by the same devil, Daniel, but God will be his judge," I said. "We can only try to forgive him."

"That is true, Ada," Daniel said. We both cried, lamenting the loss of our former selves. But we held each other close and agreed that we mean to march only forward now.

Daniel slides closer to me at the rail, and we look west, waiting for the coast to show itself. I feel giddy of a sudden and do not wish to witness our approach to Ireland.

"Will we go below until we dock?" I ask.

He shakes his head, wanting, I suppose, to see Dublin loom through the murk, to make sure it is real. These last few weeks, I have been passing from one moment to the next, keeping watch on Daniel, allowing myself only small sallies in my mind into the days and months ahead. Now, as the boat slips in past the piers that are like two arms outstretched in welcome, it is as if I am releasing a long-held, jagged breath. A smattering of laughter rises from the passengers beside us, and I grip Daniel's arm tightly, needing his body close to mine to stay me. We look at each other and smile, and anticipation surges through me.

Dublin is washed with showers, not made clean by them but made gray and grayer. The city smells of itself: a hoppy, thick, smoky smell that I find pleasant and restorative. Gulls as big as dogs careen above the harbor, letting out eager cries. We stand on Queen's Road looking back at the boat, trying to adjust ourselves to the feel of solid ground under our feet and the familiar, easy air of home.

༈

Rose meets us in our boardinghouse on Sackville Street. She embraces me, then stands back, holding my arms to take me in.

"You seem well, Ada. You've lost weight, but you appear strong in yourself."

"And you, Rose, have budded into a young lady while I've been gone." It is true; my sister looks composed in a way that she never used to. Maybe I had to get out of her path in order for her to grow up. Her eyes flick shyly to Daniel.

He steps forward and offers her his hand. "How do you do?" he says.

"Very well, thank you." Rose shakes his hand and looks at me. She knows who Daniel is, for my letters to her have been crammed with him, but she is made quiet by his presence.

We sit into the parlor, and the lady of the house brings a tray.

"Not one letter from you, Rose, in eleven months," I say, pouring milk into her cup for her to douse with tea. "Did your pen meet with an accident?"

"Ah, Ada, I never took to writing." She knows I am teasing, and she laughs.

"Do Mammy and Daddy know where you are today, Rose?"

"I didn't say anything, like you asked in your note. But will you not come out to Tigoora? Mammy would be so pleased to see you."

"We will by and by, Rose. We are going south first. We want to get settled. Then we'll come and visit."

Rose sips her tea. "Why did you come back at all, Ada? You were getting on fine beyond. I had no notion of you returning to Dublin."

I glance at Daniel.

"Ireland is our home, Rose," he says. "There's nothing can replace that. We mean to raise a family here."

Rose looks to me, and I smile. I open the lanyards on my bag and take out my money pouch; I hand her a few notes. "For Mammy. Tell her I will explain everything when I come to Tigoora."

❧

Down Granny Dunn's mountain we come. It is my mammy's mountain, too, and that of all women, and now it is mine. Down

Slievenamon's slope I walk with Daniel by my side. The May hedgerows are alive with elderflowers, and they are like a dusting of flour over the leaves. Down we come to Killusty and past it; the high walls and ornate pillars of the big houses and of Kiltinan Castle keep us out, but the buttercup fields with russet cattle and waving ferns welcome us along the way. Our tread disturbs the morning forage of a pheasant, and he bursts across the track ahead of us, his scarlet cheeks a welcome flash in the green. A pair of swallows—intent on play—flit and dive above, keeping us company on our walk. They swoon and lift, their forked tails fanning in carefree flight.

I am hungry—we have been fasting—and my stomach growls like a hound. Last night we had beestings from the near farmer's cow; he came to see who we were. I boiled up the thick, creamy milk, and it curdled together nicely; we ate it like hungry babies. The farmer wished us well. He spoke of his regard for my grandparents and all the Dunns and the Mahers. Now my insides grumble once more, and I look up to see if Daniel has heard, if he might make a joke of it. He is quiet, the way he always is now, and his face is fixed on the track ahead. As we approach the bridge at Fethard's Watergate, he grabs my hand in his and presses it.

"By noon, Ada, we will be man and wife."

"We will, Daniel."

We pass the bridge over the Clashawley and into Fethard. We walk its wide streets to the far side of town and the abbey. Farmers and shopkeepers stop to look at us. When they take in Daniel's jacket, my red merino and my tussie-mussie of clover and dog daisies, they realize that we are going to the church to be wed. The men take off their caps; the women wave and call, "God bless you both."

Father Lonergan meets us at the door to the abbey, and we follow him to the side chapel. St. Rita stands in her shrine, a livid cut on her forehead. Before she became a nun, Rita suffered a violent husband. I will have the opposite—a decent, gentle husband, despite all. My hope is that we will get to enjoy the pleasures of marriage: having someone to face the world with, to build a home around; being able to talk about anything we please; working to help each other. We will not have much, but we will have each other for as long as God spares us. And, maybe soon, a son or a daughter to delight us, now and in our dotage.

There was a feeling of comfort the moment we opened the door to Granny Dunn's cabin; it seemed to sigh in relief and usher us in. Everything was as it was; no one had come near the place to plunder or occupy it. We tied bunches of cow parsley from every rafter to clear the damp. I washed the small windows and swept cobwebs and dust until my arms ached. We will whitewash the walls soon, and I will fashion some bright covers for our bed. It will be as gay as it was when Mammy was a girl.

Last night I hung our clothes outside, to air them so that they would not be dank or smoky for today. Daniel sat on the stool at the doorway and watched me fuss over his shirt, pinching the collar flat with my fingers.

"Are you satisfied this is what you want, Ada, to tether yourself to me forevermore?"

I put aside the shirt and knelt before him "Yes, Daniel. I am more than certain."

"I'm not a good man, and well you know it."

"What happened happened. There is no changing it." I kissed his hands.

"I left Crohan on the ground, Ada. Like an animal."

"You had no choice, Daniel. *We* had no choice. No doubt he is swaggering into Conkey's Tavern as we speak, not a bother on him."

Daniel nodded and took my hand. "And you're sure, now, about getting married?"

"Yes, my darling. Are you certain you want me?"

"I am," Daniel said. "More than any other thing."

I sat up onto his lap, and we kissed, our mouths joined in love. As ever, his lips and tongue astounded me with their fervor, heat and gentleness. We kissed and kissed, and I thought of tonight and our lying together in Granny and Granddad's old box bed. I was not scared but felt expectant and cherished and safe. I looked forward to seeing him as he was born, bare and fresh, and to feeling his skin against mine and to our caressing each other with all the fond yearning that passes back and forth between us.

I sat there on Daniel, and we rocked together until the sun slipped away, turning the blazing yellows and greens to gray and making a navy hump of Slievenamon. We sat on, and the sky grew black, as if all the crows of the world flew wing on wing together, a dark gathering to blot out the moon and stars. The wavery whistle of a gosling carried up from the farm below, reminding me of the geese who trumpeted at night on Amherst Common. The young goose went on to speak as all geese do, in gabbles and blasts and strings of sentences, and we listened to its chatter for a long time before it fell silent and the night was ours alone.

The smell of the earth rose and swirled around our faces. I pulled Daniel's head to my breast and kissed his hair, felt the subdued bulk of him under me. I thought of Miss Emily far away across the sea in her fine Homestead, and I sent a prayer of thanks to her for all her goodness toward me and toward Daniel. And as I recalled her, I wondered if freedom is possible for anyone in this life or if we are all doomed to imprisonment one way or another. But no, I thought, there is always hope. It may be small and bald at first, but then it gathers feathers to itself and flies on robust wings. Hope never stops; it warms us in cold lands and through strange occurrences. Hope asks nothing of us. Yes, I am sure—surer than anything—that hope never stops at all.

## Acknowledgments

My thanks go to Stan and Cindy Skarzynski and Jeff Kern for transport, chats, and support in Massachusetts; to Suzanne Strempek Shea for making sure I got to be in Massachusetts in the first place; to Marcella Brown for friendship, guidance, and gingerbread; to Jeff Morgan of the Emily Dickinson Museum at The Homestead in Amherst for a warm, informative tour of Emily's world and for instruction since. Thank you to Robert Olen Butler for always being such a generous supporter of me and my work. Special thanks to Maureen Sugden for superb copyediting. Enormous and heartfelt thanks is reserved, of course, for Gráinne Fox, wonder-agent, and for my super-editors Tara Singh Carlson and Adrienne Kerr, and Helen Richard, and all at Penguin. Gratitude, as ever, to my family.

Go raibh maith agaibh—thank you, all!